FUNERAL SONGS FOR DYING GIRLS

FUNERAL SONGS FOR DYING GIRLS

CHERIE DIMALINE

tundra

Tundra Books, an imprint of Tundra Book Group, a division of
Penguin Random House of Canada Limited

Library and Archives Canada Cataloguing in Publication

Title: Funeral songs for dying girls / Cherie Dimaline.
Names: Dimaline, Cherie, 1975- author.
Identifiers: Canadiana (print) 2021035173X | Canadiana (ebook) 20210351756 |
ISBN 9780735265639 (hardcover) | ISBN 9780735265646 (EPUB)
Subjects: LCGFT: Novels.
Classification: LCC PS8607.I53 F86 2023 | DDC jC813/.6—dc23

Published simultaneously in the United States of America by Tundra Books of
Northern New York, an imprint of Tundra Book Group, a division of Penguin
Random House of Canada Limited

Library of Congress Control Number: 2021949250

Edited by Lynne Missen.
Jacket design by Emma Dolan.
The text was set in Bembo Book MT Pro.

Printed in Canada

www.penguinrandomhouse.ca

1 2 3 4 5   27 26 25 24 23

Penguin
Random House
tundra | TUNDRA BOOKS

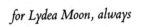

for Lydea Moon, always

LIVING DEAD GIRL

There's a film company whose logo comes on before the movie starts. It's a boy sitting in a crescent moon, fishing the sky. That's the closest thing I can think of to explain how I feel in the attic, sitting at the window watching the fog roll, or the leaves fall, or the snow chase itself around gravestones in the cemetery below. I feel like a boy with a fishing pole and a shitty sense of hunt.

What could you possibly pull out of the heavens to eat? What kind of bait would you use to hook a star? Some old people say stars were people once. So maybe you could find your ancestors out there, and yank grannies out of the dark like slick trout.

My room is like my brain—kind of messy, full of too much, organized in ways only I can decipher. Except the dog that sleeps in the actual room farts too much, and up here the air circulation is bad in the summer. And then there's the way my brain has bled the need for patterns into its space. So now I do math with the digital numbers on my alarm clock (12:34—1 + 2 = 3 + 1 more number = 4), and symmetry has become increasingly important. (I touch the tips of each big toe twice on the hardwood before I pull them into my hammock at night.)

I want to ask Dad about the patterns. I want to know if maybe my mother counted too much, or if when she scratched her left ear she maybe buzzed angrily beneath her skin until she scratched her right one, too, with the same amount of pressure. It's probably one of those conversations that would get cut short, where instead of speaking he'd just pull at his beard and slowly lean back until he felt safely removed from my quiet hysteria.

In the attic I don't have to worry about stressing anyone out. Up here, I can cry for no reason, or maybe for all the reasons. I can watch myself in front of the mirror and feel powerful and fragile at the same time. I can buy dollar-store paint and put fairy doors on the wainscoting and actually believe they'll be opened after midnight. And I can push the heel of my hand into my crotch and wonder at other hands that might give me this feeling of bruise and pinch at the same time. Up here, I am allowed the full range of sixteen that the world won't accept, without the consequences the world would demand.

I have this shitty turntable someone was throwing out, with a speaker that crackles like the music is under a constant boot heel. I play the albums my mother left behind—the Smiths, the Cure, Red Hot Chili Peppers, Tori Amos. And when I put them on and those first silent vinyl laneways slip by before the music begins, when the speaker crackles itself into life, it feels like slipping into prayer.

If my mother were to haunt the most suitable thing here, it would be those quiet divots between songs on her records, sending Morse code messages in the cracks and pops of the speaker. Instead, she haunts my father, slipping over his ribs, filling his tear ducts, pulling him away, away, away; taking his words, making him, in a way, almost as dead as she is.

And so when he's having a bad day, the kind of day when I can almost see the imprints of her fingers around his wrists, I play her records as loud as the dial will go, hoping to lure her up here, hoping to trap her in the shiny trenches of her own anthems. Maybe in the pause, she would learn how to sing. And in that way, without a hook, with just a lure, I could yank her out of the dark.

I lived in the cemetery with my father, in a house at the end of a laneway to the right of the front gates. Our apartment was above my dad's administrative office and looked out over both Parliament Street and the foregrounds of the property nearest the chapel. We'd lived there since before I have memories, when my dad decided a cemetery was the only place he could be, not willing to really live but unable to die because he was all I had.

My father, Thomas Blight, was the chief crematory operator at Winterson Cemetery, one of the oldest in the city. I spent a lot of time with him, wandering the gravel walkways that divided the graves into silent suburban developments. But even if we had lived in a cramped condominium where he might try to make up for the lack of a mother with hand-crafted dollhouses and bright pink walls like other single dads, even if we'd somehow managed to purchase one of the million-dollar Cabbagetown homes down the street with a shared driveway, even then I would have chosen to tag after him to the dusty buildings that made up the defunct older chapel and burning chambers.

By the time I was nine, I knew two things for certain: one, people have all kinds of quiet reactions when you tell them you have dead people in your lawn; and two, cemeteries make people want to have sex.

The first time I saw people doing it I was six years old. I was sitting on a slab of marble inside a mausoleum, eating Lucky Charms out of a Tupperware container. I was still young, so my hair hadn't darkened up to the deep brown it is now and was still dirty blonde. I had a similar haircut to the one I wear now though—a blunt-cut bob that came to my shoulders, with straight bangs. Only, back then I wore it all pushed back with a plastic headband. And it had a lot more tangles and random debris in it than now—*sometimes* more than now.

The Morrison tomb was barrel-vaulted and crumbling, like an igloo molded from a scoop of damp sand. I'd snuck in to eat beside Morrison Meow, the bones of a cat in a shoebox coffin snuck in a few years ago. As far as anyone could tell, there was no family relation between the pet and the actual tomb owners. The cat being here was an act of sentimental vandalism that my dad refused to report, owing to his weakness for both loss and underdogs. Not only did he leave the cat inside, the box shut with brown parcel wrap, the Sharpie'd inscription reading *Meow He Rest in Peace*, but he also forgot to repair the broken lock, of which I took full advantage. I used that tomb as a clubhouse from the age of about five until I turned twelve, when our groundskeeper Floyd fixed the lock. I was macabre in that way only motherless children can be.

That morning the cemetery was full of mourners from Mrs. Botelli's funeral. I was inside the tomb, eating and drawing distracted lines on the sandy floor, corralling ants with my toes, when I saw a man with his pants down around his calves repeatedly pulling himself up on a woman who was bent over a grave, her dress hiked up around her waist, one floppy tit hanging over the stone in front. I was still seven years away from even my first real kiss, but it made my stomach hitch up with something like dread, that feeling you get after you do something terrible and are waiting for punishment. That horrible, exciting feeling. I crept to the window and watched. And then I was caught, sort of.

The man looked up and turned his head toward the mausoleum. We locked eyes, my mouth so full that milk dribbled out over my bottom lip like smoke.

"Holy shit!" He jumped, detaching himself, and then yanked up his good, pleated pants.

"What the hell, Joey? What's wrong?" I ducked, but their voices carried through the cracked walls like spearmint gum–scented wind.

"A little kid, I swear to God! A little freaking kid, over there."

"Oh my God, are you serious?"

"Yeah, I'm serious. Do I look like I'm joking?"

"Where'd it go? Jesus, Joey, which kid was it? Was it one of Diana's?"

"In there, in that little shed!"

The woman paused in her arrangement of nylons and panties and sighed. "Joey, for real? That's a goddamn crypt. There's no kids in there unless they're dead."

"No, Angela, I swear, I saw it. It had these creepy eyes looking straight at me. And its mouth was all, I don't know, messed up. Scared my boner away."

"Oh, real classy." She fumbled with her clothes and straightened the mass of ironed curls on top of her head. When she spoke again, it was in a gentler tone. "Let's just go catch up with everyone else. I'm sure it's just your nerves. This is your ma's funeral after all."

"But I swear, I saw it . . ."

"C'mon. It must've been a bird." Her maternal tones were squeezed shallow around a wad of gum. When I looked up again, the girl was leading him in the direction of the parking lot, slightly wobbly in her borrowed pumps, and my breakfast was spilt on the stone floor.

This wasn't the last time things got heated on the grounds; over the years there were the make-out sessions during visiting hours, teenagers jumping the fence at night to grope between the monuments, and the behind-the-chapel humping squeezed in between funerals and wakes. Dad said it was because grief did funny things to people, but I knew it was because people were just basically assholes.

In my head my dad was seven feet tall, played for the Toronto Maple Leafs, and never had to sleep. When it came time to replace the flagstones in the walkway, he trimmed them with karate chops. At night, if I screamed that some hideous monster was drumming its branch fingers on my bedroom window, he would yank up the pane and reach outside to snap every finger from both of the beast's hands. The next night after supper we'd have a bonfire in the backyard, roasting marshmallows over the haunted timber.

But none of this was true.

Thomas Blight may have been quiet and unassuming, but he was a fascinating human to observe. First, there was the way he walked, like a loping gazelle with extra-long legs and arms that paddled like down-covered oars. Then there was the way he spoke, as if each word were depleting his personal bank account and needed to be considered. He even said my name in a compacted way, not Winifred but "Win."

Dad displayed my mother's photo on the mantel like an Oscar statue; having a woman that beautiful love him was the greatest accomplishment of his life. My grandmother, Faith Trudeau, was a mixed-blood woman from the Georgian Bay, the land named after the white sands that rolled into the green of Lake Huron like the sugary cliffs of Dover. My grandfather was Zlatcho Kalder, the son of a Romanian traveler whose family came to Canada in the last great migration of 1970. He was passing through in a rickety pickup, buying and selling goods like a traveling nostalgia shop, when they met. That's where I got my gray eyes, passed down through my mother from him, a gift from a Romanian homeland I'd never even bothered to look up on the globe.

Zlatcho's own mother had already died by then, and his father had defected from the clan, so there was no one to protest the marriage to an outsider. After a small ceremony in the kitchen of a local priest's house (paid for with a grandfather clock unhitched from the pickup's bed that morning), they were married. They lived together for the rest of their days, raising their only daughter—my mother, Mary Bax Kalder—in a dilapidated house on the outskirts of a small town.

Dad said Mom had told him all about that house. It sounded like a fairy tale, crammed with broken clocks, embroidered vests, cloudy gem-crusted cuffs, and beaded moccasins. My grandparents ran a pawn shop and took in a decent profit during cottage season when the tourists parallel-parked in the rocky driveway, eager to bring a piece of this crazy little cottage town back with them to the city. Having no idea how anyone dressed back then, I imagined them in buckskin and lederhosen. (Later, I would find a photo of them, both with long hair, looking like they had just crawled home from Woodstock.)

When Mom started walking, the shop's inventory became her toys. The scratch of old lace soothed her swollen gums when she was teething; the tinkle of bone shards broken off of animal skulls and banged against the metal bathtub made her giggle. So the Kalders began selling only the larger pieces of furniture that didn't interest their little girl, making up for the lost money with Faith's filleting skills.

Fishermen from around the bay would drop off boxes and bins full of the day's catch to be filleted, a task my grandmother performed with methodical precision and great pride, marking each fish with a small cut in the upper tail to indicate its designer, an incision that made two sharp turns before ending down toward the ass-end of the fish like the letter Z, for Zlatcho. And so, by carving her love into each fish, she inadvertently became the Zorro of filleting. After I heard this story, I pictured her in buckskin and a black eye mask.

The universe was kind for the next nineteen years and they were happy, hidden in their sloped cottage full of treasures and riches like pirates with better hygiene. Then, the summer after my mom met my dad and decided to follow him on his travels into the Far North, Faith and Zlatcho died in a fire that ate up their home and all its trinkets in one swift gulp, as if without the third person, balance was lost and they tipped off the edge of the world.

My mother avoided that fire but died anyway, and it was me who killed her. It's a crime for which I was forgiven, since I was just a sad little newborn. But Dad never stopped mourning her.

My bedtime stories were all about Mary, her gray eyes in every princess, her temper in each dragon. I was dressed in clothes cut down to size from Mary's closet. By the time I turned fifteen, I fit them perfectly. She had been thin and short like me, her hair a heavy weight down her back. I could never grow mine that long; I was too impatient with the upkeep it would require. I felt her every day in a way much different than the way my dad felt her: a sunny heads to his gloomy tails.

I had grown on the outside of my mother's womb like a pink barnacle. My mom and dad were out on the barren lands of the Northwest Territories for most of her pregnancy. When I imagine it, I think of myself as a wad of gum some messy god stuck to the side of her guts. When I got to sixth grade, I started looking that stuff up. It turns out that if I had died but stayed lodged in my mother's dark nooks (instead of just dropping off the small edge of existence and ending in miscarriage), her body would have worked hard to contain me. Her defense systems would have labeled my corpse a threat and begun layering my remains in calcium and minerals; in short, turning me into a lithopedion—a stone baby. I was almost a statue.

In my case, I continued to grow, causing cramps and an embarrassing inability to hold even the smallest amount of pee. Not having the benefit of a nice, cushy womb, the placenta had attached to several organs: a kidney, part of an intestine, and the corner of an overworked bladder. At thirty weeks gone, my mom didn't go into labor. Instead, she passed out. By then, they'd come back to Toronto so I could be born in a hospital. My Dad rushed my mom to emerg. Within an hour, I was born through a deep cut that curved red and dangerous like an extra rib sketched by a child, and my mother was brain-dead.

"We'd just gotten back from up north," Dad would say, working his way through the painful tale with small sentences and careful words. "We knew you were there, just not where exactly. Just assumed, you know? Didn't have time to get a doctor. Everything seemed fine. Then, that's it. One day. It's over. And it was just you and me."

Each word was a felled log he had to carefully extract from his memory, lest the water push the entire dam down and he lose control.

"I waited three days before I let them unhook her, waited for you to be able to leave the nursery. I knew when I put you on her it was over. She didn't move. If she were still there, she'd have held you at all cost."

I'll admit that, when I was younger, I became obsessed with the idea of lithopedions, stone babies that could go undetected for a lifetime. I read as much as I could get my hands on: old medical texts found in used bookstores, encyclopedias from the library, and—the best resource for the truly bizarre—the internet. I was all-in obsessed, coming up with all these scenarios and alternate endings. Like, what if I had refused to be born? What if I hadn't killed my mother and, instead, she had killed me, covering my fetal frame in a hard shell, like an oyster around a chunk of soft meat? I tried to imagine what it would have been like, developing into a fetal mummy, still as a tree trunk in my mother's guts. Would my fingers have fused together like the mermaid kids I found online? Would my eyelids have remained closed forever like a puppy that never aged? Would I still be there now, a tiny ghost haunting the marrow and eardrums of a living mausoleum?

I spent hours lying on my side on the far hill near the back of Winterson's oldest acre on my mother's grave, imagining the slow tucking-in of calcification. After almost being run over by Floyd's ride-on mower one Sunday afternoon, I decided to move closer to the rickety tombs that sat together like crooked teeth in a lower jaw, where the mower wouldn't fit, where I would be safe to be still, curled around the graying markers like a crescent moon in a grassy sky.

But this was all in the time before. Now I'm too busy being a ghost.

CLOSING TIME

It was days away from my sixteenth birthday, and I was glad to be leaving fifteen behind. Too much pressure. I blamed Netflix for feeling like a failure because I was still a virgin and didn't look like a well-groomed twenty-five-year-old. Not like on those shows where people my age had abs and a classic sense of style (red lips and pearls in eleventh grade, anyone?). I'd been up late listening to music, planning my life after high school, and tracing the lines of my legs where they connected to the flex and curve of hips. So I was still sleepy when I padded downstairs the next morning just before noon, driven out of my cocoon by hunger and the knowledge that there were Pop-Tarts in the cupboard.

"Hello, Winifred. How are you, dear?"

I jumped at the greeting, already settled into a lazy summer schedule. Mr. Ferguson sat in the kitchen on one of the two red chairs at the round table. He ran all the business at Winterson, from church services to equipment repair, and he was wearing his usual gaudy pinstripe suit, which would have been okay except that the stripes were three tones of green, none of them the right one. He also had a collection of vertical wrinkles stamped above his eyebrows. As he leaned his arm on the kitchen table, where all good business is conducted, I noticed he was still wearing his impossibly large, shiny dress shoes inside.

"Good. How are you, Mr. Ferguson?" He rarely came over to the crematory or the admin offices, and certainly not to our apartment above them, so when he showed up on a Tuesday at noon I was already suspicious.

"Oh, well, that's a story in and of itself now, isn't it?"

I struggled not to roll my eyes. Why did people feel the need to give such convoluted answers to the simplest of questions? And who wears shoes in someone else's house? And I was the one raised without a mother. Jesus.

He sighed, lowering his head. My father was standing against the kitchen counter. The kettle was still steaming behind him, and a couple of mismatched mugs had been pulled down from the cupboard. It looked as though he had stopped in the middle of preparations for tea.

Mr. Ferguson slapped the table with the palm of his hand and lifted himself up onto those pontoon feet. "Well, I better be going then. Let the two of you enjoy your day. Thomas?"

He held out the same, slightly palsy hand for my dad to shake, which he did, in a slow, meandering fashion. "Think about what I said. It's best to be prepared is all. We won't give out hope until the very last."

My dad nodded, a movement as slow and thoughtful as the handshake.

"Okay then, Winifred. You be a good girl. Keep an eye on the old place for us then?"

I smiled, one that didn't reach my eyes, which were still fastened on my father, leaning against the counter like a flower with a broken stem.

Mr. Ferguson navigated his huge shoes across the tiny kitchen, each step covering a square and a half of linoleum. He folded around the corner, into the tiny hall, and down the stairs. When I heard the door close behind him, I was finally able to move.

"What's up, Dad?"

He didn't answer right away. Instead, he poured water into the mugs and measured overfull scoops of sugar into each. I opened the fridge and grabbed a tin of condensed milk with two small holes punched into the top and handed it to him. I knew there would be a few minutes before he'd respond, so I sat in the chair that had recently held Mr. Ferguson. It was warm on the backs of my bare legs. Dad placed the mug in front of me and then, surprisingly, pulled out the other chair and set his mug down beside last week's paper. He lowered himself so that we were sitting across from one another, as if we might actually have a conversation.

I immediately started to worry.

"What is it? What's going on, Dad?"

"Well now, the cemetery isn't doing so well. Business-wise."

That same old battle to save and spit words at the same time; it was not endearing right now. Right now it made me even more anxious than usual, and I tried to help him along by inserting the right questions. "Business? Like you mean the cremation business?"

He nodded, grateful for the guidance, and at the same time annoyed by the increasing pace. "Everything."

"But it's not like they can shut the crematory down, can they? People need to be cremated."

"There are companies that do it cheap. Saves Ferguson the cost of repairs on the old place, this apartment." He looked up, his eyes making a circle of the kitchen. "Saves him the cost of paying your old man too."

"What? Dad, they can't run without you!" I was frantic, zero-to-sixty frantic.

"Nothing's set in stone. We find out later. End of summer."

"End of *this* summer? What the hell, Dad? How do we stay? Can he raise the price of the cremations? What about the burials?"

"Wouldn't be fair, would it? People don't need to pay more, not at a time like that."

"I don't care!"

"You do."

"No, I don't! Make them pay twice. I don't want to leave."

"Win, it'll work out. I will work it out." Each word was sculpted with even facial movements—lips and cheeks and eyebrows working the consonants over vowels like clay. It was like trying to communicate under water.

"Where would we go? This is our home! This is Dingleberry's home! What about him?" I pointed at our dog laid out across the cold kitchen tiles, frantic to invoke something other than myself in this argument. The dog barely twitched an ear at the sound of his name.

Mrs. Dingleberry was a pug-Chihuahua mix we chauffeured around in a metal wagon. The wagon was a lot easier than trying to haul his fat ass around on a leash. He'd been a ninth-birthday gift from my father's younger sister, a loud woman named Ida. Really, he was more of a "ditch and dash" situation, but I preferred to think of him as a heartfelt gesture from an otherwise selfish woman. Before the dog-gifting visit, I'd only seen Ida once, when we met her for lunch at a hamburger stand off the highway so Dad could sign some papers for his parents' estate.

We'd been celebrating my birthday with old movies and a lemon meringue pie; I'd had to keep that pie on the counter overnight so the meringue was hard enough to hold the candles. The doorbell rang and we both went down to answer it; I was hoping it was a birthday delivery and Dad was worried it was work related. Turns out, I was right. It was Ida, who declined the invitation to join us. She was in a hurry, on her way out west to meet a retired fireman she'd met on Tinder. Owing to her new fiancé's violent allergies, her overweight seven-year-old mutt wasn't going to be making the trip with her.

"So I thought, who better to take care of my own little Dingles here than my own little Winifred? You two won't be gallivanting anywhere soon, so he'll have a nice home here with yous, and with plenty of room to run around too."

We looked where she was pointing, down at her feet where an obese mass was either solidly napping or completely dead. I tried to imagine him running anywhere; it was doubtful that his legs worked—they kind of just poked out of his rolls like sticks with calloused roots at the end. I bent down and patted his tan head and was rewarded with a deep sigh. Pleased that he was alive, I hugged Ida, never bothering to ask why her male dog was named Mrs. Dingleberry. I didn't care. She turned on a green patent heel and marched back down the walkway to her ambling Buick before Dad could even say "hello." We watched her pull away in a rush of gravel and rubber, honk her horn twice, and wave a bejeweled hand out the window. Then we looked back at the top step, staring at the dog that hadn't so much as woken up for a goodbye. Dad picked him up, grunting at the weight, and carried him upstairs to the apartment, settling his pudge on the flowered couch.

I was so happy. "This is the best birthday ever." I'd meant

it. The dog didn't move for the rest of the day, even when I snapped a paper party hat on his head.

And here we were, about to make him homeless. Tiny explosions like old flashbulbs popped and sizzled in my head. I looked with sentimental eyes at everything in the small, sun-soaked kitchen, everything rendered with a touch of loss in light of the uncertain news.

And, of course, we both knew what the real emergency was—Mom was here, her ashes buried inside a small metal urn near an elegant willow that wept with lush greenery or skeletal grief, depending on the season. My auntie Roberta was also buried here, but I could visit her grave now and then without feeling like a deserter, because I'd had the real live version of Roberta for years. But Mom? How could we live without her this close by?

Dad reached across the wooden tabletop and patted my hand. "We'll figure it out. Maybe head out west to my parents' old land." He got up and started rummaging in the pantry for dinner provisions. "Spaghetti tonight?"

Spaghetti? Dinner? How could he think of food? How could he just go back to the regular schedule? I felt like I was going to throw up, and if I did, I knew my heart would be in the mess. I didn't say anything, and he sighed.

"We've been through worse."

Maybe *he* had been through worse. My trials were buried under the amnesia of infanthood. This was a goddamn emergency. My entire life was being threatened by shitty budgets and an old man in pleated trousers.

I tried to imagine my father out there in the real world. All I saw was his sad, long beard tangled with gray wiry strands as he stood on a street corner, shaking a tin can with a few nickels in it. I was playing the harmonica and shuffling out an untrained two-step. Dingleberry was sleeping on the cold cement, a sign around his neck that read: "Help me buy a wagon." Tears gathered in the corners of my eyes.

Dad put a hand on my shoulder. "Win, maybe we need change. Everyone does." He shook me a bit, as if waking me from a deep sleep. "Maybe this is our time to change."

"I don't want this to be the change we need!" I could hear myself; I was almost screaming. "Let's change in other ways—start dieting, exercise more, take judo class, learn to read maps, anything but this."

I ran out of the kitchen, into the living room, and up the stairwell into my bedroom. I climbed back into the hammock, almost forgetting to touch the ground with each big toe—almost—and folded my arms over my chest. Strung straight across the far corner, from rafter to rafter, the hammock started in on a low, even sway, and I felt better right away. I'd never had a real bed, just this hammock with a hanging fringe that'd gotten a bit frayed and dirty at the ends, strung from one corner to the other, right by the front window. I'd begged for a hammock like the kids in *Robinson Crusoe* when I was little, and Dad, being an odd parent who relied on no outside reference but his own, went right out and got one. I fit in its middle curve like someone had poured me there.

Up here the air was different and I was able to breathe again.

A stream of pale yellow sun spilt into the room through the picture window that took up almost the entire front wall. In and out of the streaming light blew feathers of dust, kicked up from the striped rug, skimming across the dark hardwood and settling on the bookshelves rammed with all my best treasures, organized in mason jars. Collecting was something, I guess, that was inherited from my grandfather Zlatcho. In my hoard was an abandoned bird's nest shaped like a straw tornado; a tiny raven's skull; two beaded hair ties from my mother's regalia, the beads getting milky with age and storage; rocks shaped like other things . . . . Beside the jars was a collection of comics and classics culled from the stacks of used books at the Goodwill store. Pencil sketches of the graves and visitors were taped up along the slanting roof, above the curly-footed writing desk and over the corduroy floor pillow where I tucked Mrs. Dingleberry in at bedtime.

The move wasn't for sure yet, but it was serious enough that Mr. Ferguson had come by to mention it, serious enough that Dad had bothered to tell me. It was just now edging into July, and we had until September to wait for the final axe blow to land. Anything more than a month is an eternity, and I felt consoled by the oodles of time still left in the tube for anxiety to gradually squeeze out. There had to be a way to stay in Winterson. Life on the other side of that wrought iron fence was unbearable. Everything was blur and scream and decisions and metal. Everything was too much out there. Everything was too much, and I was just too less to deal with it.

I imagined a hundred ways to make money, from lemonade stands to part-time jobs to garage sales to petty theft. Honestly, nothing was off the table. By the time my dad came upstairs carrying a plate of spaghetti with hot dog chunks, I was starting to feel better.

I loved summer at Winterson. The cemetery gardens between the crematory and the rest of the graveyard sprung color and perfume and bees in one long, green exhale. Me and Dingleberry resumed proper walks instead of the rushed runs we managed through the winter. In wintertime we barely made it past our small front yard. Dingleberry didn't do much in terms of physical exertion, but he sure did know how to shake, and after those walks, I would have to prop him up against the heating vent in the hallway to thaw. His tiny teeth would chatter in his fat face like teensy mice drumming their fingers on wood. But now it was warm and we were out a lot.

The trees in Winterson were spectacular, like leafy fireworks pushed out against the sky. It was a tie for which species was my favorite. I loved the willows that looked like they were crying, which was appropriate for a cemetery. Where their branches hung down, graceful and heavy right to the ground so that the smaller tips dragged like luxurious draperies on a ballroom floor, I imagined that if I walked right through the center of them I'd emerge into a different world. On the other hand, I also had strong feelings about the birch trees. My dad told me that people from my mom's community made canoes that could travel across the entire continent out of the chalky paper strips. So, I felt culturally obligated to choose birch.

So much had happened here—like my entire life, every weird, lonely day of it. When I was eleven I accidently started a rumor the place was haunted (more than just being spotted in a mausoleum). It was a rumor that spread out into the neighborhood and that the cemetery staff were asked about once in a while. Of course, we just assumed that every cemetery had these rumors, a "professional hazard," my dad called it.

It had been the last weekend before the end of sixth grade and I had gone out for a walk. The sun was streaming in the window, heating the living room floorboards to a toasty wooden grill on which Dingles sacrificed himself, sizzling away like a fat sausage all morning. I left him inside, since he was happily snoring, and got ready to go out by myself.

"Alright, Mrs. Dingleberry, you keep the house in order while I'm gone."

I'd thrown on my favorite faded black Converse and grabbed the long red cape I'd purchased from a secondhand store the week before. It was for next Halloween; I was planning on being a superhero, or maybe Little Red Riding Hood, or maybe even an old-timey magician with a curly waxed mustache. Living in a cemetery obligates you to be an ambassador for Halloween, and I was aware that, as I was newly in the double digits, I only had a few years left. I pulled the voluminous hood over my head and skipped down the stairs, cutting through my father's seldom-used office at the bottom of the stairwell and bursting out the side door, all red velvet and spindly legs.

I took the narrow path that led from our place through the garden and around the crematory, down to one of the main roads that ran across the property like cobblestone arteries.

It was the weekend, and owing to the great weather, plus the semi-high-profile funeral of a local politician, the grounds were busy with the activities of the living. I stayed off the main path and trudged up Gibraltar Lane, hiding in and around the gray structures, to the larger society-type tombs, buzzing with murmured woe at this hour. Women in long dresses or over-heating in black pantsuits held onto their children as they pulled and skidded across the cobblestones. Their hats, viewed from a distance, resembled stiff plants in a plastic garden. Men walked with hands shoved into the pockets of their good pants, staring as much at their watches as at the gravestones. I made myself small and wove in between the groups and families, the solo widows and the weeping lovers.

I walked to the Tratskoff obelisk. There was a great hiding spot back there that I loved. It was Floyd's preferred spot to teach me boxing moves on days when he'd had enough to drink that he felt social, but not enough that he remembered he hated every living thing. Behind the knotted willow was an old cellar, built right into the ground. Grass covered the door like a rug so that it was almost invisible. I wouldn't have even noticed it if not for my dad pointing it out one day as we did a walk-through.

"Careful there. Old storage for the shovels."

I approached the obelisk and dropped to my knees, which were barely covered by the tops of my socks, so the grass tattooed itself there, leaving the patterns of its needle-tipped landscape. I held the edges of the red cape closed over the faded David Bowie T-shirt kept from my mother's stash. Because the grass was so harsh here, I lay my head on the lip of the monument instead. I needed to feel safe; there was too much shifting at eleven years old already. I'd lost what friends I'd had at school, and now there was new dimension to my chest and hips that I couldn't make sense of yet. I felt without an anchor, and so I searched for ground. And what came back, from the depths of memory, was a shape, a soft curve. I lay on my back, lifting scarred knees up, curling shoulders down, fetal now at the base of the obelisk. I tried to stop breathing for long minutes at a time, to become the lithopedion that could have saved my mother; the stone child that had chosen to keep its eyes closed, tiny fists thoughtfully poised under a dimpled chin, forever. Forever.

I couldn't help it. Whenever I thought about my mother, whenever I imagined the tragedy of her death, there I was—little, pink, seemingly innocuous Winifred, like a soft, fuzzy time bomb.

The cape's hood fell over my cheek and muffled the noise of the day. My hands curled like rosebuds underneath my chin, and my knees attached to one another at an angle that made my toes touch and the bones of my ankles rub together. My stomach tightened up and hitched along the bottom so that its round-ness disappeared in the tension. And my spine curved like a tense hand: a flesh-and-bone bumper on the edge of a stone-base monument. My breath became small, running a circle in the space between knees and nose. I closed my eyes tight.

"Peter, look at that beautiful sculpture over there, on that grave up there."

"Oh my, that is something, in full color. Jesus, somebody spared no expense. I saw something like this in Germany last year. Let's go check it out."

"No." She lowered her voice to a whisper. "It's a woman; she's asleep on a grave. Must be her family member, or, oh, maybe a lover. How beautiful. Hang on, let me get a picture for Instagram."

"Is it a Little Red Riding Hood homage?" Peter, not paying the best attention, was a few steps ahead of the woman I pre-sumed was his wife, and the shuffling of his feet over the crum-bly grass alerted me to the fact that I was no longer alone.

"Peter, it's not a statue. Give me my phone. I gave it to you when I went to the washroom, didn't I?"

"I don't have it."

It was this couple that started it all. Not that they meant to. They were on one of those "hop on, hop off" tour buses and ended up strolling the Winterson grounds. Winterson, being adjacent to the Necropolis, the oldest cemetery in the city and an official part of the tour, was often inadvertently included on the tour by those who were easily lost and did not notice the gate between the two lots.

"Peter, I can't find my phone. You didn't leave it in the restaurant, did you?" She sounded frantic. Peter turned back and stuck his hand in his back pocket.

"My bad." He handed it to her, smiling apologetically. By the time he turned back, I was gone.

"What the? Wasn't it right there, on the tall one?" He pointed across the yard, past the half dozen markers between them and the obelisk, now empty except for grass and stone.

"Oh my God! Peter, you know what this means?" The woman put a shaking hand over her burgundy-colored mouth.

"I don't see anyone anywhere." Peter jogged across the narrow road and climbed the gentle slope that gave him a better view of this swatch of the grounds.

He whistled. "Not a darn thing in sight."

"I wonder why the tour guide never mentioned this place was haunted," the woman said. "Maybe they don't know. I'm going to mention it. Too bad we didn't get a picture of the damn thing. Might've been some dough in it for us."

I heard them above me, from the shovel cellar behind the willow, as I was locked in an accidental staring contest with a hairy spider hanging from the center of its considerable web. I waited ten more minutes before emerging. I didn't mean to freak them out. I just was embarrassed, I guess, being so vulnerable, so stupid, laying around in a Halloween cape. This was exactly the kind of weird shit that made me a pariah at school. I had no idea what this one moment of refuge, and the split-second decision to hide afterward, would end up doing. I certainly had no way of knowing that, that very day, tourists who thought I was a ghost were sharing their excitement on the bus. And I certainly couldn't have known that a man named Chess Isaacs was one of those fellow passengers, a man who, now four years later, had started as a partner in a ghost tour business. He'd carefully stored the story in his mind and, years later, would return with a plan.

Now that I know better, I wonder if the real ghost was there, sitting in the corner of the storage cellar, smirking through a curtain of dark hair, watching me set off the sequence of events that would bring us together.

GUILD WARS

If I'm going to talk about my life, especially my life before I was haunted, then I need to talk about Jack.

It wasn't always like this—just me and my dad and the random cemetery staff members who made up a kind of morose extended family. Up until fourth grade, this wasn't my life. I had real friends. I went on playdates. I even went to a sleepover birthday. And I know I shouldn't care that they all left me—some gradual like fading colors in the sun, others like they'd been shoplifted out of my life as soon as my back was turned. I mean, all the good characters in every book and movie, they never give a shit. I should've been okay with the solitude. And at first, I could convince myself for short periods of time that I was. I did this when it got too dismal. It was like pausing to dump confetti out of a jacket pocket; it was distracting and sometimes felt a bit special, but then, eventually, you had to keep walking and the rest of the sidewalk was just gray. Back then, I didn't know what it was like to read a book in the bathroom during recess, or to wait for the teacher to pair you up with someone in class when you had to have a partner. But then I made a mistake.

For English class, Mr. Gutt asked us to write a short auto-biographical essay and present it to the class. It was our first unit on oral presentations, or Tiny Toastmasters, as he called it. I'll admit, I didn't even think about my essay being a problem. There wasn't a moment of hesitation when I wrote it and not a sliver of hesitation when I slipped out of my desk chair to read it at the front of the class.

I live at Winterson Cemetery in historic Cabbagetown, home to the Riverdale Zoo and the Bloor Viaduct, better known as the Suicide Bridge. I live with both my parents. My father, Thomas Blight, burns bodies in the crematory and lives with me in a two-story apartment with a cool attic where I sleep. My mother, Mary Kalder, died when I was born in the wrong spot and is buried in what we call our front yard, but which is actually the gravesite.

I waited for the applause everyone had been afforded, even Joe Johnson, whose entire presentation was one and a half sentences long and punctuated in the middle with a burp that sounded like it smelled. But there was none, only silence, even from Mr. Gutt.

That was the day they started calling me Wednesday Addams. That went on for . . . well, it's never really ended.

In fifth grade, things changed again. I had Ms. Soul as a teacher that year. When I first read the final fourth-grade report and saw her name typed out in the "Next Year's Class" box, I was excited. *Ms J. Soul.* I looked at the name and imagined a young woman with dreamy green eyes and an aura of wispy blonde curls. I pictured her in flowing skirts and tinkling brace-lets; teaching meditation for phys ed and having the kids count the meters in a poem for math. Instead of cursing when she'd slam a finger in her desk, she'd say, "Oh Goddess!" and for lunch she'd eat petals plucked from the head of a daisy.

So, on the first day of school I was actually excited and showed up with my straight brown hair coaxed into a long ponytail, a new pair of white Keds, and a small bouquet yanked from Mrs. Howard's plot on the way out. But the Ms. J. Soul who greeted us at the side door at the final bell was a much different sort of creature altogether.

She was no taller than the median size of her class, and walked like an overweight Hitler, hands clasped together behind her back, just above the bulbous mound of her butt.

"Let's get one thing perfectly clear. Summer *is* over." Her sentences had an uneven rhythm that threw even the most perfectly mundane statement into dangerous disarray. "This is the beginning of the real school *year*, and as such, I intend for you all to *get* right to work."

I slowly folded the stalks and stems of my childish bouquet and rammed them into my back pockets before they could be seen. I counted up to ten under my breath and then back down again, tapping the pads of my thumbs against my thighs with each number.

I laid low for the first few weeks, making sure I did her work and paid attention, which wasn't all that difficult, since it had just been the year before when I'd read my fateful report and was dubbed "the weird kid."

During the second day of class, Ms. Soul handed out pastel-colored notebooks, forty-eight pages each with floppy covers stapled together along the narrow spine. Every student received five, one of each color: green, pink, orange, blue, and yellow, all muted and institutional. We also received two HB pencils and a gummy pink eraser for our "little errors," as Ms. Soul said. "And I do expect you to catch and eventually, over time, *dismiss* all your little errors."

The alphabetically ordered seating chart had my desk right next to the window. My dad said it was like putting an alcoholic in charge of an open bar: a big window to stare through, a sharpened pencil, and a total of two hundred and forty creamy lined pages of fresh landscape to populate. I resisted, just barely, for the first week. Then I started designing in the margins—vines and flowers and twisty gray branches, each side symmetrical, each number exact. By the second week of school, lead forests framed each page covered in lines of sloping letters and careful numbers.

"And just what kind of *spelling* is this, then?" Ms. Soul snatched the book from the cradle of my arms. Painfully, I had only finished four of the planned five rectangles, two rising in height to the largest shape in the middle, and then another descending. But that was only four done. It was uneven, not complete. It made my muscles tense.

"Uh, I was just . . ." I couldn't think of a damn thing to say, mostly because I'd never been that physically close to Ms. Soul before.

"Just what?" Her eyes narrowed as she spoke. "You *were* 'just what.' Ms. Blight?"

"I was just drawing."

It was barely a whisper, pushed into the empty cradle of my arms. Ms. Soul reached out with a finger and inserted it between my chest and chin. I felt that finger, clammy like the dank sprig of a lake plant, and panic jabbed into in my chest, making my arms twitch as if I'd been pinched instead of touched. Ms. Soul pulled her finger upward, my chin still attached. I'd never been touched with anger before.

"You will look *at* me when I am speaking to you."

That's right about when I started shaking, and right before I found out how much weakness made Soul's anger stronger and more venomous. The glare in her eyes sharpened and color flushed her cheeks, a deep, ugly burgundy that spoke of ill-health and bad omens.

Oh no. My bladder pinched up with sudden urine. I looked over each of the teacher's unaligned shoulders and saw my stupid classmates watching with a mix of fear and amusement. All I could think, still stuck in the vise grip of shame and a hooked finger, was *don't piss your pants, don't piss your pants*.

"I thought this was art class too!" The whole class gasped and shifted in their seats so that a sudden wave of material and breath filled the room. Ms. Soul released my chin and turned to face the student who had dared to speak. "Look, I even drew a portrait of you, Miss."

Jack Yeffen, a short boy with dark hair and small eyes but giant teeth, held up a piece of lined paper. The image of a fat pig with stick legs and Ms. Soul's thick-framed glasses snapped the class out of their shock, and the room filled with hysterics. Ms. Soul sped to Jack's desk. In that moment I got up and ran, straight out the door, down the hall, and into the girls' room.

I forced myself to return after the lunch bell, filing in with everyone else. Safety in numbers, I supposed, even though these numbers shuffled around me whispering into cupped hands, collecting words for the recess yard where they would throw them about like gossipy farmers planting sentences into the dirt so rumors could grow.

Assholes. My cheeks hurt with an intense flush.

Jack wasn't in class the remainder of the day. I assumed that he was dead and mourned him quietly, the brave boy with the huge teeth. But there he was, back in his desk after the last bell. He and I ended up in detention for the rest of the week—both during recesses and after school, under the careful security of Ms. Soul and her heavy anger. We couldn't so much as look at each other without a ruler coming down hard on her desk to shock us back to work—writing out each and every line of the multiplication table up to twelve, over and over again. All those even numbers were a small comfort.

On the final day of our sentence, we were allowed out for afternoon recess, since Ms. Soul had a meeting. We walked down the hallway toward the metal double doors in silence, beaten voiceless for now. He opened the door and held it for me, smiling in the sun like a prisoner let out of a box, which was mostly true. We walked out into the yard and stood there, hands on our hips, watching the kids run and yell around us. Not us; we were hardened and matured. We regarded them with the nostalgia of the old. Jack broke the silence.

"Hey, why is everyone at this school part of the same guild?"

"Huh?"

"It's, like, everyone is Ascension. And somehow, we're the only Asylum. It's a damn good thing we have mage-level abilities, or we'd really be screwed."

I didn't play computer games like Jack did, but still, I understood completely. We were surrounded by hostiles—invisible to most, despised by others—but at least we were together in this dumbed-down elementary prison.

From that day onward we were kind of thrown together by virtue of our oddities. Jack was, by all accounts, an internet-gaming nerd with bad teeth and the shoulder width of a newborn, but for some reason he refused to give a shit. He was

skinny, dark, and was both loud and confident. It made people
nervous.

And me, well, I lived in a goddamn cemetery. Physically,
there was nothing unusual about me. But, like all kids, the
students at Regent Park Elementary could feel the loneliness.
And the Addams Family taunts were still going strong, regular
enough to be part of the daily routine but new enough to make
me flinch. I guess wearing my mother's old clothes—faded con-
cert T-shirts with beadwork—didn't exactly help.

After the pig portrait incident, Jack and I didn't suddenly
become cohorts in mischief or anything; we didn't plan any
pranks and were not known for being a bad influence on one
another, but still, after that glorious fifth-grade year, we were
never together in the same classroom again. We had to resign
ourselves to recess, lunch, and a couple afternoons a week of
hanging out after school. And at the end of each excruciating
year, we were set loose on the summer months.

The July we were both thirteen, the summer after eighth
grade, Jack arrived on his BMX and we sat on the couch in the
living room, the dog smashed in between us, watching *Ghost
Hunters, Inc.* It was Jack's latest obsession. Dad, who thought the
show was nonsense and let us know by sighing his way through
the first fifteen minutes, headed up to bed early.

"Hey, Win. Can we go for a walk?"

After the gates closed I became an inmate at Winterson as
much as the Pierros (1920–1994) and Baby Boy McCoy (1987).
I was thirteen, but my dad was still cautious to an extreme.
I didn't give him much to worry about with my sedate social
life, so it hadn't yet become a struggle. But I knew Jack meant
we would wander the grounds. He was, after all, a freak like me.

"Sure. Let's go."

We carried Dingleberry and our sneakers down the stairs to the bottom foyer, settled him in the wagon, and yanked our shoes over sweaty feet. The dog was about five pounds lighter back then but was still a narcoleptic butterball. It was cooler outside, and the hiccupping and scraping of summer bugs punctuated the drone of the cars from the road, only the buses whining and screeching above them all like predatory birds.

"Which way do you want to go?" Jack was stretching out his long arms over his head. It made his T-shirt lift up, and a slice of pale belly peeked above the waistband of his jeans.

"The Peak?"

"Perfect. Let's go, D-Man." He grabbed the wagon handle and started pulling Dingleberry.

When I was little, I'd thought the graves by the cliff, the ones in that section known as "Widow's Peak," needed a family, and so I became somewhat of a matriarch. I felt sorry for their neglect—long grass covering the crumbling inscriptions on soft rock; unworn pathways barely delineated from the fields; flowerless plots and unappreciated statues rounded by time and weather, guarding the long-forgotten bones.

Every Saturday for years, right after dinner when Dad was retiring to the front room to watch the news, I'd carry Dingleberry downstairs and put him in the wagon. Then we'd roll down the front walkway, back around the house and up Soldiers' Memorial Lane. The Peak slouched off behind a collection of willows that grew together so close that their branches were braided and their boughs shared one set of gnarled, gray skin. It was a small piece of land that ended abruptly where the ground dropped off into a ravine eighteen feet below, bordered by pines and shopping carts. Down there was where the teen-agers partied, on the banks of the stream littered with crinkled chip bags and broken glass glittering through the branches like jewelry on a sad woman.

Summer evenings are best for this kind of visit. A gentle sort of gloom settles over the tombs and statues like the thinnest layer of jam—sticky and opaque, making everything appetizing and appalling at the same time. Moisture collects in the shadows, dripping warm and cool until morning. Insects sing louder, ser-enading the sun down behind the ravine like a sleepy toddler hanging its bright head. Purple and blue muscle their way out of the green-gray landscape, and slippery trails from fat snails snake across the stones. This is the time when the ghosts come out, sliding from under earth, pulling faces against the purple sky. You couldn't really see them exactly; they lived in that spot in the corner of your eye that skips out of existence when you turn.

The only thing I liked better than visiting the graves at night (which is one of the reasons I wasn't invited to parties) was playing marbles with the glass eyes left over from cremations (definitely a reason I wasn't invited to parties). Truly, I lived a fairy-tale childhood. Like, a Grimms' fairy tale.

"Are you sure you've never seen a ghost here?" Jack asked.

"I think so, not like a movie ghost or anything, that's for sure."

"I wanna set up a few things while we're out. Is that cool? I have to go to camp tomorrow and I haven't had a chance to try out anything yet." Jack was itching to test the homemade ghost-hunting devices he'd been piecing together. We were both aware that time was running out for us to be able to follow our own weird whims. Soon enough we'd have to conform. It was sad and exciting at the same time. We felt the panic of real life pulling at the edges of our imagination-built fortress, like a rainstorm or a monster. Yeah, more like a monster.

We pushed through the bushes to the Peak and spread one of the blankets from the wagon over the sharp grass so we could sit there and watch the night fold itself dark. "You really think ghosts are real?"

"Sure, why the hell not? I mean, we're just skin bags of bones and flesh, and we're real." He demonstrated his animation by punching at the air in front of him with brave little jabs. "That's the *real* spooky shit."

Jack's parents wanted him to grow up to play football and date blonde girls named Madison, so it was better they didn't know he was at the cemetery with a weirdo. He told them he was at the movies. In a way, added to the potentially embarrassing nature of our infantile pursuits, him sneaking over here made things exciting.

We walked over to the patch of green between the graves and the drop-off to the ravine. "If you want to see ghosts," I said, "I think this is your best chance."

"Right now? Uh, okay."

I detected a bit of hesitation, now that we were actually going to hunt ghosts. "Are you scared or something?"

"No." He tucked a curl behind his ear with his long fingers. "But can I stop at the washroom first?" He was joking and lightly punched my shoulder to make sure I knew it.

I spun again, smiling, then sank down on crossed legs to the grass.

"I don't think there are ghosts here. They can't be bothered." I sounded stupid, I knew it.

It was bright under the moon and I wished there were more clouds. I felt exposed. I smiled too much, too big.

"Uh, so, is this where your mom is buried?"

Well, that took care of the smiling problem. "Yeah."

There was a moment of silence. "She was cremated first."

"Oh." He coughed. "Cool. I mean, not cool, but like . . ."

I put a hand on his arm, letting him know he could stop.

Jack walked around, checking for spots to put his equipment. It looked less trashy down in the ravine now that the humidity had coated everything in a layer of green and the seasonal rains had made the area too damp to enjoy as a party plot just yet. It looked almost pretty; even the ragweed was lush and tropical. I felt a stab of pride when Jack threw his arms out and walked the area with a goofy smile on his face.

"This is so cool. Honestly."

Then he walked over and grabbed my upper arms in his hands, talking into my face. "I can't believe you get to live here! This is, like, the best place ever." My stomach broke loose from its moorings long enough to flip over once and readjust.

Jack let me go and unpacked his backpack. Then he hung bells from the tree branches. Next, compasses and magnets were placed on top of alternating gravestones, and an old AM/FM radio was tuned to a spot between stations so that a steady stream of static poured into the grass.

"Uh, what is all this garbage?"

"This is not garbage. These are the tools of the trade, my friend. In light of not being able to get my hands on an actual EMF reader and the like, I make do. Now help me set up this tripod."

We finished setting out the camera and trip wires and powdering the stones and then lay on the blanket propped up on our elbows, side by side. Crickets sent codes through the tall grass.

"So, what exactly are we waiting for?"

Jack pushed himself up a bit. "Listen, Winifred, if you're going to be a ghost hunter, the first thing you need to find is some damn patience. Seriously, woman, you need to just breathe in, and let it go." He demonstrated, and then lay back on the blanket, hands folded over his chest.

"Whatever." I rolled my eyes but joined him on my back, aware of how close our arms were. "This is a weird hobby. I mean, shouldn't you just be locked in your room watching porn like every other thirteen-year-old boy?"

Immediately after I said it, I wished I hadn't. Mentioning sex at all was awkward, but masturbation? *Jesus, Winifred. Awesome, just amazing.*

"Yeah, right. But if you're the one who's bringing it up . . . what kind of porn do you watch, Win?" I thought he'd be sheepish or embarrassed, but instead he was eager to talk. "The kind with story lines? Or the compilations?"

"Compilations?"

"Yeah, you know." He was on his side again. I couldn't look at him, so I kept my eyes on the weighty moon. "Compiled scenes, like 'Ten Best Money Shots,' or 'Greatest Gang Bangs of the Year.'"

Why the hell had I brought this up? "As if." I snorted—actually snorted. "I don't watch porn." But of course I watched porn. I watched porn more than I cared to admit to myself, and not just out of academic curiosity. But that wasn't something I was going to talk about. I tried to keep the counting made in my movements small so that he wouldn't notice: I tapped my thumb and forefingers against one another seven times, then swung my ankles in circles—three full turns in one direction, then three back the other way. There. I was okay.

"I hear girls like watching lesbian porn. Is that true?" He reached across and poked me in the arm twice.

"What? Are you reading porn research sites? God. You're so dumb." I wished he would stop. But more than anything, I wished he would poke my arm just one more time, so I could match up his three to my threes—the ones I'd made with my ankle rotations. *Dammit!* As an emergency solution, I crossed one arm over my chest and poked the opposite arm twice. There. Now there were matched sets.

"You can tell me. We're the same guild, remember?"

I softened, remembering our friendship, the close ties that bound us together underneath this new attraction that was distracting me to math.

"Okay." I sighed. "Of course, I've seen porn. But I don't, like, actually *watch* it or anything. I've just *seen* it." *What the hell does that mean?*

He laughed, just once, and then settled onto his back again, arm pushed up against mine. I felt like I'd handed over something valuable and had gotten nothing in return. I felt ripped off in a way that gave me vertigo, like I had lost my footing.

The underside of the willow extended above us like a green circulatory system, so I turned my attention to that. It was hard not to feel like there must be magic, that there must be spirits and ghosts and just "something else" out here, just for us, even just for now. I closed my eyes and tried to listen. I matched my inhales to Jack's inhales, struggling to exhale just as long, just as full. It was making me light-headed to keep up. It wasn't synchronicity, but it was as close as I could make it.

Bells. The snap and flash of the camera.

"What the hell . . ."

Jack was already on his feet while I struggled to my knees.

"We got one!" he yelled, bounding over a row of compasses set out in a rough plus sign and toward the entrance to the Peak. He stopped, the excited color draining from his cheeks.

"Oh, shit. I'm sorry about that, sir."

When I reached him, Jack was helping a man in a red jogging suit to his feet. Apparently, he'd tripped over the wire, which had then set off the camera.

"Well, Jesus. What is all this?" The jogger brushed off his knees and yanked his earbuds out of his ears.

Turns out he was more startled than hurt. Thank God—not that I'd get in trouble. Floyd would just tell him it was his own damn fault for being there at night, after visiting hours. And running, and not from anything giving chase, of all the asinine things to be doing.

Jack launched into his ghost hunter's spiel and then apologized to the jogger, gladly showing him the makeshift ghost-detection laboratory set up in the Peak when asked. They shook hands goodbye and we watched the red suit jog off up Remembrance Lane.

We settled back in to wait.

"I read that dogs are great at spotting spirits." Jack stretched one foot out to nudge Dingleberry. He was splayed out on a towel at our feet, a baby bonnet slipping over his eyes, tongue sticking out the side of his mouth. "Jesus, where does he even get these clothes?"

"Flea markets. Garage sales."

"But, I mean, why?"

I glanced over at Dingleberry, snoring ungracefully through his nose. "It suits his personality."

We kept trying to pretend this was just another Saturday, ignoring the fact that Jack was being dragged to camp tomorrow, but it came up now and then.

"It's such bullshit." I flipped over from my elbows onto my back, ripping a dandelion to fluff. "That you have to go away. Total bullshit."

"Yeah, I know." Jack also flipped over, leaving a walkie-talkie on the ground above his head (the matched handset was attached to a string dangling in a hole we'd dug beside the one of the graves). "I mean, it's not horrible, I guess. Soon I can take the leadership course and be a counselor."

I thought about all the blonde Madisons who might be there with him, in their bathing suits and easy laughter. "Yeah, I guess so. But I mean, I suppose this ghost-hunting stuff isn't too sucky either."

"Yeah, and hanging out too." He cleared his throat a little aggressively. "I like hanging out with you."

I caught my breath. *Don't read too much into it, Winifred.*

"I wonder if there'll be other ghost jerks at the camp?"

"Uh, I doubt it. This is a sports camp my dad makes me go to every year to try to get me to 'man up.'" He followed this with a sarcastic flex of his arms.

"Ha ha, put those noodles away." I punched his bicep.

"Noodles of steel." He growled in a baritone, rubbing his arm.

"The only thing steel about you is in your mouth." I didn't mean to be unkind, but his face fell a bit.

"Hey, soon enough my braces will come off." When he had finally grown into his teeth they'd started getting crowded, so these last few years had been lip cuts and orthodontic appointments.

"Awesome."

"Yeah, no more snacks for days stuck in the tracks."

"Sick!"

Dingleberry sighed and shifted his head a little.

We flipped over onto our backs. After a minute, Jack cleared his throat again and remarked, "I'm just kidding, of course. It's not that gross. I take care of them."

"Whatever, man. I'm not your mom, I don't care." I cared. I cared about anything he wanted to tell me.

"Yeah, I know. I just didn't want you to think I was nasty." He turned on his side and started digging a distracted hole with his finger.

He looked a bit hurt. "Relax, I believe you. I'm sure your hygiene is impeccable."

The air felt heavy, and there was something else there too. At first I thought it might actually be a ghost, but then I realized it was Jack. Something was off. He was acting strange.

"Are you nervous about camp?"

"Camp? Nah. I can handle myself." He ripped up blades of grass and put them on the blanket in a small pile between us. "Besides, it's only for two weeks."

"Okay, what's up then? You're acting all weird. Is it school? Because we agreed we weren't going to stress about that until the last week of August."

He sighed, grabbed the grass pile he'd made, and threw it straight up so that grass rained down over us both. Then he rolled over onto his side and reached for me. I was shocked, it happened so fast. And I realized I'd been waiting for this since summer began. I smiled to let him know it was okay.

There was a tremor in his hands when he pulled me closer. He leaned in and pushed his face down into my neck, moving my whole body into him. And then he exhaled into my neck, so that the breath found voice, so that it snaked down the back of my T-shirt and filled my ear at the same time.

There are some sounds that make the whole world turn. On days when I'd wake up to rain, I'd run outside to put china teacups in the garden, between the mums, underneath the peonies, because the sound of rain plinking into a teacup ran across the roof of my mouth.

And then there was the sound of the dog's wagon, grinding under his considerable weight, crunching fallen leaves and slicing through the squishy gray muck on the gravel paths like spoons in a bowl of cereal. This sound made my breath feel huge, like it reached every part of me, all the way to the backs of my knees.

But *this* sound, Jack's breath in my ear with one hand in my hair, the other on my lower back, this sound made me open up. This sound was added to the orchestra. My lips parted, my eyes rolled, I lay the weight of my head into his palm and he pulled back a bit. That's when I went for it, before I could lose my nerve. I pushed my face forward and kissed him.

How could this be an option in everyday life? How were people not kissing every moment they were awake? How were they not joined together in sleep, lips between each other, breath cyclical, the electricity of bodies into one another? How could anyone work or read or dream while this was a possibility?

I latched my hands on the back of his neck and lay back so that he was pulled on top of me. The hard weight of him with the soft searching of his mouth made my back arch. His tongue was slow, hesitant. I turned my head to allow him more access, desperate for more, more, more. I wasn't demanding; I was too full of ache and flutter to act on the aggression that was centered in my lower stomach. Everything was so slow and delicate and agony. I couldn't even think straight. This is why people close their eyes when they kiss; there's no way to focus when all the blood and thump and pitch is below the waist.

It couldn't be more than this, this was everything. And then he slid a hand up my shirt. In my head I had played out this scenario. I was pulled out of the moment to stress about the size and proportion of my breasts. Were they enough for him? They were enough for me. I loved the way they fit in my favorite shirts, the way they jumped to attention under my own fingers. But now they weren't just for me, were they? I was worried about making him love them, love everything about me.

God, did I love him? If I listened to my body right now, filling up and finding new ways to knot into him, it would scream *love, yes, we love this boy!* But a body isn't a reliable source. It's impressionable, easily influenced, too mechanical to trust with emotion. Still, I said it, like a complete idiot. "I love you, Jack."

The words were like fingers snapping, and we came to. His face pulled back and our eyes opened. "Ahh, Freddie." He smiled. "I love you too. You're the best friend a guy could ask for."

Fuck.

BREAKING APART

On the day I turned sixteen, Jack was the first person I thought of. I was finally old enough to want real love, and young enough to run at it—like, head-down, arms-spinning kind of running. And even with all the abandon I put at my heels to push forward, I still needed a safe impact. I needed to not die from it. I had decided years ago—that night, after we kissed at the Peak, after we talked about sex in a way that made me acutely aware of heaviness in my thighs, a weight that made it difficult to bend my knees—that Jack could hold the brunt of my impact. Jack would be my first. I was sure. And I wanted it to be tonight, the night I turned sixteen. That was the kind of shit that happened to the girls on Netflix, so why not me?

Once again, it was only me, Dad, and Dingles for my birthday. Once again, I pretended I was okay with it.

"Think we should go to a movie tonight?" I tried to think of ways to make the day last longer or more special, so that it stood out the way movies let me know sixteenth birthdays are supposed to.

"If you want."

"We can just stay in and rent something."

"Whatever you want."

My dad read the paper while I ate. His cake slice sat untouched on its paper plate.

"Maybe Jack can come over?" I tried to sound casual.

He nodded, out of words, which tended to happen quickly these days, even more than usual.

"I'll give him a call then."

I left him and the dog in the kitchen and ran up the narrow steps to my room in the attic. It was my favorite place in the whole world, except for maybe the Peak. Both were quiet as a cup. Both held me in their hollow like milk.

I climbed into the crocheted hammock and held my phone for a minute before dialing Jack. This had started happening near the end of ninth grade—having to take a minute to pre- pare before calling someone I'd been best friends with for years. I wasn't sure if it was the awkward second-guessing that had started popping into my day like pulled stitches, or if it was because I'd started thinking more and more about the kind of love I was pretty sure I needed.

They say that loving yourself is an act of rebellion. I wanted to be a rebel. I wanted it in ways more than just wearing Cure T-shirts in a sea of pastel or braiding my hair so tight that my eyes looked more like my mother's. I wanted to love myself so hard I felt whole. I wanted to love myself so big I felt entombed. I wanted a love so beautiful there was more to my belonging than just the curve and grip of a hammock holding me or the ways in which I could touch myself to gasping. And sometimes, in this love, it was more than just me. Sometimes there was Jack.

→))))-

The summer between ninth and tenth grade, the puberty fairy had visited Jack, fallen in love with him, and bestowed all her best gifts in such a frenzy, he was left with stretch marks. He had nothing to wear for a month, until the great transformation ended. His mother drove him to the mall dressed in his father's gray sweat suit to buy new separates that would fit over his six-foot frame, filled out to symmetrical and blemish-free perfection. He got a better haircut and his jaw seemed to widen. The only small piece of the old Jack that remained lay embedded in his braces, and then those came off halfway through the year.

Things changed after that. Suddenly, Jack had more friends than time, many of them girls. This made me jealous. I told myself it was because there were a hundred new dumbasses competing for his attention and I'd started taking a backseat to them. And it was that, for sure, except there was something more too. Something that made me pause before I called him, all the familiarity pushed out of simple movements.

This is stupid. Don't be stupid, Winifred. I dialed his number, and he picked up right away.

"Freddie."

I hated being called Freddie. Every time someone said it, I had a flash of Freddie Mercury in a lamé jumpsuit hitting a high note. Not that I didn't appreciate Freddie Mercury, just that it was distracting and usually not an appropriate time to be having a mini Queen stroke. "'Sup?"

"Nothing. 'Sup?"

"It's my birthday."

"I know."

"Wanna come over?"

"Sure."

He hung up and I lay back in my hammock.

I swung the hammock with a push of my toes, singing an old Smiths song and thinking about the way he laughed. Jack was all angles and awkwardness when he was forced to sit still or catch a ball in gym class. But there was this thing he had, this grace, when he forgot to fit in, like when he laughed, big and with his whole body involved. Jack made being a misfit graceful. I imagined the way he must move when he slept, probably with arms thrown up in wild abandon, sweat on his smooth skin, naked from the waist up under a *Star Wars* duvet. I squeezed a pillow between my knees, thinking about him in his too-small bed.

I got up and jumped in the shower. Then I brought the razor back into my room and sat in front of my desk in a towel and switched on my laptop. I went to a porn site and referenced the women from girl-on-girl scenes, the same ones Jack accused me of watching. These women were hairless except for the explosion of curls and waves on their heads like the feathered crowns of Vegas chorus girls. They looked like they would topple over, and then they did—into each other, onto beds, across couches. But there was always a man. No matter how much they held onto themselves and each other, there was always a man. The frame on pause, I concentrated on shaving my pubic hair into a bit of a punctuation mark like one of the actresses. Then I worked my shoulder-length bob into a full sweep that left one eye covered, a purposeful handicap.

Jack showed up around eight. I met him at the side door with a blanket.

"Let's go to the Peak."

"Sure thing." He was always so casual, so nonchalant. I was full of chalants. Enough for both of us. Enough to make me awkward. Adding to the awkward was the fact that my crotch was already itching from my less-than-expert shave.

"Can't believe it's finally summer—woot woot!" Jack was kicking rocks and snapping low-hanging branches as we walked.

"Yeah, thank God school is done. It's the literal bane of my existence."

"Oh, c'mon, Winifred, it's not that bad." He pushed me slightly. "You're a smart egg."

"Yeah, it's not bad for you maybe. I'm smart, but the system itself is whack. I mean, how are we still living in a time when every book we study is written by a dead white guy?" Frig, I was really not setting the mood here.

He tossed a rock into the trees with a tight jump shot and laughed. "Classic Freddie."

We pushed through the bushes and into the clearing. There was a quarter-moon embedded in the sky like a comma, a pause before the connecting sentiment. More punctuation—I was sensing a theme here.

I spread out the blanket in the center of the gravestone arc and sat. Jack threw himself into a recline on his side, his elbow bent, propping up his head in a hand. "What are you up to this summer anyway?"

"Uh, this, I guess." I indicated the cemetery around us. "Helping out and reading. I might look for a part-time gig in Cabbagetown—a coffee shop maybe." I was lying.

"Cool. Yeah, I leave for camp counselor training tomorrow, but only for July. I'll be back for the last half of summer at least." He lowered himself onto his back and folded his hands over his chest. "It's not so bad. Camp is fun, and at least next year I'll be on salary."

"Cool." Not cool. He was leaving tomorrow? It was now or never. Well, at least now or not until August. And that was too far away. I'd spend the next month stressing about it, over-thinking it. I couldn't casually tap and count and fidget the patterns that would be required to try to cage in that anxiety. I'd have to count in fractions.

I let him go on about his parents and their expectations. (Poor Jack, expected to go to a good university, to work at his dad's law firm, to travel and be healthy and show up for sit-down dinner every night at a real dining room table with placemats and centerpieces and everything.) I lay down beside him and began moving over, pretending to be uncomfortable, until my head was on his shoulder.

Now or never.

I popped my head up and rolled onto my stomach when he paused. "Hey, so, I was thinking . . ." He turned to look at me. Nerves bubbled up my throat and I tried to push them down with a loud swallow. "I mean, you know how you were my first kiss?"

He laughed, pushed his arm out, and scooped me in toward him so that I was half on top now. "Yeah. How could I forget? You were mine too."

"Wellll, today is kind of a big deal. Sixteen . . . . I was kind of hoping you'd give me a gift."

"Oh shit, I'm so sorry, dude. I didn't have time to get anything. Besides, what the hell do you get a legend?"

"No, I mean, I was hoping you could take something from me?" Was I really saying this? Asking this? I wanted to stop now, but the words were already out there and the look on his face showed he was puzzling it out.

"Take something?"

"Yeah, take 'it.' You know what I mean?"

"It?"

I raised my eyebrows, trying to will him to understand.

"Wait." He sat up, and I rolled off him. "Do you mean, your virginity?"

I covered my face with my hands. "God, you don't have to say it out loud." It sounded so transactional. "Plus, I mean, virginity is a myth, really. There is nothing to actually take . . ." I rambled on, already losing my nerve.

"Are you serious?" He was genuinely shocked. He even laughed a bit, incredulous.

"Jesus, no, forget it, okay." *Shit. What was I thinking?*

"No, Freddie. I'm not laughing at you." He pulled my hands away from my face. "I'm not, I promise. It's just, unexpected, you know? It's not something that gets offered to you on the regular."

He scooted over closer and, still gripping my forearms, pulled me up so that I was sitting beside him, still folded forward in embarrassment.

"Hey, I'm honored to be considered for the job." He let me go and then did the stupidest thing ever, the thing I will remember forever about my sixteenth birthday—he fucking punched me in the arm and said, "So how do you want to do this? Should we kiss? Or like, get down to business, or what?" Like we were discussing an art project. Or a heist. Transactional. Like an equation we . . . or rather, I, had to tackle. Two minus one equals one.

"What the hell, Jack? How do I want to do this? How do I want to do this?" I moved away.

"Oh, Jesus, sorry. I guess I should take the lead since you're the virgin here." He scooted back over and reached for my hand. I yanked it away.

"You're not a virgin?"

"What the hell, no!" He said it like I had insulted him.

"When did this happen? I thought I was your best friend?" Why was this the hill I was willing to die on—not that he was treating my proposal like a casual suggestion that we grab a pizza, but instead, that I was out of the loop? Not that he didn't know me well enough to anticipate what I would want, but that he didn't know me well enough to tell me about important things anymore?

"It's nothing." He tried to smile, managed a small one, and then rocked backward so he had enough momentum to push onto his feet. He brushed at the seat of his pants with his hands.

What the hell was he doing? Who the hell just gets up in the middle of, of whatever we were doing?

I stood up too. Once I was on my feet, I wasn't sure what to do. Anger started to fill in the uncertainty. I felt humiliated. I felt like someone was watching and I was being judged. Except it was by me; I was the judge, and there was no escaping that.

He looked anywhere except at me, and when he did, he just giggled a bit and said—of all things to say—"It's just that, I don't know, sometimes you're . . . weird about stuff."

"What do you mean?" I moved back. This wasn't going anywhere good. What had just happened? "I'm weird?"

He of all people knew how this one word—this one stupid word—had isolated me, had made me a pariah at school while people like him got to think "school's not that bad, dude."

"Freddie, listen, people change is all. And we don't, you know, it's just that it's not like 'you and me against the world' and shit anymore. We're not little kids."

Jesus, this hurt. I squinted my eyes so I didn't have to see everything at once. I wished the dramatic hair sweep had worked out, wished I only had one eye to view my own humiliation with. "You're a real asshole right now."

"C'mon, Freddie. You'll always be my friend because we grew up together, just not the day-to-day 'tell each other everything' kind of friends. Don't get crazy about it." He fussed with the drawstring on his shorts, avoiding eye contact.

I wanted to laugh. I started to. "I don't know what you do with your other friends, but, like, this is kind of a big deal for me." I grew shy. "It, it was going to be my first time doing . . . anything."

He laughed, turning to face me. "Wait, like, anything? I'm not the only guy you've kissed, am I?"

That was it. I was zero-to-a-hundred pissed. "Why is that so hard to believe? Maybe it meant nothing to you because you're going to your camp tomorrow to fuck some of your friends there?"

How did I get here?

"Maybe I already have." He wasn't laughing anymore. There was a hard edge to his jaw; his teeth were clenched like he was rolling spit or keeping something stored in his cheek. "You don't know everything in my entire life, Freddie."

I was mortified, embarrassed beyond belief. I had thought he liked me. I'd thought the best moment of my life was about to happen. But it wasn't even enough of a moment to slip inside a baby food jar on my shelf.

"Fred, just come here." He tried to reach for me, but I was already walking away. "Come on. Let's talk at least. Maybe we're not friends like that anymore because we can be something else, or . . . I don't know."

I turned back and he was standing there with his hands held out, head tilted. Wasn't he offering me what I had asked for? My desperate want, even now, sat like serrated knives in my chest. His shorts were kind of low on one hip and I saw that beautiful handle of bone and the start of muscle. His hair was messy and so perfect. But why did he have to add that "I don't know" to the end of "maybe we can be something else"? He was feeling something, and obviously it was pity. I filled my lungs with air and closed my eyes as I spoke, so I didn't have to watch the words land.

"Fuck you, Jack."

I stormed away, rubbing a hand over my lower belly, resisting the urge to scratch at my excruciating attempt at grooming. The path was longer than usual; I couldn't leave the Peak behind quickly enough, couldn't get away from the wrench humiliation had pushed between my ribs and turned sideways. I slowed my steps and listened, hoping Jack wasn't following me, and hoping Jack was following me.

Footsteps—a light crunch and roll at the side of the asphalt.

I turned my head, not quite stopping. The grounds rose on the curve and Jack and the path to the Peak had been swallowed in green and there was nothing but space and the rub and pull of insect songs. I turned back and walked quicker.

Crunch. Crunch.

I looked quick over my shoulder. Nothing. The hair on the back of my neck moved.

"Hello?" I whispered, not wanting Jack to think I was talking to him.

No answer. Oddly, the silence was the right answer.

Already humiliated, feeling torn apart, I decided I didn't care if I was being followed. So instead of rushing, I slowed right down, counting the steps that were not coming from my feet. They were even and exact, the perfect sound for counting, and the numbers I mumbled under my breath loosened the wrench in my ribs. Thinking back, I don't know what I thought it was—maybe my imagination, maybe another midnight runner. All I know is that by the time I passed through the gate into my front yard proper, my breath was even as math.

This is how I left my best friend, who was definitely not my best friend anymore, under a willow in a cemetery—followed and alone at the same time. This is how the stage was set for something bigger than the both of us. There was some kind of new potential being placed on the ground. All it needed was the right prayer to make it grow.

THE SHAPE OF A FACE

The first time I talked to anyone about sex was with my mother's aunt Roberta while we waited for the cable guy to install her new router. I was twelve and she was like a hundred and six.

Roberta lived at Wigwamen Terrace, the seniors' building beside the Friendship Centre. Roberta liked to tell fortunes with a deck of cards, only they were regular playing cards instead of the tarot ones you're supposed to use. Her apartment always smelled like mini donuts, the kind you get at the midway, but I never saw her cook. And once a month, I would go over to her place to dye her hair blue-black with a box kit so she could cut down on the number of times she had to wash her hair, even though I explained that it shouldn't.

My favorite thing about visiting Roberta was the way she talked so much shit about her neighbors.

"The Inuk man on the first floor is a hoarder. I seen his place, boxes right up to the ceiling. Could go up like a Roman candle at any time."

"The Inuk man" was actually the superintendent, and the apartment she was so worried about was the building storage room. Also, he was from Singapore.

"Can't stand all the scooters parked in the damn hall. It's like a bumper car rink in here."

She was just salty because disability hadn't approved her for one yet. She blamed this oversight on her "dancer's calves" being too strong to fail a medical exam. "I was a great powwow dancer back in my day, boy I tell you. And not traditional style neither. I danced fancy shawl right up until I had to retire." Retirement was powwow code for "until I got too fat to fit into my regalia or to make it to the end of a song without hyperventilating."

My least favorite thing about visiting Roberta was when her daughter Penny would show up. She was old, like at least thirty, and skinny in a way that sharpened her to mean. She took enough time with her makeup that it made you suspicious. *Like, what are you hiding, lady?* She always had a different job. One summer she worked in the Friendship Centre kitchen, so she slept most nights next door at her mother's. That winter she was taking a paid training gig through the employment center, learning how to collect data and report on it. But by spring she was a janitor at the women's transitional home. The one thing she kept constant was a part-time phone job as a psychic. She couldn't even predict where she'd be working a week ahead, so I didn't know how she could help anyone else.

"It's a soft con," she'd explained, watching me stripe Roberta's head with creamy dye. "Nobody gets hurt and I get paid. It's a win-win situation."

"Yes, yes. Until you tell someone the dead sent a message and the dead don't like what you said. Then you deal with them." Roberta huffed, crossing her arms over her low breasts under the sheet we'd draped on top of her housecoat to keep it safe. "Not me, no siree. I don't need that kinda trouble."

We tolerated each other, Penny and I, in that tiny apartment, and on Easter and Roberta's birthday, both of which we celebrated at the Swiss Chalet. I didn't like her impatience with her mother, especially when Roberta started getting more forgetful. And she didn't seem to like that I took up any physical space or the annoying way I needed to breathe air.

Since Roberta's funeral, I hadn't spent time with Penny; that was over a year and a half ago. I did see her one time, at her mother's grave, smoking in a pair of oversized sunglasses taped at the side. I turned down the first lane that split off the path and pretended not to notice her. She did the same. Small kindnesses, I supposed.

I went over on the day Roberta was having a modem put in for cable. She couldn't wrap her head around the need for this black box just to watch her shows. "What the hell do I need a computer attached to my TV for? I can watch *The Young and the Restless* without a computer." Roberta was sulking, and sulking for Roberta meant being loud and argumentative and moving around the small apartment with arms like chicken wings— short and flappy at her sides.

"That's how TV is now, Auntie." I said it around an Oreo that coated my teeth in grit.

"There's always something more now. Everyone has to add something to something." She was barely making sense. This was the afternoon I noticed her beginning to change. But instead of sinking back into herself like other old people had the decency to do, she turned herself inside out, showed me the thick parts inside. "Can't even screw without extras anymore."

"Auntie!" I was genuinely shocked. I'd heard her cuss, but not in a way that talked about the things people did to each other, not in a personal way. It hadn't even occurred to me that she knew the choreography of these things.

"S'true. Every damn show has people doing it in different ways." She snapped her arms down hard so that they clapped against her padded hips, then she rounded the small kitchen table where we did puzzles. "And it's only gonna get worse with a damn computer sending more shows in here, more people doing it."

The cable guy pretended he couldn't hear her, but a slow creep of red colored in the space between the bottom of his sweaty hairline and the roll of his collared shirt. I felt embarrassed, but not enough to walk her out of the room, into the bedroom maybe, or out onto her tiny balcony just big enough for two bodies if they faced one another.

"My girl, people only need to want to hold onto themselves and someone else at the same time and they'll figure it out, put things where they fit. You don't need no equipment or sexy words to convince you to do anything. No one needs convincing. You do or you don't." She fluttered to the couch, tried to sit and then stood back up right away. This man in her house with his small tool belt and spools of wire, doing things she didn't understand, had her flustered to mobility.

"You do or you don't what?"

"Want it."

I thought she was speaking in absolutes. Either a person was one who had sex or a person was one who did not, there were no in-betweens. I thought Penny was the kind of person who looked like she wanted it. I thought Penny looked like she *thought* she wanted it but then was the kind of person who halfway through would look over a shoulder and decide that this was not what she wanted at all. It made me feel sad for her.

-------»»»»-

That same afternoon of the cable guy and the lecture about sex, Roberta told me something else once we were alone—a story about love, which felt to me like the opposite of sex sometimes.

She was supposed to marry a boy from Wisconsin. They'd been pen pals since they were twelve, back in the days when you had to use paper and stamps. They met at a summer camp run by the Catholic Church for poor kids. Their parents had agreed to let them get married when she turned eighteen. That's how things were—just all matter-of-fact. Roberta assured me that eighteen was hella old back then; eighteen was time to start thinking about mortgages and college funds.

So, when she turned eighteen, he took the Greyhound from his rez with his mother, a younger sister, and two first cousins.

"I knew as soon's he stepped off the bus he wasn't for me."

"Was he ugly?" I couldn't imagine my great-auntie in this grand, cross-border romance.

"Nah," she answered. "He was handsome, alright. Looked good in his suit too. But still, I knew."

"How?"

"Someone else had the right-shaped face." She stared out her kitchen window at the totem pole on the front lawn of the Friendship Centre. A black squirrel sat on top, staring back at her.

"What do you mean, the right-shaped face?"

"Huh?" She looked at me, confused for a minute, then picked up the thread once more. "For the hole in my chest. I didn't feel unlocked." She made the motion of turning a key with her right hand, as if she were opening a door. The squirrel had caught her eye again and her voice wavered in volume. You could map out her concentration this way, with volume—like a musical score. She snapped back after a few seconds.

"But all his family was there, and all my family was there, so, I didn't say nothing. And then it was the day. And I was shit out of luck." She left the window, squirrel forgotten, and settled in at the table. I took the seat across from her. The cable guy worked quieter now, straining to listen.

"I let my sisters get me ready and my dad came in off the trapline. It was just gonna be a small thing at Ste. Anne's and then a meal at my parents'." Her fingers longed for something to do when she told a story. Sometimes they braided the fringe on her placemat. Or they folded the corner of every page in her recipe book. That day, they pushed their tips like burrowing roots into the soil of her ficus in the margarine container in the center of the table.

"We even drove over there, to the church. Borrowed the car from my cousin Tim. I made it there—oh, I loved driving, me. Made it to the parking lot. Made it to the double doors. That was as far as I got." One final push, all eight fingers buried up to the webbing in dollar-store dirt.

"I didn't even run. Just walked away. A few people hollered at me, but my sisters, especially your grandma, they held them back. They knew." She extracted her fingers and started cleaning them off on a dishcloth folded on top of the stack of placemats.

"I walked all the way home in that white wedding dress, dragging ruffles through the mud. It got caught in the screen door when I got back and ripped. I let it rip." She laughed small but full. "I went to my bedroom and pulled it off. I put on a black jumpsuit I made myself out of one of those Sears patterns. You know those?"

I nodded. I always agreed, even when I didn't know exactly what she meant. Such was the gift of Roberta's tales. She just forgot you were there and sang stories into life with you as a witness.

"I put on my black suit. Every stitch put there by these hands." She regarded her blackened hands, soil caught in the deep lines and ancient hangnails. She looked at them with such appreciation, these gnarled things covered in cheap soil, holding nothing but the memory of a failed love. "And I walked down to the shore. I sat there, on a rock over a nest of snakes too small to hiss. And I ate a peach. By myself."

"Shit." It came out in a sigh. It was the most romantic thing I could ever imagine existing. Because she knew. She held onto herself and she just knew. There was no sharp rejection, no sting of being turned away, not for her anyway. I always thought I would do that, that I would be the one leaving and not the one being left.

Maybe Jack's face wasn't the right shape after all.

The night of my sixteenth birthday fiasco, I checked my window every few minutes, waited until Jack's bike was gone so I knew he had left, waited until my father's snoring trickled from under his door like loose gravel out into the hallway, then I crept out the side door and ran across the lawn in bare feet.

Night was so still here—the absolute absence of presence. I wandered out of the little patch of lawn we delineated from the regular green expanse by a small fence, and tiptoed over the paved pathways, avoiding the soft circles of milky light thrown by iron lampposts. I hurried around the chapel with its administrative offices closed up tight for the evening and kept walking back, into the density of the grounds, away from the street, away from my house. I went over to the memorial wall, stepped up onto the low stone fence and walked its curve, the ground dropping into a scoop of valley filled with mausoleums.

I thought about my great-aunt's story, about ditching a nice boy with a good suit at the altar, about waiting for the person with the right shaped face to unlock her. Maybe such a face didn't exist for me. Maybe there was no one who could free me from being alone. I'd never felt locked up until Roberta told me you could be unlocked.

I jumped from the fence to the nub of a gravestone, as worn down as a night grinder's worry, sticking out of the gummy earth like a slanted molar with a nicotine-yellow core. I counted the cracks in the crucifix across the pathway. It was like a stone dagger jabbed into a side of a hill. The moon was still hanging like a fingernail, dividing the night in a small way I thought was just for me.

Tomorrow, Jack's parents would drive him to Muskoka for forced social interaction and allergic reactions. Maybe this was the last time I'd see him ever. I just knew he would spend August avoiding me. How could things have gone so bad?

"Twelve. Fourteen. Sixteen." The cracks were highlighted by the green moss that grew in the defects.

For some reason, counting by twos was the most calming. I let my arms hang by my sides, brushing against the skirt of the long white sundress from my mother's wardrobe. It hung to my ankles and I'd worn it because it made me feel grown, beautiful. There was a picture of my mother in the dress, laughing on the damp sand up on the bay, rocks slipping under the water behind her. That was before she grew a thumb-sucking assassin like a splinter cell. Before she was burned into ash because my dad couldn't bear the thought of putting his claustrophobic wife in a box under the ground.

"Twenty-two, twenty-four."

That was it, all the snaking fault lines that made the crucifix so dangerous, fault lines that kept Mr. Ferguson paying into the insurance and hoping for a windfall in plot sales so he could remove the hazard; all these worried cracks amounted to the same as the number of hours in a day, one measly day. He needn't have worried; it would be nearly ten years after his own peaceful passing of old age while riding the train to Washington, when it finally crumbled directly on top of a priest visiting from a Swedish parish. His church buried him with stony scales embedded in his skull, evidence of baptism by masonry. No charges, no press. They thought it might reflect poorly on the order, being smited by Jesus, and all.

I stood very still in the eyelet dress, slightly old-fashioned in design, face turned toward the fading sun, hands dangling at the end of too-skinny arms. It felt very suddenly like I was waiting for something; that some odd thing like Easter morning was slowly marching over the blurred line of the horizon dotted with root-bubbled graves. And my heart ached under my mother's dress. God, I missed Roberta.

The last Christmas we'd had together, she came to our house in a cab. She always took the same one, calling specifically for Abdi at Beck Taxi to come get her. By this point she had forgotten he was a taxi driver and that she was a customer and was contractually obligated to pay a fare.

"Bye! Don't forget to pick me up after poker." She closed the passenger door and waved goodbye. Abdi waved back, blew her a quick kiss, and then waited for me to run out a ten-dollar bill and to let him know what time he should head back to pick up "his girlfriend."

Roberta brought my dad a baseball cap that said "Native Pride" across the front with an embroidered feather. She'd forgotten he was white, or refused to accept it. I got a red journal with embossed flowers on the cover and a real lock with a tiny key to lock it up. It was a bit kiddish for fourteen, but I loved it anyway.

"That's where you write your secrets, like who you want to snag up and whatever else you want to tell your mom." She was thoughtful when she was thinking straight.

We ate ham and cranberry jelly and sang her favorite Christmas carols, including "Grandma Got Run Over by a Reindeer" and "Sweet Child o' Mine," off-key and at the top of our voices. Soon enough, Abdi was outside, honking twice. I walked her down the stairs, going first so she could hang onto my shoulders for guidance. It had started to snow, a soft flurry that looked like glitter under the yellow streetlamps. I brought her to the car, loaded her in with a parcel of leftovers and hand-made decorations for her living room, discreetly handed Abdi a ten-dollar bill to cover her fare, and leaned in the window to kiss her goodbye.

"Hey, my girl. Do me a favor?"

"What's that, Auntie?"

"Don't forget about me when you're all grown up and in love, eh? I won't be here to see it probably, but just don't forget. That's when you're really alone, when you forget. And I don't want neither of us to be alone."

"Okay, Auntie, I promise."

She looked out the front window, her face lit up by the green glow from the dashboard gauges, making neon lines in her wrinkles so that for a moment she looked like a cat. "So lucky, you, to live in this place with so many people. Imagine a world without your dead? It'd be so lonely walking around by yourself like that."

She sighed big, then swung her head to look at me. For a moment I could see her eyes skip over my features, trying to place my face, and it made my heart hurt. Then recognition came and she smiled, her smooth gums pink and wet.

"Alright then, mister." She patted Abdi's arm. "Let's go home." I stood in the drive, watching the red taillights turn onto Parliament in the tinsel twist of snow, feeling full and very empty at the same time.

I felt pretty damn alone now, even with her memory still holding onto my shoulders. I thought about Jack, about everything that had happened just hours before. A sudden wave of embarrassment pulled through my guts. And then the memory of the footsteps returned. And for a second, I saw her face—not Roberta's, but my mother's, the face frozen in the picture on the mantle. I wouldn't allow it to settle in. I jumped down from the grave and into the shadow of the stone fence, landing on my feet and falling to my knees. I stayed there for a moment and closed my eyes.

At the same time, Noreen Dunn, visiting from Niagara Falls on the occasion of her sixty-first birthday, turned onto Soldiers' Memorial Lane. She was lost, another tourist who had started in the Necropolis Cemetery, which was open late for tours, and somehow wandered too far and ended up here through the unlocked back path.

"Jeez and jumpin'. How the heck did you do it this time, Noreen," she asked herself out loud.

So much for a Widower Buffet. Damn Lana Jefferson—she should have never listened to her to begin with. This trip was a bust so far. But then, she stopped. There was something up ahead, something strange up on the hill above—a girl, or a woman, hard to tell from here, standing on a grave, staring into the moon like a werewolf. It was striking, so strange it made Noreen certain she was witnessing something supernatural. A glimmer of excitement wrapped in a cocoon of fear swelled in her throat, and she almost choked on her butterscotch mint. In a throwback to her Catholic upbringing, Noreen reached for her rosary wrapped in a damp tissue at the bottom of her purse. When she looked back to what she was sure by now was a ghost, it had disappeared.

Noreen had rushed back out toward the streetlights and found herself at a closed gate. "Winterson Cemetery," she read. So, she was somewhere else after all. She remembered her Girl Guide days, put her right hand on the fence and followed it to the end, down around the side, and finally came to the meandering laneway that brought her back to the Necropolis and the tour. The bus was parked out on the street, waiting. Noreen was greeted by the guide, a short man with a large head named Chess.

"Where you been, Mrs. Dunn?" He was obviously distressed. "Now, you know we have a 'no man left behind' policy, but you were pushing it there." He helped her up the steep steps.

"It's *Miss* Dunn, and I was lost." She smiled, leaning into his face and clutching both his hands. "But then I was found. Mister, I would pay twice the $29.95 if I'd have known I'd get to see her."

She had barely taken her assigned seat before bragging about her supernatural experience to the couple beside her. Chess crouched in the aisle to listen, though he should have been talking about the Wandering Wailer of the Windsor Arms, which they would be passing in just a moment.

To her, it was obvious that she was some sort of chosen one. No one else had wandered into a different cemetery. No one else had seen a real ghost in a white gown staring into the moon. No one but little old Noreen Dunn, that's who. Just wait till the girls of the Quilting Quartet heard about this! Lana Jefferson would especially be jealous, always trying to be the most important person in the room, giving bum advice on finding men and taking credit for quilts with patterns she stole from magazines. This was the best gift Noreen had ever gotten, and she would never be the same for it.

Two days later, the Winterson Cemetery also received a gift that would change things forever.

GHOST OF A CHANCE

Two days later, at around eleven, after the morning stroller moms zipped through with their Starbucks and yoga pants, but before the noon-hour widows arrived, a small man walked into Winterson off Parliament Street. He had a large head but a short torso, the kind of haphazard anatomical pairing that changes the way a person moves. I was hanging out with Floyd, hoping he'd be up for some boxing lessons in what he called "the back forty," by the old storage cellar. Instead, he was taking a switchblade to a huge dandelion by the front gates, which, for the time being, was just as amusing. The large-headed man walked over. Floyd didn't acknowledge him until he spoke, too preoccupied by the simple pleasure of wielding a sharp knife on a warm summer's morning.

Each Tuesday the lawns were mowed by Floyd Flynn, except in May, when Dad hired a lawn care company to take over while Floyd was visiting family overseas. Floyd drove an ancient ride-on mower that looked and sounded like a mechanical Frankenstein. For the tighter spots where the beast couldn't fit, he'd undo the bungee cords behind his duct-taped seat and take down the push mower he kept sharp with a grinding stone rigged up in his shed. This was usually when he and I spoke, while he was sharpening his blades. It was the only time he was really approachable. The rest of the time he was perfectly mannered to be surrounded by the dead.

"Winnie, ya don't keep the grounds tidy for the living. Nah. Not even for the living who visit. They're already customers. Ya do it for the new ones ya wanna hook. The confused sons of bitches who think they'll care about gladiolas and hedges while the worms are eatin' their eyes." Each sentence was punctuated by the swipe and release of stone on metal.

Shiiing.

Shiiing.

Shiiing.

I would sit still, listening, and watch him smoke. Floyd chain-smoked in three stages. Walking, he clenched the cigarette in his ham-fist like a spike on a set of brass knuckles. Gesturing, he'd bring it to his mouth, angling the lit smoke close against his pointer finger, at not more than a twenty-degree angle, so that you were waiting for him to burn holes in his dirty skin. This is when the cigarette looked like an inflamed hangnail. And, lastly, once the cigarette started to creep toward the filter so that the brand name barely remained, he would pop it between his thin lips, in the small space left in the center of his grizzled goatee, and smoke it straight down to the filter. You could almost hear the sizzle of heat-blisters. He smoked while he worked. He smoked when he talked. He was smoking the day he taught me how to ride a bike when I was five, pushing me down the hill by Remembrance Lane and yelling to "brake" before I smashed into the Olsen memorial, which I did anyway, rubbing the skin right off both elbows. War wounds, he called them, tousling my hair with pride. He probably smoked when he slept.

It was Floyd Flynn's opinion that the reason behind the grass's curious consistency was all the bones buried beneath it.

"Roots are tiny wee funnels, you see. They suck up what they can from where they can reach. Makes sense then that it comes in like it does." He didn't really have a theory about the weeds. He just hated them. They were like a middle finger pushed through to bloom yellow and personal in his face; thus the switchblade.

"I'd like to speak to someone about the Winterson ghost," the man said.

"Huh?" Floyd turned his head, squinted against the sun to take in the visitor, and spit. "Listen, no crazies allowed on the grounds. Ya here to visit an inmate or ya get lost." I laughed. I know it was rude, but sometimes Floyd just cracked me up so hard I forgot about manners. Besides, he was the one who was supposed to be the adult.

The man gave me some serious side-eye before addressing Floyd again. "I assure you I am not crazy. My name is Chess Isaacs. I run the Toronto Haunted Ghost Tours." He produced a cream card from an inside pocket and extended it between two fingers like a magician's rose. Floyd moved his eyes only, looking down at the embossed card, and sniffed. Eventually, Isaacs retracted his hand and put the card back in his pocket.

"There have been two sightings reported here and I would like to speak to the manager."

"Two sightings? Of ghosts?" I couldn't help it. I immediately thought of Jack. Maybe this was a way back in. I still had some of his old ghost-hunting equipment from the year that was his thing. I kept it in a closet by the back door—the string of bells and a walkie-talkie on a rope. Then I remembered I wasn't talking to him. Still, maybe we could fix things, say, over a ghost hunters' reunion . . .

The adults ignored my questions.

"That'd be Ferguson." Floyd grabbed his spade from where it was leaning against the gate and pushed the tip under the dying weeds.

"Okay, well. Can you direct me to where I might find Ferguson?"

Floyd sighed. He didn't have time for this shit. "Well, he'd either be in one a the graves, shoveling ash in the furnace, or sitting at a desk in the building that's marked 'Manager's Office' over by the church. Hard to say."

Chess Isaacs pushed out his jaw and nodded. "Well, I can see you moonlight as the PR man around here. I'll just be moving along then. Sure I'll come across the office eventually."

"Only if you walk with your eyes open." Floyd leaned the spade back on the fence and picked up the knife, stabbing the ground again, twisting a wrist and slicing the jugular root of the weed with a satisfied grunt.

"I'll take you over," I volunteered. Normally I avoided people, especially outsiders, at all costs. But I had to know what was going on.

Mr. Isaacs looked me up and down and gave a stiff nod. I walked him along the driveway, working up the right way to prod for intel. We followed the driveway when it turned in toward the church, and, once standing in front of the Gothic structure, tall steeple decorated by spiny gingerbreading, as on Brothers Grimm staging, I asked, "Do you know for sure there are ghosts? Did it come from, like, you know, reliable sources?"

"My dear, people rarely lie about these things. They're going to be called crazy by some—not me, of course—and that isn't something to take lightly." He chuckled to himself. "No siree. This is no joking matter, especially not when there's money involved."

"Money?"

"Listen, you haven't seen any ghosts or the like around here, have you?" It was the first time he'd looked me in the eye. It made me nervous. What was the right answer? I hadn't, really, other than the feeling of never being alone. And then there was last night, the footsteps, the feeling of being walked home. Should I try to explain that?

I paused too long and the man lost interest. "Never mind. That's for later anyways."

He stepped away from me and went to the door, knocked twice on the heavy wood and then pushed, already extending his other hand for an expected handshake. He found Mr. Ferguson behind his wide leather-topped desk reading the newspaper. I walked in a few steps behind him, slipping into the office, hoping to be unnoticed.

"Ferguson? Sorry to intrude on you. I'm Chess, Chess Isaacs. You may have heard of me through the industry grapevine." He grasped Mr. Ferguson's hand before it had fully released the paper; the sports section shook and crinkled like an origami rattle.

"Ehrm, no, I'm sorry, I haven't."

"Hmm, that's odd." Chess seated himself in a wingback near the back window, beside a fireplace stacked ready with wood but unlit. "Though Winterson isn't really known for being progressive or involved now, is it?"

"Uh, yes, Winifred?" Mr. Ferguson asked, looking over Isaacs's shoulder. "How can I help you?"

Dammit. "Oh, I was just walking our guest over to make sure he got here okay."

"Well, yes. Thank you. You can go now."

I looked around, frantic to find a reason to stay. The men watched me, silent. No chance they'd just keep talking then.

"I'm going to see if Mrs. Prashad has any magazines." I pointed to the hallway on the other side of the room, the one that led to the waiting room and receptionist we would have passed through had I taken Chess on the public route to the office. Sometimes I took old issues from there for school projects and just out of general interest in things like *Cosmo*'s sex advice or *Hunters Inc.* wilderness survival tips—subjects I found related to one another in many bizarre ways.

Mr. Ferguson waved me off and I crossed the room quickly, walking up the hall and stopping just before I would fall under the watchful gaze of Mrs. Prashad, who generally had no time for me or any other non-customer visits. I hugged the wall and leaned in. I could still hear and see from here; I just had to stay hidden.

"Involved in what?" Mr. Ferguson refocused, folded his paper, and leaned across the desk toward the strange visitor.

"The community, of course. The death community."

"Death community?"

"Yes, the community built around, for, and, some say, by the dead. I myself run the city's largest ghost tour company." He dug out the card he'd unsuccessfully offered up to Floyd and slid it across the green expanse of antique desk to rest against the knuckles of Mr. Ferguson's clasped hands.

"And seeing as how you seem to have a haunted cemetery here, I think it's about time you got to know this community, and I am just the man to make introductions."

"Haunted?" Mr. Ferguson's eyes narrowed at the word. I wondered if he would even hear him out. Turns out, he didn't have much of a choice. Isaacs barreled on.

"Yes, Mr. Ferguson. And frankly, I'm surprised you didn't contact me sooner. I'm sure you're aware of how much money there is to be made from running a cemetery that is on the haunted city tour?"

"Money?" Aware now that all his answers were stuttered questions, Mr. Ferguson tried again. "How exactly would one make money from claims of a cemetery being haunted?" It was still a question, just better stated.

"Well now, there are several ways. I myself make upward of six figures with my own company. But that takes time and luck and more than the average number of balls."

"So, three then?" Mr. Ferguson said this dry as fact. Isaacs ignored it. I cupped my hand over my mouth to stifle the laughter. I'd never imagined Mr. Ferguson capable of dick jokes.

"I also happen to have taken and now teach a very well-attended Learning Annex class on entrepreneurial opportunities, so I'm familiar with the ways in which a ballsy man can make a buck."

He hooked his fingers in the fold of his jacket's lapel like an old-timey politician, impressed as hell with himself. "But anyway, as the cemetery manager, you can certainly capitalize on this opportunity. For one, you set up a website advertising the place and it's a well-known fact that your sales will increase."

"How's that?"

"How's that? Why, who wouldn't want to bury dear Aunt Marjorie in a site known for helping to rehabilitate the living-impaired?" He settled farther into the chair.

"I'm listening."

"You bet you are, and that's just the beginning. You set up a donation box right by the front gate. Our guides will make sure we give the spiel right by that box and that we point it out, with the usual 'save our graveyards from corporate greed or soon the only way you'll be able to see ghosts is at the movies' speech."

Chess produced a handful of nuts from his jacket pocket, silently offered them to the befuddled manager, who shook his head, and then jammed the lot in his mouth. As he spoke, a spray of crumbs peppered the carpet. *What kind of person carries around random nuts in their pocket? Apparently, a man with pants full of balls.*

Finally, Mr. Ferguson asked the question I was dying to know the answer to.

"And you say this cemetery is haunted. How do you know?"

Chess pulled a small notepad from the inside pocket of his suit jacket.

"Let's see here." He made small music with his mouth while he flipped the pages.

"Can I help you, Winifred?"

"Jesus!" I jumped. It was Mrs. Prashad, and she was standing right behind me. I should have smelled her coming—she wore an overabundance of Chanel No. 5—but I had been too busy eavesdropping.

"No, I'm good." I tried to buy time, shuffling my feet and shrugging my shoulders. She pursed her red lips and folded her arms akimbo, raising both eyebrows.

I smiled this broken half smile and remembered my lie. "I just came for magazines. But I can come back later." I made for the reception area behind her, taking care not to touch her angled shoulders in the small hallway. Frig, she was mean. I went out the front door and followed the brick wall back to the side of the building, where I'd brought Isaacs in. They were standing in the open doorway when I rounded the corner, so I pushed my back up against the wall.

"By the way, the surly groundskeeper I met up by the front?" Mr. Ferguson pumped the extended hand of his new partner. "Oh no, no, don't mind Floyd. I can talk to him. A reprimand maybe, about his, uh, disposition."

"No, no, not at all." Isaacs laughed, perhaps remembering the way Floyd had stabbed the ground like he was committing murder. "He's goddamn perfect the way he is. It's straight out of an episode of *Scooby-Doo*, for Chrissake."

"Oh, good." Mr. Ferguson was relieved. It was clear he didn't have more than the average number of balls and wouldn't have been able to reprimand anybody.

Isaacs took a few steps from the door, back onto the path. "Oh, and one last thing. We really want to make sure the ghosts stay active. The more active they are, the more active your guests will be in requesting this stop be added to all the tours. More tours, more *denaro*, got it?"

"Yes. Got it."

"But." Here he pointed a chubby finger at Mr. Ferguson. "Absolutely no funny business. We get one fraud complaint and the whole operation, MY whole operation, looks like a sham. So, no managers in sheets wandering the grounds, strictly the real deal, or we're out."

Then he walked his big-ass head up the road toward the gate.

INVOCATION

I left the admin building and walked over to the Peak. Something about the grubby and the austere back here put me at ease, even if it was the site of my recent humiliation. I passed the willow, kicking the blanket we'd left in a crumpled ball overnight.

"Asshole." I wasn't sure if I meant Jack or me.

I sat on the edge of the drop-off, feet dangling, even though the hill was gradual and, if you really tried and had good shoes, scalable. I wished I was wearing heels so I could balance one on the tip of a toe.

I'd always wanted to live in a *Vogue* photo shoot. I didn't want to be a model and I didn't want to live in New York City—I don't think anyways. I just wanted to exist in the kind of world where a six-foot African girl in a voluminous fuchsia gown could ponder the fish being unloaded at a stinky wharf. I wanted to be friends with the Swedish twins with no eyebrows in gold tutus and painted breasts climbing a ladder into the clear Arctic sky. I wanted to pass by an albino boy on my longboard while he sat on the edge of a water fountain wearing a leopard-print suit and a raccoon-skin hat holding the biggest fist of blue cotton candy, but not eating any. I would host the best parties, if only to see them all, these beautiful people draped over the cracked headstones like ornaments. All these beautiful people, all these living people rubbed smooth of the cut and corners of live people; people set into positions and angles; people without words that would hurt me, without real lives that would end.

I thought about Chess Isaacs and the idea that Winterson was haunted. Damn Mrs. Prashad. Thanks to her, I'd missed out on hearing about the sightings. I mean, the whole thing had to be a hoax, right?

"It has to be a hoax." I said it out loud to hear the words. But still, the image of my mother came to mind before I could push it away. It caught my breath in its grip and squeezed. Had she come back to save us? To help us stay here next to her well-tended grave, the only one with climbing vines of magnolia.

I cleared my throat.

"Mom?"

The word was dusted with rust in my mouth, so unused.

"Mom, if you are here, really here, can you let me know?" I looked around. Maybe I should close my eyes for this. I snapped them shut and tried again.

"Because if you're here, you need to let me know, please. There's this man and he wants to bring tourists through. I don't want to sell you out or anything, but there's a chance it could mean me and Dad can stay. With you, at Winterson."

I thought I heard something, but it was only the wind playing empty chip bags like tambourines in the trees.

I cleared my throat, then spoke a little louder. "Because if it's not you, then that's okay too. It's not like you need to just be waiting around or anything. But I need to know what to do."

This was a precipice, and I teetered at the edge. "I need to know what to do so bad, Mom. Everything is fucked up. School sucks. I'm pretty sure I just lost my best friend and I think it's my fault. Dad is so sad all the time. And now we might be getting kicked out of here? Just tell me what to do."

I was over the edge.

"Please. Please come to me. I need you." My voice broke over the words, consonants hitched on a sob, vowels filling the breathless spots. I waited.

"I'm so stupid." I opened my eyes and grabbed handfuls of grass, tossing them down the hill. "So fucking stupid!" What was I waiting for? What were we always waiting for?

The afternoon here was scooped out of the rest of the day. This place was all absence and want. No one would visit these graves. No one was coming for any of us—not the dead, not me, and not my father. No one would save us, not even my mother. It was a safe place to cry, and so I did, face in my hands, shoulders hunched, leaning forward, rocking backward. I was more alone here than anywhere else. I was on the outside of a womb, clinging to a half life with no way to escape.

And then I wasn't alone anymore.

Noise at the bottom of the cliff like animals climbing trees, all nails and pull. The wind stopped and the garbage lay flat in the grass like retired banners. I raised my head and watched. Two crows hit the sky like exclamation points and settled on the fence separating the far edge of the ravine from the road.

And there she was, walking through the tall weeds, dragging her palms across their tops like she was petting soft fur. Her head was bowed, her dark hair long and tangled, hanging onto each overgrown bush, every low-hanging branch like a thing alive, like black confetti on a gray sidewalk. The birch trees held the strands in twiggy fingers like a cat's cradle weave. There was something stilted about her pace; like she was on a film sped up or slowed down, just enough to exist in a stutter. Just enough to make me yank my feet up from where they dangled, enough to make me stand, hands balled up at my sides.

She cleared the brush and stood now on the path that led from the ravine, up a zigzagging path on the hill, over a long-dilapidated low-barrier half ground into the overgrowth, onto this ledge, and straight to me. She paused.

She wore army pants, tight to her thin legs, and low, flat boots. Her dark T-shirt was worn to a muted gray, and despite the heat, she wore a black leather jacket creased with a long breaking-in. Her arms hung at her sides and her nails were painted black. Her head still drooped, her hair loose over her face, down her shoulders.

I knew in my gut that this was not who I had called for, not my mother. What if this was some skid I'd woken from a nap in the bush? What if this was a stoner looking to get back up into the cemetery to head home? What if it was someone dangerous?

"Hello?" I called down.

She raised her head, hair falling away from pale cheeks, eyes finding me at the top of the cliff. She flickered, just enough to push fear into my knees, just enough to give me pause that it might just be unreliable eyes. And then she smiled, a closed-lipped grin that moved at an impossible pace—sped up and then played back in slow motion. Whoever this was, they were not alive.

"Holy shit."

I scrambled to my feet, turned and ran, not stopping once to look behind me. I ran straight through a funeral procession, through the empty chapel, and all the way home. I locked the door behind me, took the stairs two at a time, and slammed the bedroom door. Then I rushed to the window and watched the field for any signs of her, this thing that was not my mother.

COLLECTING

Last year, our history class went on a field trip to the Royal Ontario Museum. Most of the group just goofed around, trying to find ways to slip out of the building and bleed into the cityscape. But I liked the museum. It was full of old stuff, dead stuff, and things that were used and held years ago. At school I felt out of territory, but here, I was comfortable. This was more my speed.

"Hey, Wednesday Addams, better get to the Egyptian floor so you can see your mummy," some jerk-off with a sideways Jays cap loud-whispered. A few giggles. I shrugged so that he could see his lack of impact. Truly, I did not care, or I shouldn't have, anyway. What I did care about was the guide who came to meet us, stepping out of a back door beside the members' desk, his white lab coat a crisp, unexpected cape.

"My name is John Leung, and I am a curator with the early Canadian galleries." He was short and handsome and wore spectacles that were made of such thin wire the planes of glass seemed held by floss. But it wasn't him that interested me; it was his job title: curator. Walking through the first exhibit, I pulled out my phone and googled it.

Curator: a keeper or custodian of a collection; a content specialist with intricate knowledge of the artifacts under their care.

That was basically me in the cemetery, in my life. Surrounded by all this stone and green and grief, I was a content specialist. Was this how I called her to me, the girl from the ravine? And was I the one who called to her? Maybe she'd been there all along. I would know for sure if Mrs. Prashad hadn't caught me in the hall.

I didn't leave my bedroom window for hours, but there was no sign of her. I had to pee so bad, but I didn't want to abandon my post. What if I went to the washroom and came back to find her swinging in my hammock, dragging an axe across the floor? Oh God, what if she was waiting behind the shower curtain in the bathroom? I didn't want my dad finding my corpse on the toilet, pants around my ankles. How embarrassing. Jesus Christ, I had to get a hold of myself or I was going to piss my pants.

I remembered what Jack had said about how dogs are sensitive to spirits. Dingleberry could be a kind of fat alarm system!

"Dingles!" I called him in a singsong voice, whistling between beckons. "C'mere boy! *Diiinglebeeeery . . .*"

In what world did I imagine he would jiggle his way all the way up the stairs? Well, maybe he could act as a guard from downstairs then. I shook out my sleeping legs, cringing through pins and needles, and made a mad dash to the bathroom. I slammed the thin door, as if it could stop anything, punched the plastic shower curtain to the side to check the tub, and then struggled to get my shorts off in time.

"Ahhhhhh." Relief.

Midstream, I heard it; a small, muffled bark—so unusual it took a minute to recognize.

"Shit." I forced myself to finish quick, pulling up my underwear and shorts without wiping. I had a few seconds of paralysis. Should I run to my room? Take my chances in here? Try to make it down the stairs? My number one pet peeve about horror movies were the idiots who put themselves in places with no escape. Why did they always run upstairs? Or hide in a corner? But what choice did I have now?

I decided to get to my room. I flung open the bathroom door and sprinted to the attic stairs, scrambling up as if chased, and maybe I was—I didn't pause to double check. God, I wished these were folding stairs so I could remove the opportunity to get up here altogether. But Dad had built them after I claimed the attic, so they didn't have any fancy features. I slammed the hatch closed and swung the hook into the latch. Maybe if it couldn't see me, it would leave.

I sounded just like an idiot from one of those movies, acting as if ghosts see with regular eyes. *They can cross over from death but they can't figure out where a loud, breathing human is huddled?* The low rumble of the dog's best growl reached me through the floor. Panic pushed needles back into my legs and I scrambled to find safety. Maybe I could escape out my window, drop to the ground, and make a run for the crematory. Why hadn't I gone there first?

Another bark.

"Shit!"

I searched the room. If I'd had a bed, I would have crawled under it. The wardrobe was packed to overflowing. The curtains around the window were sheer. Where else, where else . . . I scanned the small space. The bookshelf of jars. The beanbag chair. The stack of papers and books piled up by the hammock. The desk.

The desk!

I got on my hands and knees and half crawled, half slid across the floor and under it, pulling the wooden chair in tight to try to block myself. It was feeble, but it was the best I could do. Then I listened.

Dingleberry was quiet. But that meant nothing. He'd probably just dozed off after his huge outburst of energy. There was a creak. Then another. I flattened my spine against the wall and lowered my head so that it rested on my knees. My breathing was too loud; all I could hear was the greedy pull and ragged release in this small space.

In and out.

In and out.

And I couldn't take my eyes off the hatch, the small square of hardwood cut into the floor covered with a piece of fake Turkish rug. Could. Not. Look. Away.

Creak.

Right below me, I was sure. Then an odd scrape. Something being dragged? Something heavy?

Oh my God, what if it was Dingleberry? I pictured him limp at the end of a rope. I put a hand over my mouth.

Thump. A foot on the bottom step.

I squeezed my fingers into shapes like fists only useless. *Make it go away. Make it go away.*

The slap of a hand on the wood railing. I tightened the bend in my knees, shuffling my feet back so that there was scarcely room for my lungs to fill in the fold. My breathing became quick and shallow.

Thump, thump.

I could burst. I could die from the thousands of pins sailing through my veins.

Thump.

Top step. Why couldn't I look away? Why did I need to see it? You don't need to see the truck's headlights before it hits you to know you're fucked. Why was I searching for headlights?

The coarse shuffle of skin on hard grain—a palm on the hatch. And then the low groan of wood and metal where they resisted connection. The latch caught and held and the hatch was raised four inches up, the length of the metal hook at full extension. And in that opening, there was darkness, a shifting, ombré darkness.

My breathing was a siren under the desk.

Then there was a glimmer, a small glint of something catching the light, held still. Minutes dragged by like this—the hatch stayed lifted, no shake or drop, and that tiny glint in the dark . . .

I leaned, chin over knees, trying to make it out, trying to see in spite of the fear that turned my guts to sludge. What was that? I pushed the chair to the side—a long screech as it slid. I waited again. No movement from the hatch. I put hands on the ground and leaned farther, lowering into a crouch, unlocking my knees and resting my weight on their wobbly caps. I stayed like that, frozen.

I was eight feet from the opening, on hands and knees, rear end still under the desk, when movement from the window made me flinch. A bird, a small crow, watched from the ledge.

"Shit." It was a hiss.

I swung my head back quick, expecting claws and maybe teeth in an open jaw. But there was only the dark of a four-inch gap and that small pinpoint of light.

I swallowed hard and placed one hand out, moving toward the opening, the corresponding knee nudging forward. Other side. The distance shortened by half a foot. I couldn't go farther and, still, there was no making out what held the hatch up. What was it?

I stretched out my neck, squinted into the dark. I felt every vulnerable inch of my throat, each flex of pulse. I crawled on hands and knees, one more pace. I was halfway between the desk and the hatch—vulnerable. There were shapes in the opening. Something propped open the hatch, and at floor level was a small crescent moon of pale white, almost blue, and the shine of wet black. I squinted. It almost looked like . . .

And then it blinked.

I screamed, so loud, so hard, my eyes closed. I skittered backward on my palms, sliding my ass across the hardwood, back under the desk. The hatch slammed shut, dust and sound pushed up in a puff. Thumping on the stairs, on the downstairs floor, the door slamming—I heard them as second thoughts beyond the reach of my panic. The scream devolved to a whimper as I rocked it out of me, head buried in forearms across my knees.

A fear like that lets you know we are all just a pair of pants and a utensil away from being feral. If I could have scratched through the wall I would have. I lost even the understanding of language in that moment, the soft mechanics of syllable and hard *r*. Panic rolled over the floors of my linguistic factory like acid, eating everything, corroding the rest. All I had was the scream.

The bird in the window tapped its beak against the glass. *Tap. Tap. Tap.* Three times.

Three.

"Three, six, nine, twelve, fifteen . . ." I whispered the multiples into the crook of an arm. "Eighteen, twenty-one, twenty-four, twenty-seven . . ." The multiples soothed the panic to a dull fear. My dad came home and was forced to bust the latch open to get in. He found me this way, rocking under my desk, somewhere around 630.

"All this talk about haunting."

Dad was sure that's why he'd found me under the desk, why I had insisted we smudge the house with sage ASAP. I'd blathered on about Isaacs and what I'd overheard and he was convinced this was the root of it. Not that he went so far as to say he didn't believe me; he would never say that, even if I told him aliens had landed in the bathtub. He sat beside me on the couch while I cradled the dog in my arms, trying to calm down.

"Someone followed you, someone camping out down there, probably. You just scared them off. We'll lock the front door during the day. I'll tell Floyd to repair the fence. Next week."

"I don't think so, Dad. It felt like . . . something else."

"Listen, I spoke with Ferguson." He smiled. It was such a rare movement it looked mocking on his face. "He had good news."

"About the ghost tours?"

"He thinks we can spin it. To make money. Enough money, maybe."

"Enough for us to stay?" I hefted the dog to my side and grabbed my father's arm. "Really?"

He nodded. "Maybe. We'll see."

I asked about the reports. He told me that years back there was a sighting of a woman in a cape. "Laying on a grave. Then—poof—just gone."

A cold lump jumped into my stomach, solid and seamed like a peach pit. "Cape?"

He nodded. The lump got heavier, pushing its ridges along the soft guts it nudged out of the way. "Which grave?"

He shrugged and kept talking. "Then, just yesterday. A girl in a white dress, a long one."

The pit displaced my liver, put pressure on my intestines. "Where?"

"Didn't ask." He patted my hands, still locked on his arm, and wiggled out of my grip. He walked to the kitchen and yelled back through the opening into the living room. "Probably nothing."

A disappearing woman in a cape? I remembered that October, staring at a spider, a big one, hanging from a web, and the cool ground of the shovel cellar. Voices above. There had to be a different girl in a cape, maybe even a dead one. But then, I'd worn my mother's long white dress last night. It was possible . . .

The kettle whistled like an alarm. A small shard broke in my stomach and pushed its way into my throat, blocking all chance of voice. "Either way," he called back, "could be good for us."

He made me milky tea as a token of comfort and then took the dog outside for a "walk," resting a heavy palm on the top of my head before he left. I couldn't move. This new, cold tumor was a heft in my joints, pinning me to the couch like a grotesque paperweight. My teeth chattered.

Our living room was a bachelor's space, the TV held up by milk crates, a string of multicolored Christmas lights staple-gunned around the perimeter year-round, an old couch that smelled like the dog and something organic on the slow roll to decay. Every surface was clean though, and the rug was vacuumed down to its back-netting. And each wall had a piece of art. My dad worked hard to give me some kind of connection to my mother's family, to my blood. There was a Norval Morrisseau print of two bunnies connected by a throat vine like a nickname strung between them. Above the TV was a map of Georgian Bay with Honey Harbour and Wasauksing and Penetanguishene—names I repeated like pieces of a Latin sermon I couldn't understand but felt in the flex of my muscles: Beausoleil behind my knees, the islands down the ladder of my spine.

Behind me, above the couch, was a tree line scratched out in acrylics on canvas, frantic and blipped like a nervous breakdown on a heart monitor. But it was the photograph on the far wall that kept me focused right now. It was a print of my mother Dad had blown up and placed in the best frame Ikea sold. In it, she is looking at him while he takes the picture. He didn't say so; I can just tell. When Thomas Blight loves you and is close by, you take up all the space he holds for you. Her arms are thrown up and her chin tilted back and she is smiling like her whole head is being choreographed to support it. Plus, she has this look in her eyes. It's impossible to look at that photo, innocent and sweet, and not know that she wrapped her naked limbs around her husband every chance she got. It colors me with embarrassment. In fact, I normally look at this portrait in small sips, a few seconds at a time, so as not to be drawn into that private look. But right then, I was staring. In the picture, with her wide arms and her smiling face, standing on the tundra, breathing out clouds of summer mist, my mother is wearing a dress—a long, white dress.

I was wrong about that mass in my guts; it wasn't a pit, wooden and harmless in the soft meat of a fruit. Instead, it was a bomb, because right then it exploded. I held my lips shut with both hands and made a run for the kitchen sink; the toilet was just too far. I threw up all over my breakfast dishes, a kind of disgusting irony when the rainbow chum landed back in the bowl I had eaten from.

It was times like these that I hated the compulsions the most, the obsessiveness. Stomach churning with a pitched sting in my throat that made me gasp, still, I kept my head hung over the metal sink, counting the cutlery scattered at the bottom like silver sardines, then the few dishes splashed with sick, held aloft by tines and spoon handles like ships at sea.

"Is it me?" I asked the last bowl. It answered me with its splattered empty *Fucked if I know.*

I ran the faucet to clean out the sink, cupped a handful of water and rinsed out my mouth, then walked the stairs into my room. I sat at the window, the humid evening spread even and thick over the grounds. There was no sign of my father and Mrs. Dingleberry. It was unlike him to take the dog any farther than the front yard. There was no point, really.

I hardly slept that night. Instead, I sat at my desk, trying to sketch the girl's face. It was like trying to remember the make of a car driving by you at sixty miles per hour—too much movement to be recalled as a still thing. She had stood at the bottom of the Peak, but even then there was a kind of blur. I remembered her hands, the muted clothes she wore, but not her face. There was just a feeling. It was like trying to draw the way cold feels under the skin.

I wanted to avoid the other thing, the thought that made me puke, the thing that took my terror from the spiritual home invasion of the day and tied it up in intricate knots that I couldn't find the sequence of moves to undo. But I couldn't. Clearly, I was the damn ghost people had reported seeing. Both sightings had been me. Me laying around in that stupid cape. Me standing like a damn howling wolf on the fence, of all things. Me. I was the ghost of Winterson Cemetery. There was only one other option, and I wouldn't speak it out loud. Besides, if it was my mother, wouldn't she come to us and not some assholes lost from a bus tour? I wondered if the thought had occurred to my father.

I threw the pencil on the desk. Of course it had. When had he ever taken Dingleberry for his nighttime walk? When had he stayed up past 10 p.m. at the kitchen table, playing solitaire and watching the door like he had tonight? He'd spent the years waiting around, but not like this, not with this specificity and optimism, the kind that gave him more words and fewer sighs. Not with this quiet focus.

"Goddamn it, why can't we stop waiting?" I leaned back, head tipped over the wooden rail on the back of the chair, and stared at the ceiling all cracked like a tapped egg. What was the game plan here? What could I do—run around the grounds in a white tablecloth with the eyes cut out?

I wished I could talk to someone. I would have wandered over to Roberta's grave, but there was no way I was going outside tonight. Instead, I put a Smiths record on low. I tiptoed downstairs past Dad's bedroom. He'd finally turned in an hour ago but his light was still on, leaking out from the bottom of his door. In the kitchen, I grabbed a roll of paper towels and cleaner from under the counter. I climbed the stairs again, pausing to pass my hand over the railing where the girl must have touched. I'm not sure what I was expecting, but its continued ordinariness was surprising. Then I ascended, keeping the hatch door open behind me, and settled in front of the bookcase.

I pulled each jar down and wiped the shelves clear of dust.

I examined the jars one by one, wiping the glass where it was cloudy, and then put them back. There was one empty jar between the collection of cicada skins and another with the pencil nubs I'd found by the front gate, each one carefully sharpened almost straight down to the metal bank and pink eraser. They'd excited me, thinking of the hand that held them so hard they were each curved like a fishhook. I unscrewed the top and held the empty glass to my chest, concentrating on the possibility of staying. I thought about the relief and the comfort and the certainty of safety here: of me and Dad, of Dingleberry and Floyd, of the graves holding the women of my family, and this whole cobbled-together place right in my chest. Then I put the jar to my mouth and exhaled. When it was full of safety and full of Winterson, I screwed the cap back on and slid it back in place on the shelf. No one was going to take this away from me, not a ghost and not a budget cut. I would not be moved.

In the dream, she sits on my windowsill, perched like a great black crow. It is the cicadas that pull me from oblivion to the window, little violinists cracking their own backs for the octave. Her wings are tucked up into shoulders and arms that spindle out, fingers splay on the glass leaving prints that look like half-moons—all shape, no ridge. I lean in until my forehead is against her forehead. It is cool as glass anyways. Then she wraps me in those wings and we drop to the grass, tippy-toed jewelry box ballerinas, turning around and around on a graceless axis.

"You have to get out of here." She shouts into my face, but her words are whispers that barely move an eyelash.

Our timing is all off. We are slowed down and words come out wrong. We are in a bad facsimile run through a dry copier machine, all fade and cut. It makes me giggle. The laughter is bubbles around my head.

We walk to the front gate. She holds my hand and I pet the pads of her fingertips with my own, searching for the whorls that will show me her DNA. Proof of life, of belonging to some code or mother. I feel full of tears, but then the most marvelous thing happens. Our feet through the long grass push grasshoppers from slumber and they jump at small heights like popcorn kernels. They pelt our legs, and we coo to them, wanting to hold them, to pluck them up and pop them in our pockets, in our cheeks.

The gate is open, pushed wide to the street that hums with traffic. I skip onto the driveway before she pulls me back.

"Not there. You'll never make it." She points to the fence instead, taller than I'd ever imagined it. Impossible.

"No, it isn't," she says. Then we laugh until we have to hold onto our knees—each other's knees, like artist dolls with elastics slack and bust, because she can hear me without me having to speak the words aloud.

She gives me a boost and I hook fingers and toes into the chain links. The pressure of wire holding my body weight with a collection of tiny bones is unbearable. Then she passes me and I pull and balance and climb after her.

Why? I think it. I know she'd hear. *Why do we have to go this way? We can just walk out the front.*

She is so far ahead now I can just see the bottoms of her shoe soles above me. There are letters there but I can't read in this place. Language makes its own arbitrary rules here and it chooses to remain hieroglyphic. I stop climbing and she stops climbing.

I'm going to walk out. I lower one bare foot and catch the link below it. That's when she turns like a spider on a web and curves around, catching link by link in a smooth arc, and then crawls down directly above me, upside down. She moves fast like a puppet held by strings. And then her face is so close to mine I can see my reflection in her dark eyes, her feet up above her head, arms bent to hold her there.

"You won't walk out of here."

Finally, the loop rights itself and her words match her lips and the effect of the distinct voice and the impossible arachnid angle at which she hangs make my stomach clench. I can't hold my bladder and the piss running down my legs make my feet slick and my toes can't grip the fence anymore.

And then I fall, like a spool of ribbon toppling off a table, becoming unwound, falling into piles and folds—yards and yards of myself, all the way down.

I woke up with my fingers and toes tangled in my hammock, my pinky turning blue. I used the paper towels and glass cleaner to mop up the puddle under me, running in warm rivers across the slanted floor all the way to the window.

DEAD LIVING GIRL

The next day it rained. Rain always felt like a low conversation. Snow was a whisper, but rain was a fistful of voices negotiating a dozen languages at the same time. My dad was gone by the time I got up, and the house was too quiet. I watched the water streak the stone outside through the living room window. The grounds were empty. Even Floyd had buggered off somewhere dry.

I was obsessed with watching the grounds. I went to every window at least three times before lunch. It was maddening. I couldn't think of anything else. I didn't want to eat and I held back from going to the washroom as much as possible, which worked out because . . . well, no food. Finally, I knew I had to do something or I'd go crazy. Maybe it was better to force things to a head. Roberta always said that. I hated it. It made me think of pimples.

"I think I have to go back," I told Dingles, who couldn't give two shits where I went as long as he was left in peace to sleep. He was stretched out in front of our old gray corduroy couch, head propped up on an empty slipper.

"Don't try and talk me out of it." I let the front curtain drop back into place and went to find my rain boots.

The grounds were squishy and the horizon lost. There was no

clear line between the snaking path and the sky; everything was a shade of gray. Water hit and pooled off the yellow hood of my raincoat, and I pulled it forward so that I had a small awning. I watched my feet, trying to keep them moving forward.

I have to know, I convinced myself. *There's no point in hiding. This is my home.*

I pushed through the wet trees and slid into the clearing of the Peak. The rain started to thin, melting into a weighty cloud of moisture and stillness. I walked to the edge, past the graves, over the patchy grass, and looked down into the ravine. She was there—still or again—standing in the same spot as yesterday, hair in front of her face, hands at her sides. My breath was a storm in my throat, spinning around instead of in and out.

I don't think I could have done anything other than what I did then. Eyes locked on her dark figure, I lowered myself to the ground and sat right there, right where I was the day before, legs dangling over the edge. And I watched.

The rain cleared away, but somehow, I could still hear it like the soft crackling of a thousand plastic bubbles, pinging off my rubberized hood. And then the sky got dark, too dark to see anything beyond my own hand. And I was cold; I shivered inside my oversized coat.

Then her name filled my head, bypassing my ears. *PHIL.* Full and stretched like a yawn. I put it in my own mouth and whispered it back.

"Phil."

Saying it out loud pushed the goosebumps back to smooth on my skin. I felt safe, somehow, made calm by the very object of my fear, this personified smudge at the bottom of the hill, staring up at me under a shifting sky.

And then I can't explain it. In something like a blink that closed out the whole world for the briefest second, I was standing at the bottom of the cliff, beside the girl who was really just the shadow of a girl, somehow exact but still only an idea of what a girl should look like. Up close her hair was greasy and her skin pale but solid. Her lips were thin and she was wearing a soft pink lipstick made thick with time and glitter. She wore a silver ring on each of her middle fingers, both sized with grubby tape wrapped around the band so they wouldn't fall off. She was maybe a little older than me. Her eyes were dark as dead stars, as dark as my mother's, and framed with thick black eyeliner, top and bottom, so that she looked sore. I imagined this face now, her wide, clear face, pushed into the space between the floor and the attic hatch, watching me cower under my desk. She gave me this smirk, a half smile that was both defiant and comforting in its humanity, and then she popped a cigarette between her lips.

"Phil?" She didn't answer.

"Are you Phil?" I tried again.

She pulled a matchbook from the pocket of her jacket and lit her cigarette, maintaining eye contact through the movements.

And then we were walking.

She shows me the ravine, clear of shopping carts, with the submerged skeleton of a BMX upside down, handlebars anchored to rebar at the bottom. She shows me the same trees, smaller, less dense, and two others that in the real world had long since begun a soft slouch into mulch. In this version of the creek, they were still standing. I touch them as I pass and feel the pull of mourning. Already an invasive caterpillar is eating dark into their bark like rot.

It's damp here. Water pushes between the hard pack of

ground and the looser topsoil, making sponge, and I feel the suck of it under my feet—wet cotton and thick weight. *Where are my boots?*

She shows me the beer box full of empties, a needle jammed between two brown bottles like a splinter. She shows me an upended crate, a broken pail open-side down, a stack of creaking pallets all set around an ashy firepit with a kicked-in perimeter. She edges me past a pile of old clothes decayed to pulp and dull buttons, now tiny round thrones for the slugs that settle over the snapped thread loops holding them to the mucky mess.

She shows me her hand, like a busted tulip opened too far, reaching from the base of a tree. I don't want to see more. My knees hit ground, squelching into the mud, leaving indented cups for raccoons to drink rainwater from. I pick up the bloom of her grip and lower my chin so that it fits into her cold palm. And I close her fingers on my face, her arm a dark stem.

I'm too chickenshit to see more, to see her eyes rubbed gray like scratch tickets, to see her hair as seaweed around a dead man's pallor. So, I make her hold me like this instead, her stiff fingers closed clumsy on my weak chin.

"Oh, Phil."

I spoke her name and the fingers became just my own and I was alone again, feet dangling over the Peak, rainboots neatly at my side. I counted to seven before I stood. I needed the space the unfinished number allowed—not quite a group of even sets, more than a handful of fingers.

She was gone. I placed my feet on solid ground and felt the cold of wet fabric. I looked down. My soles were black with wet mud. I didn't bother to run home this time. This time, I knew it wouldn't matter where I was. She'd find me. I picked up my boots, small puddles of rain in each, and walked away. I was halfway home before I noticed the rain had returned. I lifted my hood and pulled the sleeves down over my wrists.

Then a thought occurred to me—that maybe my dad's job and our home were safe for now. With a real ghost around the tours could actually work. In the back of my mind, behind the elation of home, was the small joy of having news for Jack. Maybe this was my way back in, maybe this was the way we became normal again in our own fucked-up way. Now all I needed was for her to show up when Chess's tours came by . . .

Wait. How the hell does one train a ghost to appear on schedule? How could I ever be sure she would show up when we needed her to? I thought about her hand, lying pale and broken in the mud. Goddammit, I might have to keep playing ghost, except it was different now. Before, it was an accident, a stupid misunderstanding. But now, now I'd be setting it up and playing it out. No take-backs.

And then I thought: What if this ghost had showed up for the very purpose of punishing me for playing ghost? Was that even a thing? This was unchartered territory. And, of course, it could only happen to me—meeting an actual ghost who may or may not have returned from the grave to avenge my own false haunting, which may or may not save my home but may or may not also drive my fragile father to madness thinking his dead wife had come back.

Jesus. I grabbed the ends of my sleeves in fists and pulled the coat hard until it was tight across my back, until it constricted my throat.

It was clear I needed someone who knew the intricacies of both deceiving people and the paranormal world. I stopped short on the path when the answer came to me.

"Dammit." I punched at the rain. "Shit!" I turned in circles, stomping soaked socks into the wet ground. If one of Chess's tourists came by now, they might report a childish sort of spirit, a tantrum ghoul. Or maybe a hysterical woman, something dangerous. At sixteen, it could go either way.

I sighed and walked the rest of the way home slowly, like delaying my return would delay the inevitable.

Because the truth was, I had to call my cousin Penny.

I was already logged into Facebook when I opened my laptop.

I typed "PENNY FORYOURTHOUGHTS" in the search bar under Friends.

Her profile popped up, the picture a cheesy design you'd see on a T-shirt in a gift shop—a drawing of an Anglo-looking Native woman with a headband and feathers curving at impossible angles in her long hair. In her cupped hands she held a glowing light in shifting hues. All the colors of the wind, I supposed. I clicked Message.

> Hey Cousin,
> Hope you're good. Haven't seen you lately. I was hoping you would stop by the cemetery. I need to talk to you about something.
> Love, Winifred

I reread it, deleted *Love*, and pushed Send.

I filled my cheeks with air, leaned back in my chair, and released it slow and loud. Even messaging her made me uneasy.

Penny had never been discreet about her feelings for me. I was annoying, a nuisance. I never asked Roberta for anything and so, by comparison, made her look bad for always needing a couch to crash on or twenty dollars for whatever she needed twenty dollars for. And then, after the funeral, I got the one thing of value Roberta owned, her emerald engagement ring. She'd left it to me in a handwritten note she had her neighbor Thelma witness, both wobbly signatures scratched out on the back of a Walmart receipt detailing the ring's destiny. She'd left it tacked up on her fridge with a magnet from Niagara Falls, a place she'd never been. That was the last straw for Penny. Cleaning out the apartment, my father had shown her the note while she rummaged around in the credenza drawers. "What a bitch," she yelled and stormed out. I never knew if she meant her mother or me. No one would ever call sweet deaf Thelma a bitch, so it had to be one of us.

Maybe she wouldn't bother to respond now. Even in my predicament, this gave me some peace.

Ding.

There was a reply. I opened the Messenger box.

About what?

Christ. She wasn't going to make this easy.

Well, ghost stuff I guess.

There was a brief pause and then the three dots let me know she was typing.

I'm $35 an hour for ghost shit. That's work. Some of us work.

I sighed.

Is that the family rate?

I finished it with a winky-face emoji.
Dots right away, and then her reply.

Yes.

"Of course, it is. Asshole," I said into my room. I thought for
a minute, tapping my front tooth with the nail on my pointer
finger. I had eighty dollars saved up from allowance for an emergency and I was pretty sure this qualified. I had serious doubts
about getting any real value for my money. Still, what choice
did I have?

Okay

I typed.

Tomorrow good?

A longer pause, then:

Two o'clock. I only have an hour available. And I'm charging
you for my bus fare to get there. $41 total.

Jesus, what a dick. Seriously.

Sure—sounds good. Meet by the chapel?

No response. I could only assume it was agreeable. Dealing with Penny was always assumptions and guesses. Unless she really wanted to make sure you knew how she felt. Then she was as subtle as a shotgun.

"They hired this new white bitch to run the Friendship Centre." I remembered that day—two years ago now—so clearly. Penny had tossed her giant purse on the dining room table and a bottle of hairspray rolled out, coming to a stop against my mug of tea. Damn near took out the corner of the jigsaw we'd been working on all morning. "What kind of colonial bullshit is that?"

"Jeez, my girl. You come in here like weather." Roberta waved her arms above her head in circles, like small tornados. "Want tea?"

"No." She plunked down in the wooden chair across the table from me.

"What's going on over there?" Roberta lowered herself back into her seat. She slurped from her own mug and set it back down with a thunk.

Penny was agitated. I watched her fingers pick at each button on her jacket. She looked tired. She was always extra bitchy after a night out.

"I just came back from the Annual General Assembly . . ."

"Oh! They're having a gathering? Are they playing prize bingo in the cafeteria?" Roberta put her hands on the table to stand again.

"No, they are not." Penny was exasperated already. I wondered why she'd bothered to come at all. And then I remembered it was check week in the building. End of the month. The older woman settled back down, her face fallen, and started matching puzzle pieces again. "What they are doing, Mother, is taking over our damn community center and letting white people run it. Well, nearly white people."

"What do you mean? The whites over there aren't people?"

"No, Mom, not nearly people, nearly whites." She lifted her eyes and watched me for a second. I pretended not to notice, and snapped the end of the beak onto the largest duck in our puzzle.

"They have half-breeds over there in all the best positions. The new director is damn near blonde. Can you imagine?"

"Oh now, Penny. Maybe she's a bottle blonde like Arseface Annie."

Arseface Annie lived above Roberta. My auntie was convinced she had a pogo stick instead of a walker.

"Yeah, well, how do you explain green eyes? Real Indians don't have green eyes." She didn't bother to pretend, looking me straight in my light-colored eyes across the table.

"Well, maybe she'll know how to show up to work enough to fill out a report, though." I couldn't help it. Everyone knew Penny's problems weren't half-breeds.

"'the fuck do you know about anything, kid?" She grabbed her purse and stomped off to the bedroom, slamming the door behind her so that a pile of housecoats and flannel pajamas fell off the hook and crumpled on the floor.

Roberta punched me in the arm, chuckling. "Good one." Then she pointed to the pile of pieces by my elbow. "Hey, pass me one that looks like a nipple, wouldya?"

And now I needed Penny's help. And she was not going to make this easy.

A TINY HAUNTING

Later, when there were more visits to compare, I would realize that Phil was different at night. But the night of that first visit, the night she began her haunt in earnest, I had no idea.

It wasn't that she had multiple personalities. It was more like, at certain times she was more colored in, more present. And not just that. It was like she regained memory or personality or both. Night was when she was all smudge and feeling. Night was when I felt her sorrow, or her loneliness, or her longing; these were not things she allowed during the daytime. The daytime was when she mentioned things offhand, like her preference for heavy metal or the games she played with her two younger siblings. These things she told me in her loud voice in answer to my questions, and sometimes just to fill a silence. These things seemed less important to her than the pull of the ravine or the ways in which she could tease me to surrender, till I whined at her like a little kid. Then she'd laugh, kick some rocks, and start the work of bringing me back to happiness. But at both times—during the day and through the night—it remained impossible to have a linear conversation, and difficult to make sense of her motives and movements. And at both times, it was impossible not to be pulled in.

It began the night after she revealed her death to me, after I Facebooked my asshole cousin for help, back when I still didn't know her. She was just a girl who had lived and died in the ravine. Thinking about the image of her body turning soft near a party camp changed my heart rate, pushed small drips of adrenaline into my blood, and I couldn't sleep, couldn't even really settle. Instead, I made equations out of the digital alarm clock numbers for twenty minutes, straightened all the jars on my shelves again, and washed my face three times, just to be sure, just to appease the numbers and sequences that could pop the stitches of sleep if they wanted, if I didn't address them and put them into some sort of order.

I dragged out *The Mists of Avalon*, a bent-up paperback from my mother's collection that had come in the box with my entire inheritance—beadwork, clothes, records, and a few books, this one included. But this one was my favorite. It was worn because she had loved it. And her name was printed in neat letters on the inside of the front cover: MARY BAX KALDER. When I'd carried the book over to Roberta's as my bus read, she asked me to mark off the "sexy pages" with sticky tabs and lend it to her when I was done.

I had just read her name out loud, moving my finger over the indented blue letters, when the desk chair moved, its legs scraping across the wood. I caught my breath. Was she answering me?

"Mom?"

"Dude, why do you keep calling me that?"

"Jesus Christ."

"Nope, not him either."

The voice sounded close, but I couldn't see her. "Where are you?"

"I'm waiting until you promise you won't freak out. Are you going to freak out?"

I couldn't promise that. "I don't know." There was a few seconds of silence. "Are you the girl from the ravine?"

"Yes."

Oh Jesus. Oh Jesus, Mary, and Joe. I took a few breaths. "Have you been . . . Hanging around for a while now? Maybe peeking in the hatch?"

A sigh. I had no idea ghosts sighed! "Yes. I was trying to come up slowly, to give you time not to freak the fuck out. Didn't really work."

"Sorry." I honestly did feel apologetic. I had truly freaked the fuck out. But in my defense, a member of the undead had been trying to get into my bedroom.

"Okay, so are we good now?"

I nodded, not really sure if we were good at all.

"Alright, I'm going to come out now. Do not scream."

I closed my eyes tight, like a baby who thinks if he can't see you, you can't see him—a false protection. I counted four full breaths. Four was a comforting number, small, compact, and completely symmetrical. Then I opened my eyes.

I expected to see her hovering over me, her dark hair dangling inches from my face. But she wasn't there. I looked around, and besides the chair being pushed out from the desk, everything was as it should be. Oh God, what if she was under the hammock? That's how it went in movies. I swallowed hard, hooked my fingers along the netting and pushed it to the side so I could peep through the holes.

Hardwood and empty air.

"Where are you?"

Three solid taps at the window. I jumped and focused. There she was, perched on the ledge like a great black crow. I put my feet on the ground and sat, keeping my eyes on her dark figure then stood. "Why are you out there?"

When she answered, her voice was inside the room even though her body remained in the night, on the other side of my window. "I don't want you to lose your shit."

She was right, my shit probably would have been lost if I'd suddenly seen her in this space.

"Phil, right?"

She nodded.

I took a step toward her. The moon was full behind her, all muted and gauzy like it was a wound held with bandage, like it was half shot on painkillers and full of sleep and that's why things like the dead wandering around were allowed to happen. The moon was off-duty.

"What's that short for?"

She snorted. (More sounds I didn't think a ghost would make.) "That's what you want to ask me? There's a dead girl at your window and you want to know her full name? You're messed up, kid. And that's a lot coming from the dead girl herself. *What's that short for?*—great question, genius." Her sarcasm was edged in anger.

Maybe she was right. Though I did notice she hadn't answered the question. I took the remaining steps in the weakened moonlight to the window bench and slowly sat. It was like moving around a wild animal. I didn't want to get bitten. And I didn't want her to run off again.

I wanted to touch the glass between us, but there was something too intimate about that. She squatted on the small ledge in black boots, her knees pressed up against the glass, arms resting on them. When she moved them, I heard the leather of her jacket creak. It was too big for her, worn-in by someone else. She turned and I saw her face in profile, backlit. I don't know why I was surprised at how beautiful she was. Maybe it was zombie movies. Or maybe it was something else about how we are trained to see brown girls, but she was remarkable.

"Where are you from?" I needed to know. Roberta had told me this was Indian geography, figuring each other out by the land we belonged to.

"Here." She kept still.

"Toronto? But I mean, where is your community?"

She laughed now. "Not all of us are from the bush, you know. Maybe the city was my community."

I didn't want to offend her. I felt like a child. That's about where my understanding was anyways—very childlike—when it came to us as a people. I tried to apologize with information. "My mom was Métis from the Georgian Bay. It's not very far from here. Maybe you know the place?" What if she was related to me? What if this was my own relation? I got excited.

"So, what are you then?"

I was deflated by her response. "What do you mean?"

"You told me your mom was Métis, but not what you are." It was a challenge, and I didn't know the right answer.

"My dad is white. British, I think." This split identity was why I didn't feel confident "enough" to sit in one definition, so I avoided it. And this made me feel really bad. I wasn't ashamed of my father, but it felt like his part of the family equation was to subtract from my mother's whole number. Penny would have agreed. She would have called me a remainder.

"Again, that's your dad. What are you? What do your bones say you are?" She leaned in, resting her forehead on the glass.

There was no breath to fog up the pane. I took the movement as an invitation. I had a memory of this and so I leaned in, forehead first, closing my eyes and moving my head, anticipating contact. When it bumped against the cold glass on my side, I was a bit disappointed, though I couldn't say why.

I was quiet, inelegant with breath. *How do you listen to your bones? With what voice do they sing?* The glass was growing warm under my skin. I knew I was building condensation that erased her face. I tried to breathe smaller. It should have been easy to spit out one answer or the other—there were only two, really. But I couldn't. I squinted hard, asking the question in every cell, but there was only silence.

"I don't know. Nothing. I can't hear them." I felt sad and wanted to move on, to get past me and back to her. "Why did you die so young? Did someone do something to you?"

She laughed without mirth. "Starting with the small things, eh?"

I blushed. "I'm sorry."

And then she started her story. Her voice was low and as smooth as the glass between us and I closed my eyes—

Honestly, I never thought I'd end up the only body in the cemetery without a grave. I thought I'd have a hole to rest in. Isn't that how it's supposed to go? We die and are buried, right? I mean, they say it's "going to your eternal rest," for fuck's sake.

"People acted like it was inevitable—that my destiny was a ditch outside a cemetery from day one. But that's not how I was born. That's not how I lived.

My mom, Rose, was so charming she couldn't leave the house without someone giving her gifts or offering a ride into town or proposing. That's what Grandpa Amos said, anyway. Grandpa told us stories about how he had to take the shovel out of the shed every day and fill holes left around the front porch from all the men fainting at the sight of her. He said that's why the roads were so bad on the rez.

"S'like Rose's a damn lumberjack, just cutting straight through the men," he'd chuckle. "Don't stand a chance, them." He was proud of his middle daughter, even more for her gentle nature than her famous smile. "Come to think of it, there were some bird-sized holes too. They fall from the clouds just to be near her feet."

My mom was not a small woman. She liked to cook and loved to eat even more. She was short and soft. And she didn't give a good goddamn about it. She was perfection in a pair of XXL jeans. It was probably that that made her so damn irresistible, the fact that she loved herself with the same kind of gentle ferocity that she loved her kids with. There were three of us, a small family by community standards. Our dad died when I was ten and my sister Leaky was three and Baby Boy was just one. It almost killed her, but then she remembered that there were many days in a life and not all of them would be so painful, so she kept moving forward. At the wake, she asked everyone to make sure to tell Baby Boy stories of his dad, so that he'd have those memories through them since his own wouldn't be that easy to call up.

"Phil, you're the oldest, so you're really, really important," she'd say, enunciating each *T* to slow down the words, so they stuck. And I felt important. I had work to do now, work for the family, work that my dad couldn't do anymore. That fell to me. So, I taught Leaky how to ride my old BMX and stopped stealing candy from Wanda's Corner Stash. I had to be a good example. Well, as good as I could be while still being myself. I still didn't do my homework, expect for art class assignments, but I showed up every day, which is the kind of compromise I could live with. Because, you see, I was still living back then.

Puberty was a fucking horror show. I got tall and ugly and all my underwear was stained. I hated it. Hated the boobs that started to grow and then stopped growing—just big enough to get noticed, just small enough to get teased. "Shit or get off the pot!" I'd yell at them in the bathroom mirror flecked with toothpaste, because apparently everyone needs to watch themselves brush their goddamned teeth.

This is important. I need you to remember this: I was loved. I was profoundly and fully loved. This is critical, because people like to tell a version of stories where we were born to be neglected or forgotten or hurt.

But when I was born my mother refused to cry because she didn't want me to ever see her like that. She held in all her tears and maybe because of it, her milk came in fast and hard. She had so much love, she could feed me for two years and a few of my cousins when she babysat. My father built a doghouse-sized church in the backyard because he wasn't sure how to show his gratitude. He wasn't even Christian. My grandparents sang songs in the old language so that my ancestors would know that I had arrived safely.

By the time the cancer started eating my dad, one cell at a time, I only had one grandparent left, my mom's father, Amos. It was probably for the best. I don't think the others could have handled it. My dad sang and split wood and fished like God was handing him the scaly bodies himself. I don't think anyone but Amos could have beared to witness him wither and shrink and then be cut into pieces by surgery and depression. I don't think they could have sat by his bed hour after hour while he cried or was so full of morphine he forgot who we were. My mom did, though, every single day. She read him all his favorite Thomas King novels, front to back, even when he called her by his mother's name and begged her to smother him with his pillow. On these days, I took care of the kids. Really, Amos was watching us, but he spent more time snoring in the rocking chair by the stove than making up games to keep small children occupied. It was okay, I was important—with every *T* enunciated.

I was profoundly loved, even then. Even now, maybe.

And when I opened my eyes, the ledge was empty and the moon was still full like a broken, weeping thing.

MAKING A DEAL WITH SATAN

Lets meet later. 3pm.
—P

That was it; no apology, no real explanation, just a solid reminder of where I sat on Penny's priority list—on the back of the page, not even numbered, misspelled even.

"Whatever." I closed the laptop and leaned back in my chair. Maybe this delay was for the best. I hadn't been able to wrap my head around last night's visit. The idea of plotting with my dickhead cousin over how to use Phil was starting to make me feel like *I* might be a bit of a dickhead as well. No, I had to keep my wits about me on this. Phil was the answer to our problem, the thing that could keep us from being homeless, from having to leave my mother. That had to come first.

I took the spray bottle and paper towels to the window and cleaned the greasy rectangle I'd left there last night. There was no twinned smudge on the other side, just mine, just my gross, greasy living side. I wondered about the rules of her world. When was she able to visit? Was there even something or someone regulating her? Was she here for good? Could I just talk to her like a regular human being, maybe try to convince her to "show up" when I needed her for the bus tours? I remembered her sarcasm. I had never been good with figuring out even regular human beings. I hoped Penny could help. That hope made me nervous.

I took my time in the shower, then counted out the money I needed to bring and decided to take the dog with me. I ate half a jar of near-expired kimchi and four Timbits for breakfast and rushed outside with Dingleberry. I wondered if I'd see Phil on the way to the chapel. Not that I wanted to, I told myself, just wondering is all. But then why was my heart beating fast and hard and spastic? I wondered if Phil's heart beat in her chest. I wondered if her chest could hold such a thing as a heart. I wondered what it would feel like to lay my ear against her ribs, wondered if the movement that echoed out would be the steady thud of an amorous pump or the slow drag of worms. I decided I'd be okay either way as long as her eyes were clear and she smiled. If she smiled I might be able to keep my fear tucked in the muscles of my back where it slept.

The dog peed right away and I plopped him in the wagon. Then we squeaked our way down the path.

What Penny and I had for each other was the kind of hate that's grit in your guts. It took time and concentration to add layers to the grain, to make it so that you could carry that hate in your dark parts with less of a sting. Of course, as soon as we saw each other we started pulling at those layers like scabs. It's the kind of hate that is unique to family and people you once told secrets to. It's the real danger in developing friendships—the potential of this hate.

I was in no hurry to see her, and even less so because I needed her. "Never need nothin' from nobody," Floyd said once, coming out of Mr. Ferguson's office with medical insurance forms he'd been asked to fill out. Floyd was a wise man when he wasn't urinating on the rose bushes that grew out by the back fence, the ones he was told not to cut down like the rest, since they'd been planted by a prominent family with many plots.

I arrived at the chapel first and found a spot a few yards away to park the wagon. I didn't want to expose Mrs. Dingleberry to Penny's negativity. She had a way of sensing what was sacred to you and then shitting all over it. I didn't think I could take any comments about my dog from her. I sat on the front steps and picked up a small stick to draw patterns in the shallow grit between my feet. It was a series of eights all looped one into the other like links, like a perfectly dividable chain.

I heard her approaching but refused to raise my head. I didn't want to have to offer up even a wave. She dragged her feet to a stop right in front of me, kicking small stones over my work.

"What's up?" It wasn't a casual greeting. She wanted to get right to it.

She wore her hair in a low ponytail, wisps puffed out by her ears like a baby bird where the hairspray missed. She was dressed in black jean shorts and jelly sandals, her toes painted a bright green that had grown out to show slices of yellowed nail in the beds. She was tall and her back was flat from her neck to her thighs, so that the seat of her shorts drooped. "Long back," Roberta used to tease her. She wore a too-big plaid shirt unbuttoned to show the top of a black bra and the gleam of a thin silver chain. Over her shoulder was a small purse. Large sunglasses covered half her tanned face and made it difficult to read her, which was exactly the point of Penny: difficult.

I dropped the stick. "Hey, Penny. Thanks for coming."

She responded by holding out a hand and then opening and closing her fingers, the universal sign language for "give me money." I handed over some bills crumpled around a handful of coins. She sighed and opened each one, counting it out. She slipped the newly folded bills and coins into her purse, snapped it shut, then crossed her arms over her chest.

"Alright. Go then."

Jesus, why did I bother? But, this was what I had to go with right now. With my dad not being reachable on the best of days and this weird shit with Jack, she was all I had.

"There's a ghost in the cemetery."

She snorted. "No shit, eh? In the cemetery. You don't say."

Oh my God, I wanted to spit on her reflective lenses. "Yes, but for real. And I need help."

"Getting rid of it? I don't do exorcisms. I'm not some damn Catholic."

"No, I need help knowing how to make her listen to me."

She uncrossed her arms, found a pack of cigarettes, a pack of gum, and a lighter in her purse, and sat down beside me. She popped a green cube out of the gum package and into her mouth. Then she retrieved a cigarette and lit it. "They don't sell menthols anymore," she explained, even though I hadn't asked. "A girl's gotta improvise."

We sat there a moment, side by side, not speaking. It was as amicable as we could manage. I hoped Roberta was watching from somewhere, just for a moment, just long enough to see us together like this. It was all she had hoped for. And then Penny opened her damn mouth.

"It's your money, so talk. I have to leave right away. This isn't a social call."

"Right." I explained the first sighting, sitting at the Peak and seeing Phil in the ravine. I told her about being visited in my room and that my dad thought it was just my imagination.

"He's not really one for thinking outside the box now, is he?" She ground the cigarette butt under her clear heel and blew smoke out of her nostrils, acrid and stuttered. She was definitely tugging on a scab. I tried to ignore it. Otherwise, she'd keep her payment and I would be left high and dry.

"He's practical." I tried not to sound too defensive, or she'd pounce.

"He still pining over Mary, or what?" she asked, then looked away.

I watched her profile for a bit, trying to figure out the real meaning behind the question. "I don't know. I guess. Why?"

"Jesus, just asking." She snorted. "Not very practical. It's been forever."

"So . . ."

"So there's a ghost; what the hell do you need to establish connection for?" She turned her head whip quick. "You're not trying to push in on my game, are you? Because you'd be piss-poor at it. You can't even look interesting, let alone be interesting."

"Christ, Penny, I don't want to take your business. That's you, not me. I'm not the taker!" I was on my feet.

"Listen, Winifred." She drew out the syllables of my name like a belch. "I'm here for you, little cousin." More sarcasm. "So don't get all high and mighty with me. I'm just trying to figure out what the fuck you're up to."

Hands on my hips, I took in the grounds. Our home was beautiful in its own way. The landscape of Winterson seemed accidental in vision, like debris out on the water—driftwood bobbing about on the waves. Gravestones and peaked mausoleums snaked up and down the rolling green expanse with curving geometry. The trees scattered on the property were bent and hobbled, like the widows who tended the nicer sites. I remembered what was at stake and sat down, resigned to the fact that not only would I have to have patience with this asshole, but that I would have to tell her more about my life than I really wanted to.

"We might get kicked out. And this is our last chance." And then I told her everything, leaving out the part where I was inadvertently haunting the place myself; that she didn't need to know.

She was quiet after, taking out more gum and another smoke. "Well, that's a fuck of a thing, isn't it?" She sounded, almost, sympathetic. Maybe she'd changed. Maybe I'd underestimated her.

I nodded and pushed out a small, sad laugh like a sigh. "Yup."

"I might be able to help. But it's gonna cost you."

Of course it was. It already had. How could I have ever thought it wasn't going to be about the opportunity to make more money? I can be such an idiot.

"I don't really have much money, you know. What I gave you is basically it. I have enough for another hour."

She stood up this time, brushing off her flat backside and straining to straighten her back. "So, let me just make sure I have this right. You need this place to be haunted so some tour guy can help the cemetery make money. That would mean you could stay. And you've found an actual ghost?"

I nodded, then hung my head, waiting for her insults, or worse, her laughter.

"And what you need is to learn how to, like, operate this here ghost, so it shows up when it's supposed to? Hmm. Well, first of all, I think you'd better introduce me to this Isaacs dink. Sounds

like he could use someone with my"—she snapped her fingers—
"talents."

My head popped up, eyes focusing on Penny, who stood with
one hand on her hip, the other bent so she could examine her
broken manicure over the rim of her huge glasses. "Does this mean
you're going to help me? Because you're right, it would be a great
opportunity for you and you could make money off working with
him, maybe. I guess I was kind of like a broker on that, eh?"

She held up the examined hand. "Not so fast there, Tonto
from Toronto. Hold up. Don't think you're getting this for free.
You're going to give me back my mother's ring. I'll take that as
payment. Then I'll help you with your little Casper issue."

Not ten minutes together and I had been hustled out of the
one thing of value I owned. I hoped Roberta wasn't around to
watch this part of our reunion.

I sighed and sat back down. "Can I think about it?"

She was already walking away. "Think fast. It's a limited time
offer. And you don't have much time left, I'd imagine." She
stood up and walked off, throwing a quick wave over her shoulder, headed for the front gates.

"I hope you get herpes," I whispered. I grabbed my dog and
walked toward the Peak. It was exhausting finding the ways
to not slit her throat when in her company. Penny angered me
to the point of murder and then insulted me so that I doubted
I could pull it off. We were just past the last spire of the chapel,
near the Soldiers' Memorial wall, when someone called out.

"Hey, jerkface."

I stopped short, the wagon rolling to a stop against my
heels. Phil. I turned and there she was, perched on top of the
Silverstein family stone like a messy gargoyle in creased leather

and faded camouflage. She smiled—thank God. But then dread poured into my belly. Had she been near the chapel? Could she have overheard my conversation with Penny, where I basically asked a sadistic arsehole the best ways to control her?

"Where you going?" She held her arm out at waist height. In her hand was an unlit cigarette, which she then tossed up and caught with her lips. Fuck, she was cool. She knew it too. Even dead, even trying to be nonchalant, she was pleased with herself.

"Taking him for a walk." I indicated the snoring dog behind me with a tilt of my head.

"Yeah, thank God." She jumped down and strode over, crouching into a squat to softly slap Dingleberry's haunch. "Better run this boy quick. Wear off some of his energy before he tears up the place." He farted in response. She laughed.

"He just fell asleep. Just now." I don't know why I felt I had to explain. "He's pretty old. And obese. So he sleeps a lot. More than average. I think."

Christ, why was I talking like a verbal machine gun? She was so jovial, so different from last night.

"Yeah, well, let's go then. We don't want to keep him waiting." She stood beside me, sweeping her arm out in a gentle-manly gesture, and waited for me to walk. She lit her cigarette with a match that didn't smell and blew O's out in front of us like a slow tunnel.

We were rounding the curve into mausoleum territory when I realized her footsteps were a rounded crunch, even and clear. Clear as math.

"Phil, where did you come from?"

"The ditch."

"The ditch?"

"I showed you, dummy. The other day? Down the hill? Remember?"

I tried again. "No, I mean, where did you come from, like, before?"

"Same as you."

"Really?"

"Yeah . . . from a vag." She literally slapped her own knee when she laughed.

"Oh."

Maybe she heard the disappointment in my voice.

"I don't know, Win. I just was, then I wasn't, then I was." She stepped off the path to turn a quick cartwheel, cigarette clamped in her lips like a sparkler. Her pants pulled away from her feet and her ankles flashed, thin and vulnerable above her black Reebok high tops. On the soles of her shoes she had Sharpie'd words: "MINISTRY" on the left and "PANTERA" on the right.

She wasn't so good with serious, I was learning.

"When were you?"

"What?" She jogged back to my side.

"When were you . . . alive?" I wasn't sure it was polite to bring it up.

"I was born in '75. I kicked it in . . ." She poked herself in the forehead with her finger while she thought. "I guess it was 1990."

"You guess?"

"Jesus, I don't know. Who cares anyways? You writing my autobiography?"

"That would be a biography. Autobiography is when you write it yourself."

"Nerd." She slapped my butt and ran ahead, slipping into the trees that bordered the Peak. I was shocked at the solidity of her touch.

"Wait!" I was struck with sudden panic. What if she was disappeared? What if she was going back to wherever the hell she came from in the first place and the last thing I had was being called a nerd and a nervous tingle from her touch?

I jolted ahead, Dingleberry's body shifting to the front of the wagon like a bag of water. He gave a sharp snort and tried to struggle to his feet while I dragged him behind me up off the path and over the grass.

"Sorry, boy."

He was settled back into his regular croissant shape by the time we pulled into the clearing. Phil was there, leaning against the willow, languidly smoking. I was filled with a relief that was still tinged with guilt from my meeting with Penny. It made me quiet. I slowed down and took a moment to resettle the dog on top of his bunched-up blanket. He sighed his displeasure and I patted his wrinkled head.

"Easy, big guy."

"You know, you should really get him checked for diabetes." She pushed smaller smoke O's through the larger ones, both fading out into the shade like bursts of light.

"We did. He's fine. Kind of." I left the wagon under the awning of branch and sat in the sun in front of the smallest grave, an unnamed infant who'd lived for three days a full ten years before Phil was born, twenty-five years before she died. It was the beginning of me counting in this way, around the existence of her.

I tried to ignore her, looking out over the cliff instead. It was still early enough, and in the glare of the late afternoon sun there was nothing romantic about the ravine. I saw it for what it was—brackish water trickling over debris, weeds grown feral grasping garbage in prickly fingers, a broken chain-link fence covered in raccoon shit and clotted with dandelions, and a hidden grave behind a cluster of trees.

"Did they, did they find you?"

She didn't answer. "I mean, you're not still . . . down . . . there . . . are you?"

"Fuck no." She blew smoke out her nostrils. "Jesus, you're so macabre."

"It's just, why are you still here then?"

She pulled in her cheeks against bone with the last drag and then flicked the cigarette butt onto the grass. It never landed. Instead, it was just gone without the act of going.

"Did you want me to leave? Am I disturbing your hectic day or something?"

She was growing angry, impatient with my questions. I'd finally gone too far. I really needed to slow down. But I couldn't; everything was bubbling over. I had no idea how to adult anything.

"No, it's just, don't people haunt the places where their bodies are?" Once more, the idea of my mother was behind my questions.

I turned around, but she was gone.

"Phil?" I stood. "Phil?" I looked over the edge into the ravine. She was nowhere. So then why did it suddenly feel like she was everywhere?

FIND ME

Dad kept some of my mother's ashes under his bed. He didn't think I knew, but I knew. I found them collecting laundry last winter. Laundry was my job; cooking and the dishes were his. I also vacuumed, and we split the bathroom because no one needs to do that shit job full time.

I followed a trail of balled-up socks across the floor, tossing them in the basket like an old-fashioned farmer. I got on my hands and knees and checked under his bed. One more sock, and a suitcase.

"Sweet!" It was old, definitely vintage. Pale blue and hard-sided with a pearl plastic handle on silver fittings. I pulled it out.

There were clasps on the front and I slid them up and over the hooks with satisfying snaps. I pulled it closer, so that it sat between my outstretched legs. I wasn't trying to snoop; I already assumed it had belonged to my mother so considered it fair game. I probably should have taken a minute to consider why Dad hadn't shared it with me, unlike everything else of hers. But I didn't. I just pulled it out and yanked it open.

Ashes are just calcium phosphates, potassium, and sodium, with a few other minerals. They're everything that allows us to stand, taken down to particle. I think about this when people are so grief-stricken they have to sit down. We keep a lot of chairs around the chapel. People sit in the cemetery all the time. Some families have started to make the gravestone markers into benches.

I was already sitting, so I was good on that front.

She was in the standard plastic bag, reinforced and durable. I knew it was her right away. People are always shocked in both directions—by how many ashes are left, and by how an entire life can be reduced to so little. There's enough to split among family members. There's enough to, say, bury in an urn in the cemetery where you live with your unsuspecting daughter and also keep some under your bed.

I think this is where my father's words were too, locked away in a little blue suitcase. I think he kept them here with her, for her. There was nothing left for me.

Roberta used to say she didn't care what happened to her body once she was done.

"Who gives a turd? I'm not using it anymore. Let the worms open a disco in my skull if they want." I thought about that at her funeral, pictured her eye sockets glowing with pulsing strobe lights—a worm bouncer perched on the bridge of her nose—and laughed out loud. People assumed I was grief-addled, and someone patted my shoulder in comfort.

I didn't say anything to my dad about finding the suitcase. I let him keep it like the last secret between them, but there was something unsettling about it too. It felt like an anchor.

After the haunting talk began, Dad was quiet during dinner and retired to his bedroom right after. He'd been wandering the grounds at night. Searching. I knew it was getting bad when Floyd knocked on the door one afternoon looking for him.

"He's not at the burner. Wanders, these days. Let him know Ferguson's lookin' for him if he comes this way."

I stepped outside in bare feet, onto the front stoop. "Floyd, can I ask you something."

He didn't say anything but sat down on the step and reached for his cigarettes. I sat beside him.

"Does it seem weird to you, all this ghost stuff?"

He lit his smoke and laughed out a cloud. "In here? Nah."

"Does my dad seem weird to you?"

"Thomas? Nah, he's a good head, that one."

"I mean lately. Always out, walking around . . ."

Floyd smoked quietly for a moment. I let him. I was used to the silence of men.

"I think he's hoping the ghost is my mother." It sounded crazy once I said it out loud. Crazy and cruel. But Floyd allowed it, not even raising a wild eyebrow.

When he was almost to the filter, he spoke. "When I was back home, I had a shite job delivering for shops. It was horrible, I had to talk to everyone and make nice—ugh—but it was money. I socked it all away, every last penny after helping my ma with bills. And after a year, I had enough to buy a boat. A boat was an investment, you see. It meant I could join the fishers. It meant I could be a captain. It meant I was free." He pointed out toward the yard with the smoldering butt. We both watched that far-off spot as he talked.

"So, one Saturday, I went down to Bantry and made my way to the landing. There were two boats for sale. I'd already heard about them and talked to the fellas. Both were near my price. One was near new and all sleek and kitted up. The other was an old wood clunker, the kind that breaks trailers and grows mold.

I'd made up my mind before I got down there, of course. But then I saw it: dark green hull with a bright blue interior. A mast so tall and so thick it looked like a tree stripped of branches. And on the side, in this kind of mustard color, was the name *Odin*— God of War, that is. I knew it was mine when I saw that." He whistled through his teeth, smiling, and took another drag.

"Boy, I took some ribbing for that one. The boys thought I'd lost it for good. How could I take on the clunker? The radio was all held together with tape. The wheel stuck and started. There was one life jacket so flat it was turning to sludge on the deck. But I was smitten. I would drive that war machine to hook the kraken himself. I'd hang his ugly hide from the pole like a hideous flag. I spent every day for the next twenty years on that soggy deck, and it was the love of my life. And every day I heard from the boys about it. Said I must be deluded to drive that beast."

He turned now to face me. "Sometimes the best thing to sail by isn't the North Star. Sometimes it's your own delusions. At least then, you're sailing in some kind of direction of yer own makin'." He stood, both knees popping in protest, and walked down the laneway toward the main road, uncurling from a hunch as he did. At the gate, he tossed his butt into the driveway.

"But what's even the point then, if it's that hard? And what if you're going the wrong way?" I asked him.

He smiled again—I'd never seen him do it twice in one day. "Girlie, I'll be the captain of the God of War to the day I'm in the dirt and that's right by me. It's a damn good life's story."

I didn't have the heart to ask what became of the *Odin*. I didn't want to know where delusions sailed you to.

That night, I decided I had to try to tell my dad about Phil again. I sure as hell couldn't tell him the past sightings had been me. Thomas Blight being Thomas Blight, with his stubborn sense of truth and no-nonsense living, would march me over to Mr. Ferguson right away to have the tours canceled, blowing our only chance at staying.

I knocked on his bedroom door.

"Dad? You awake?"

"Mm-hmm."

I opened it up. He was sitting on the edge of his bed, fully clothed.

"Whatcha doing?" I tried to be casual, but I imagined he had been whispering to the suitcase, beseeching the dust for coordinates to a secret meeting place.

He held up his empty hands to indicate nothing.

"Dad, I need to talk to you about the ghost."

His eyebrows lifted.

I sighed, sitting down on the bed beside him. "I talked to her."

"Who?" Too much hope in his voice.

"The ghost. The spirit that's haunting the cemetery. Her name is Phil."

More eyebrow action. I barreled on.

"She died here. She's my age, almost, I guess . . . if you don't count dead years."

"Win . . ."

"Dad, listen. I know you think I was just scared before by a person, but I wasn't. I was scared by her. I mean, she's a person, but she's also dead. And she's come back after that. I'm not scared anymore but she's real, Dad. She is real. I just talked to her yesterday."

"Win, there's been too much of this. You're confused."

"Oh, I'm confused?" I stood up, hand on my chest. "I'm confused? What about you?" I pointed at him. "You go out every night. Tell me you don't think it's Mom."

He stayed quiet.

"It's ridiculous, Dad. Honestly. I can't have made contact with a ghost but you still think Mom's going to show up?"

He looked down at his feet. He had nothing to say, of course.

"Fine. Have fun talking to your suitcase." His back tensed. I left before I could take it back, slamming the door behind me.

"Can you get a Ouija board?"

I jumped, dropping my pencil. "Jesus, Phil. You can't just show up like that." I put both hands on my chest. I was sitting at my desk writing in the journal Roberta had given me, after failing to get through to my dad.

She squeezed the bun high on the back of my head, which was being held in place by two pencils.

"Cute. Look at you, you big nerd."

It was a fair assessment. I had my black-rimmed reading glasses on, and an oversized turquoise silk robe covered in giant pink peonies. Underneath I wore an undershirt and a pair of boxer shorts, all thrift store finds. Still, I wished I were in camouflage and a T-shirt right now, like Phil. She was effortless cool.

"Oh, get a pulse." I shot back, getting up from my chair and going to the overstuffed closet to grab a pair of baggy jogging pants.

"Hey, hey. Ever touchy, you." She smiled. "Don't get gussied up on my account." She watched me yank the gray pants over my boxers and take a seat at the window where we had spoken that first night. If I was touchy it wasn't because she called me a nerd. It was because I was feeling worse and worse about my meeting with Penny. It's what I had been writing about it in my diary. Fuck, I hoped she hadn't read it over my shoulder.

"What's up, Phil? What do you want?"

"I told you." She sat beside me. "A Ouija board."

"What the hell does a spirit need with a Ouija board?"

"Ha, a spirit." She started to make fun of it but then looked thoughtful, as if she had never considered this before. "I dunno, just thought it would be fun. Maybe we could debunk the myth or something. I mean, I should be able to tell, right?"

Then she was up off the bench and stomping across the floor to the milk crate that held my records. "Ooooo, vinyl!" She dropped to her knees and started thumbing through them.

"Careful, those are my mother's." My voice was unnecessarily high.

"Is she gonna get pissed if someone else touches them?" She held up Björk and checked out the song list on the back before dropping it back down into the collection.

"Not really. She's not here anymore." My voice got quiet. I guess I was disappointed she didn't already know. Wasn't there like some kind of lobby on the other side? Somewhere where they could meet and talk? Somewhere where a ghost could send another ghost to check on their daughter?

Phil turned slightly. "Oh, she bit it?"

"What?"

She put her thumbnail on the side of her neck and drew a line to the other side, making a groaning tear sound, then closed her eyes and hung her tongue out the side of her mouth.

"Nice. Yes, she's dead. For a long time. Forever, for me, I guess." I was anxious about her fingers, anyone's fingers on those albums, even my own. "Here, why don't you tell me what you want to hear and I'll find it." I walked over and crouched down.

"You got any Metallica?"

I shook my head.

"Pantera?"

"Nope."

"Motörhead?"

"Nothing like that."

"So, nothing good?" She tipped onto her butt and leaned back on her arms stretched out behind her.

"I guess not."

I picked through the crate, trying to work up my nerve. I cleared my throat. "So, Phil, do you ever, like, appear to anyone else?"

She laughed. "What, you into monogamy or something?"

I blushed. "No, I'm just wondering. If you, like"—I didn't want to use the *H* word—"show up to other people."

She crossed one foot over the other, legs stretched out right beside me. It was making me nervous, all jittery energy.

"No. This is enough. Besides, it makes me feel kinda sick to be around people. I mean, other than you." I wondered if she could blush without the blood to flood her skin. "Like my bones are coming back."

I turned toward her. "Coming back?"

Her face was unusually serious. "Yeah, like, this prickly kind of, I don't know." She tapped the fingers of one hand against the fingers on the other. "Like knitting or something. But, like, inside."

I turned back to the records, biting my thumb. How could I ask her to haunt the place when it was hurting her? I felt sick now. I heard myself asking Penny how to make a ghost appear on command.

"It's like the more people see me, the more I remember dying, in a physical way. I don't want to remember." She sounded young suddenly.

"So, if I had to leave . . ." I shuffled some more records. I wasn't sure what answer I wanted. "If I left, would you still be here?"

"I would simply die," she responded, throwing the back of her hand across her forehead and enacting a slow, dramatic faint onto the floor.

I laughed and turned back around. I found something. I pulled out the Neil Young's *Greatest Hits* album, stood and walked over to the turntable. I moved the needle to the last groove and the first notes of "Harvest Moon" filled the room like fabric run loose off the bolt. And then she was beside me. She touched my arm, where the wide sleeves of the dressing gown draped, her fingers finding a bruise so small I couldn't remember getting it. She felt like no temperature could, like lightning itself bundled in the cold of a cloud.

"Are you going to stay here for a while?" My voice was small, a sound trapped in a seashell you had to put to the side of your face to hear.

"Are *you* going to stay here for a while?"

I saw writing on her wrist, a hand-poked tattoo with three letters, *KWE*, in uneven capitals. It was underlined by a scar raised white and keloid. I remembered her thumb at her own throat. She ran a fingertip over my bruise, found the darkest center and put pressure there. That sweet ache hit all my muscles at once and I closed my eyes. Her fingers released a kind of electricity traveling the laneways of my ribcage, zipping along one rib, jumping to the other, settling in my breastplate like a burn.

She started up her story again, and I leaned in to make sure I caught every word—

I don't have a coming out story. There was no dinner where I choked out a confession around dry pork chops or gathered family together to cry and beg for understanding. I just was, and that was that. I never had to tell anyone. My mom knew from day one, and she said it wasn't anyone's business but my own, and if I felt like whispering it to people I trusted or screaming it from the front porch, that was all it was—my business.

"I never had to make an announcement that I liked guys. Why should you have to make one?" My mom snorted when I asked her about telling Amos. "Besides, if your grandpa doesn't already know then he's more senile then we think."

Just being was enough. At least at home. It was empowering and normal and maybe set me up for failure. Because school was a different kind of thing. School was shit.

We were bused into town, in our kilts and blazers and button-up shirts. We looked like a choir heading to regionals. But we weren't. We were just brown kids barreling into town in a busted-up yellow bus to attend St. Francis of Assisi Secondary School. I didn't bother to change, not really. How would a different version of life even be worth living? So, I found a way to survive—stay low, don't talk too much, and just get through the day—each and every monotonous day. But then, in tenth grade, Jennifer happened.

Jennifer was a light-skinned half-breed, so she "passed." And she lived in town. But man, did she ever have a mouth on her—like straight off the rez potty mouth deluxe. She could make you love and hate her in the same sentence, and I did. Jesus, I hated her. And holy hell, I loved her too.

She showed up the second week of tenth grade with her shirt untucked from her gray uniform pants. She had nothing to say to anyone, not even when they asked her a direct question. Instead, she'd just lock them in a stare until they turned away. I mean, she answered the teachers, but no one else. And at lunch, she sat in the caf and ate an entire big bag of Bugles herself. Like, she didn't even offer not one friggin cone to anyone. Not even the boys who swarmed her table trying to strike up conversation. All she said was, "Please get your ass off the eating surface. I don't know what you eat at home, but the only shit I want on my plate here is gonna come from the kitchen."

I was sold. I was all-in.

I watched her in the hallway all day, following her into the gym and walking a few steps behind her as she sashayed out the side door to smoke. I was late for every class. It was worth it. I picked up valuable intel. She sang to herself when she walked and smoked Player's unfiltered. She didn't move for oncoming pedestrian traffic and she sure as hell didn't stop to chat. She was a hero in high school—all balls. No fucks given.

I watched her walk across the field after school with headphones on, backpack over one shoulder. She headed into the back woods, slipping through the perimeter of thin pine. That probably meant she lived in the complex. Kids who lived in the complex had worn a path through the brush that left them in the edge of the development. I craned my neck on the bus when we drove by. No sign of her. I thought about her that night while I was peeling potatoes and walking Baby Boy home from Amos's place. The next day I almost swallowed my gum when I walked into homeroom and there she was, sitting in the desk beside mine.

"Uh, that's my seat." Fucking big mouth Shelly Herring. She stood in front of the desk with her pale arms folded over her massive chest, her orange curls tossed over her shoulders, scowling down at the new kid.

"Relax, Tits McGee, there are plenty of other seats you can fit in to," Jennifer answered. I snorted at this, sliding into my own seat. This was a mistake. Thrown off by the unexpected response, Shelly turned her wrath on me, the easier mark.

"I don't want to sit in the lesbian section anyways." She stomped off.

"Good, we didn't want you turning it into a fish market," Jennifer shouted back.

If I'd had a ring I would have given it to her on bended knee. Or maybe a new lighter with a heart Sharpie'd on the side; she'd probably have liked that better. Instead, I leaned across the aisle and loud whispered to her, "Nice one." In return, she fixed me with that stare and kept her eyes locked until I straightened in my seat and fumbled around in my backpack.

I tried to build better peripheral vision during the twenty minutes of homeroom, not brave enough to outright look at her. Ms. Grady shushed us through announcements about volleyball tryouts and a reminder about the track and field tournament on Friday. Then she took attendance. (Jennifer Brubeck, right after James Beausoliel and before Cathy Connolley.) She answered her name with a double tap on her desk. The kids took notice.

And instead of replying to roll call with the usual "here," they found new and innovative ways to signify their presence. I was caught off guard, so the best I could manage to "Philomene Elliot" was a quick "yup." But Tyler Fisher stood, saluted, then sat back down. Gary Harris whistled. Imogene Monias threw her arms in the air and waved them like a wind sock outside the gas bar. By the time she got to the *T*s, Ms. Grady had had it.

She dropped the clipboard to her desk. "Look, if you're not going to answer like regular humans, then I'm just going to mark you all absent." She resumed to a chorus of "here," one after the other. But it was already done. Jennifer Brubeck, with her tight French braids, thin silver hoops, and wide-legged pants one shade darker than uniform standard, was a leader. And the kids in my school were always eager to follow.

Period three was phys ed. We were starting off the year with basketball, my favorite. We'd been running drills for a week already and I was in line for layups when Jennifer sauntered in, went over to Mr. P with a class schedule, and then took a seat in the bleachers.

He blew his whistle. "Ms. Brubeck, there are no spectators in PE. Suit up."

She tipped her head back in exasperation. "I just got my classes today, man. I don't have my gym clothes." She looked at him like he was a moron.

Jaime elbowed me in the back. "Go, it's your turn."

I stepped out of line. "Uh, go ahead." I pretended to fiddle with my laces. I wanted to watch this play out.

"I don't care. You don't need shorts for drills. Now get out here."

She sighed, loud and long. "If I end up with rancid BO, I'm telling everyone you are a child abuser." She stood, dropped her bag off her shoulder, and made her way down the bleachers. "Hey, Elliot."

I froze, standing up quick. The ball fell from my arms and bounced off the tip of my shoe. She knew my last name?

"You got an extra T-shirt?"

I shook my head. Dammit, why didn't I have an extra T-shirt? I vowed to carry one every day from that day on.

Jennifer just shrugged and started unbuttoning her dress shirt. I had no voice. I was nothing but heartbeat and unblinking eyes. She pulled off the shirt to reveal a white undershirt. Then she picked up my wayward ball, dribbled it a few times, and tossed it back to me. I caught it by instinct alone and she grinned. And that was it. By fourth period, I was smoking for only the third time in my life, out by the soccer field.

Jennifer didn't give a rat's ass what anyone thought of her, but everyone cared what she thought of them. We walked each other to class and spent lunch period eating junk food and talking smack to anyone who walked by. People would sit with us, but she let them know their stay was temporary. And in December, we were invited to a twelfth-grade end-of-term party, in town, no less. I made plans with my mom to sleep over at Jennifer's place. After the last bell, I followed her back through the bush to her townhouse on a corner lot in the complex. It was narrow and had three stories, like a turret. She lived there with her mom, who was "a real slut," according to Jennifer, one who rarely came home on the weekend. She said she didn't have a dad. Despite being small, the house echoed both our voices and the Megadeth cassette we blasted on the living room stereo. I thought it would be awesome to live like this, no old men or little kids cramping my style. I liked the idea of alone, as long as I could do it with her.

I sat on her box spring on the floor, looking at the metal post-ers and piles of black clothes on the floor in nonsensical heaps while she rummaged in the kitchen. She returned with two mugs and a half bottle of peach schnapps. She handed me a mug and shook the bottle with a smile. "What did I tell you? My mom's—only sluts drink this shit."

We laughed, halved the syrupy liquid into our mugs, and clinked them together. It burned my throat and coated my teeth with sick-sweet. But it sat heavy in my stomach and made me feel brave. "We're gonna have the best time tonight."

She laughed at me. "No, we're probably not. But who cares? We'll stick together and get through it, with a little help from our friend here." She raised her mug and drank deep.

We probably should have attempted cat eyeliner before we started drinking. We both ended up with overexaggerated circles around our eyes that winged out toward our temples like a super-hero mask. I thought we looked ridiculous, but Jennifer insisted it was "so punk." We both put on a pair of her fishnets under denim shorts and then carefully took turns ripping strategic holes in them. I put on a black fluffy sweater that hung off one shoulder and she wore an Alice Cooper T-shirt with the sleeves cut off so that it scooped low and showed side boob. We shared a red lipstick and brushed our long hair until it crackled. We were ready to go.

"We can't leave yet. It's only nine o'clock!" She was appalled that I'd even suggested it.

On the way back downstairs, I attempted to start a conversa-tion. "Where are you from?"

"Toronto. And now I'm here, in this hellhole." I followed her to the living room. She found a mickey of vodka with less than a third left and poured it into our cups. "I got into trouble and my mom, bless her whorey soul, thought bringing me back to her hometown would help."

"What trouble?"

"None of your business, nosey." She threw herself on the couch, holding her mug out to keep it from sloshing.

"Sorry," I lowered myself beside her.

She punched my arm. "Just kidding. Shoplifting. Just some clothes, nothing big. But she freaked out. And now here we are." She opened her arms to indicate the room, empty except for an old TV with rabbit ears, a flower-patterned couch, and heavy wooden end tables.

She got up to flip the tape and when she came back, her mug was empty. I chugged mine. The burn in my stomach was starting to twist. It made me want to move, so I danced a bit in my seat.

"Come on." She pulled me up and we thrashed around the room. She banged into one of the end tables and the lamp fell, casting a yellow light on our legs and feet. She laughed and grabbed my hands again. I yelled over the music.

"What was Toronto like?"

She pulled me against her and put a hand on my hip to make my movements match hers. "Heaven. Concerts and street artists and clubs you could sneak into, and punks on every corner. It was fucking heaven."

And then she kissed me. It wasn't one of those kisses where someone realizes they're kissing someone halfway through and gasps, backing away either. It was hard and deliberate. She pushed me down on the couch and we made out for forever. I couldn't have opened my eyes if I wanted to.

In ninth-grade science we learned that we're made up of millions of cells, that each one moves and vibrates and is independent, but they work together so we can exist. That really fucked with my head. How can I be made of separate things and still be me? Am I just a bag of other beings thrown together by chance, like groceries? I didn't understand how I could stay together that way. Until that moment, on Jennifer's couch, when she slid her hand down the front of my shorts and I was pulled completely apart, into a million different pieces.

We left at ten o'clock with warm beers shoved into the pockets of our winter jackets. The cold attacked our fishnet legs like the wind was carrying razor blades. The streetlights cut precise in the hard sky, throwing little pools in exact circles on the gray sidewalk. We drank the beers en route and by the time we'd slipped and fell our way to the party, we weren't sure if it was the ice or the alcohol that was making us unsteady.

We pushed our jackets into a hall closet behind a stack of sleds so they wouldn't get nicked, and Jennifer pulled me down the congested hallway to the kitchen. "Come on, let's tax some drinks." It didn't take long before one of the boys who tried to sit with us in the caf handed over two plastic cups of white wine.

"What the fuck, Bryce? Did you steal this shit from your mom?" Jennifer made a face at the contents of her cup but downed it anyways.

"You know it. Chardonnay for the ladies."

She looked him up and down and grabbed his cup out of his hand, slinging it back, then handed him the empty. "Apparently."

Within an hour, she was slurring. I went to the bathroom and when I came back she was sitting on Jim Flaherty's lap, smoking his cigarette. Jealousy flared in my muscles and I crossed the room and grabbed her arm. "Let's go."

She yanked her arm back. "What the fuck, Elliot?"

"Get up," I hissed.

"Jesus, you better go back to the bathroom and change your tampon." She leaned into Jim, who laughed with a circle of friends. Jennifer charmed people even hammered.

"Seriously, let's just go." I sounded desperate. "Let's find another drink, okay?"

A boy in the next seat handed her a brown bottle. "She can just have mine."

She smiled sweetly, popping the cigarette back in Jim's mouth. "Why thank you, kind sir." She threw her head back and drank, so uncoordinated the glass rim clattered against her front teeth. She finished with an exaggerated "aaaahhhh" and then belched and blew it at me.

"Jen, you're being a real bitch right now." I was hurt.

"And you are being a big dyke right now."

"Ooooooo." The boys loved it. Suddenly there were so many of them, and just me standing in the middle, alone, caught.

"Jesus, Jen, you're drunk."

She pulled her legs up and slung them over the entirety of Jim's lap. He pulled her in close and bit her neck. "Duh. It's a party. We're supposed to be drunk. Not giant losers," she yelled at me.

I don't really know what I did after that. I sulked, basically. I found another kid from the rez and smoked a pinner on the veranda. I pocketed a copy of 1984 I found in a bedroom. I sat in the bathtub with a passed-out kid wearing a red toque. I just killed some time, trying to make sense of everything. But I couldn't. When the hallway started to smell like puke, I decided it was time to go. I went to the closet and dug out my jacket.

"She let him finger her while Stephen watched. I knew it was a good idea to invite tenth-grade chicks!" Bryce staggered to the front door, almost pushing me into the closet. Rob Stein laughed behind him.

"Fucking sluts. I love this school!" He "wooed" loudly and they slammed the door behind them.

I pulled out my coat and Jennifer's ski jacket fell at my feet. I sighed. No matter what, I couldn't leave her here. Besides, I couldn't help but wonder if we'd sleep in the same bed tonight. Even now.

I found her in the laundry room with Jim and Stephen Morris. Jim was wearing her Alice Cooper T-shirt like a headband and Stephen's dick was resting on her bare shoulder.

"Jen! Let's go now." I rushed into the warmth of the small room, pushing Stephen into a pile of dirty clothes, snatching her shirt off Jim's sweaty head. She looked up at me, crouched and leaning against the dryer. Her cat eyeliner was smudged down her cheeks, red lipstick faded to cracks. She smiled, eyes unfocused. "Hey, Elliot."

"Fuck off," Stephen wailed from the floor, stuffing himself back in his jeans. "She doesn't want to go anywhere with you."

"Wait," Jim cut in. "Maybe she wants in on the action. Whaddya say, Phil? You wanna go?" He used his beer bottle to point down at Jen. Her bra was twisted, one cup pulled down to reveal the smooth pink of her nipple.

"Fuck you, asshole!" I stood in front of her, shielding her, trying desperately to get her to stand up. To come with me.

She reached up and took my hand, her head swaying, eyes half closed. "C'mere, Elliot. Kiss me. It'll be fun."

"Yes!" Stephen pulled himself out of his pants again, rubbing his diminished hard-on back to attention.

"Jen, come on, get up, let's just go home."

"Let's just do it here. C'mere." She pulled at my stockings, ripping one leg from midthigh to kneecap.

"I knew it! Fuck, I love lesbians," Jim said from somewhere behind us.

I crouched down on my knees in front of her. "You don't have to do this, any of this. Let's just get out of here, okay? It's not safe."

She smiled and put a wavering hand on my cheek. I put my hand over hers. "Elliot, don't be dumb. It's not like we're real dykes or anything. It's just for fun." She leaned in and licked my bottom lip.

"Woooo!"

For the second time that night, every cell in my body pushed off another, and then another, and I fell apart.

I managed to drag her up the stairs, wrap her coat around her and get her out on the front lawn, where she threw up. I piggy-backed her across the complex and got her into the house before she puked again, this time in her mother's boots by the front door. I left her on the couch with a glass of water and a blanket, making sure she was on her side so she didn't choke. Then I called my mom and asked her to come get me.

I'd have to wait until after holiday break to hear the rumors. And so at the start of the new year, when I returned to school, I was a bull dyke who hated men and Jen was the girl you wanted at every party. She passed me in the hall like I wasn't even there. Like I was a bag of groceries waiting for someone to take me home.

→))))→

She finished and scooped me up. I let her lead me in the next song; I'd lost track of how long we'd been like this, holding each other, moving now and again. I was having trouble coming back from the story. And there was a new feeling, more shameful than anger, burning at the edge of my tongue. Was I jealous?

I tried to push the feeling away, so I danced away from her, swaying in the long silk and hilariously mismatched jogging pants as I stepped, mouthing the words I knew by heart, eyes closed because I couldn't open them. I imagined her, standing by the turntable, leaning back on the shelf with that tight smile, waiting for me to stop. So I couldn't stop. I moved my arms like the music depended on my conducting, like I was the tune itself. And when the sounds abandoned the rhythm, one by one, pinging off into the greater silence, I opened my eyes, facing the stereo and the shelf and nothing more. She was gone again. And I was more alone than ever.

Sleep was evasive, but I refused to fill the hours with anything other than a gentle swing in the hammock, counting the cracks on the ceiling until they jumped and snapped into patterns.

I once read a story about a man who grew a fig tree out of his stomach. He had joined the Turkish Resistance in the seventies but was captured and imprisoned in a hillside cave with two other men. In a show of power, or maybe just being lazy in their work, his captors tossed in a stick of dynamite, throwing the men against the walls, blasting a hole in the side of the cave. The man's family searched for him for four decades, never knowing about the small fireworks that whisked him away.

Decades later, a researcher was wandering the mountains, taking in the local flora, when he noticed what appeared to be a fig tree growing on the side of a hill. He was intrigued;

figs didn't grow in this region. He approached and saw that it had followed the light and emerged out of a hole in the rock, directly inside an old cave with no entrance. He examined the tree, taking photos and drawing sketches of growth patterns and bark markings. Finally, perplexed, he decided to dig into its roots. There he found the skeleton of the resistance fighter, who had all those years before been imprisoned in the cave, but only after he had stopped to eat a fig, unaware that this was to be his last act of resistance. That seed in his stomach grew and, nourished by the decay of its host and spurred on by the spotlight of sun, had extended its woody arms toward the sky in one last, long hallelujah.

His family was so relieved to have found his grave, to know where his bones rested, curled fetal around the circulatory system of roots. I assume they kept the tree, wondering, like I did, if their brother's DNA was twisted into the bark, if each leaf that bloomed from a tightly spun bud was a word pushed from his lungs, plucked from memory. In that way, they only had to wait for autumn to sit underneath it to debate politics with him in a flurry of leaves or to catch enough of them— three to be exact—to hear "I love you."

Even in death, we do the work of being found.

So then where was my mother? How was Phil here and not her? How could she not have been the one to follow my voice through whatever crack in the ether had allowed in this strange girl? How could she have not given me a place to hear her, to hear the words she never spoke, that sat in her memory like tightly spun buds?

HOME

My dad was changing. He was farther and farther away each day. I kept wanting to talk to him after our fight, but he avoided any conversation. For her part, Phil dropped by my room every night for a week, popping up at least once a day on my walks, just to tag along, or tell me a joke or convince me that two was enough to start a coven.

Last night, we'd listened to Neil Young for the thirtieth time, since it was the only album we could agree on.

"Do you think you're going to stay here now?" I watched her, sitting on the floor, coloring in her nails with a black marker, lines that faded back to chipped polish as soon as she was done filling them in.

She raised her shoulders to her ears then back down. "I don't want to." She was getting more surly and closed off as the days went on.

"Where would you rather be?" Since the afternoon at the Peak when she chastised me for asking too many questions I was careful to dole them out slow.

She started from her left thumb again, chasing the impermanent change. "Just not here." I watched the movements of her body that mimicked breathing, a habit she couldn't let go of. She got to her middle finger, sighed, and tossed the marker back on my desk. "It's like here all I can really remember is dying. I just don't want to be dying every damn day."

I wanted to know about that, about how she died. I still didn't know much, other than her childhood and her first crush and then the image of her body going soft and stiff at the same time down in the ravine. But I couldn't ask. It felt like there were a thousand ways to rub her wrong.

The next week Dad was called to meetings at Mr. Ferguson's office. He came back with little news but let me know that on Friday there was to be an all-staff meeting with Isaacs to discuss the new developments.

Meanwhile, Penny messaged twice:

Send Isaac's number. Never mind, I'll google him.

And then, two days later, on the morning of the meeting:

He's not getting back to me. Make the intro. Unless you really want to be homeless.

Penny was making me anxious. And not the regular "Penny anxiety," either, but a new kind—sharp and specific because of that stupid meeting at the chapel. I'd told her about Phil, and about the potential of losing my home. She knew things now. Things she could use against me. I didn't know how to answer her.

"I'm going." Dad stood by the kitchen table while I checked messages on my phone and ate the last scrapings from a bowl of porridge.

"Can I come?"

He shook his head.

I wasn't going to argue, but I wanted to know everything that was going on. I couldn't help but start to feel that there were two sides to this thing now: us and Phil. And I didn't like being on this side, being part of the "us." Not when all I really thought about anymore was when she was going to appear. I'd started wearing earrings and lip gloss in anticipation.

"What time is the meeting over?"

He shrugged.

I wondered what would happen if we did leave. Who would she visit then? I pictured her by the Tratskoff obelisk, her hair tied up in a braid, jacket off, one pant leg pushed up to her knee while Floyd taught her how to throw a left hook. I was already homesick and I didn't even know for sure if I had to go.

I imagined her brown arms crisscrossed with a basket weave, her bones half complete and aching in their casings—her being knit in place one jab at a time. It was a painful image, just as bad as the one of Dingles begging for change on the corner of Parliament and Carlton. I sighed. I had to protect my home at all costs. It's just that my idea of home was changing.

My dad closed the door behind him and I opened Messenger again.

Penny—Come by Winterson this afternoon. He'll be here.

I waited on the chapel steps with the dog sleeping off under the bushes, just like the first meeting. This time, Penny showed up on time and in a good skirt.

"Is he here?" She was still walking up the path; no need for niceties with me.

"Just, come sit for a minute."

She pulled her sunglasses from her face and dabbed at the sweat lines they left. "Seriously, Winifred, is he here or what?"

"He came for a staff meeting." I pointed to the side of the building where Floyd and Mr. Ferguson and Mrs. Prashad milled about in the afternoon sun.

Penny smoothed down the front of her blouse and propped her glasses on her head. "Great, I'll just go introduce myself." She took a step toward the side path.

"He's gone now."

She stopped. "What the shit do you mean, he's gone?"

"I mean he left. Half an hour ago." The way her face twisted into the kind of shapes that would support a pair of forehead horns was exactly the reason I knew I needed to have adults close by for this meeting. Like it or not, Phil was a part of what made this place home now.

"What the fuck are you playing at, Winifred?"

"I'm not playing at anything." I put my hands up to show that I was completely disarmed, that I came in peace. "I'm going to give you what you want and then things can go back to normal. Just forget about everything I said, about there being a ghost or any kind of job here for you, because there isn't."

I dug in the pocket of my jean shorts and pulled out a piece of red fabric. I placed it on my lap and unfolded the material. In the center was a gold band with a large solitary emerald surrounded by smaller diamonds: Roberta's engagement ring. I picked it up, watched the sun throw rainbows where it hit the stones, then held it out to Penny. "It's all yours."

She stood still, eyes clasped on the ring in the center of my palm, the cuss words stuck in her throat. She moved toward me with malice and snatched the ring. She examined it and tried sliding it onto one finger after the next. Finally, it fit on her pinky, just barely. She glared down at me. "It's not just about the ring. This was about my career, not that you would understand. You're still a shitty little baby."

"I'm not a baby. I'm sixteen for Chrissakes!" She had the damn ring, but of course that wasn't enough. I felt its absence already—one more piece of Roberta gone.

"Yeah, well, you can't even do one thing to keep from being homeless, so again, what do you know?" She held out her hand and examined the ring. Her pinky was turning red.

I couldn't think of a comeback, because she was right: all I had to do was this one thing and we would be safe, and now I couldn't do it. My mouth open and shut again without a sound.

She laughed, a mean laugh that fell between us like hail. "Thought so."

I sighed and it ended in a scream. I stood up, stomped over to Dingleberry and grabbed the wagon handle. I made my way past her—refusing to break eye contact, scowling as hard as I could manage—and headed for home. I stopped to shout back at her. "I hope your fucking finger falls off!"

I realized halfway home that she hadn't agreed to anything.

A ROUND LOSS

"What's up?" Dad asked.

I'd left Penny hours ago, and the two of us were sitting at the kitchen table in front of bowls of tomato soup in this ridiculous heat.

"Nothing." I crushed five crackers at once onto the top layer, an orange skin already settling over the uneaten surface.

"Doesn't seem like nothing."

"Oh, you're one to talk. Or not talk." I snorted. He was more of a ghost around here lately than the actual ghost. He wasn't eating much more than me, just scooping up spoonfuls and letting them pour back into the bowl.

He let that one slide and we ate for a bit in silence. I broke it. "Dad, I want to know more about my family. Mom's family."

"Okay." He didn't look up.

I wondered if he felt insulted, like maybe he wasn't enough.

"Call your cousin. Maybe she can come by, spend some time with you."

"Ha! Penny?"

He nodded.

"Penny can't do anything for me. I mean, she wouldn't do anything . . . and yeah, I'm not sure she actually could even if she wanted to." I walked over to the counter and dropped my bowl in the sink, turning on the water to rinse it out. I wondered if it was a coincidence that he was bringing her up now.

"You could try calling back to your mom's community." His voice grew strained. As much as he was preoccupied by obsessive thoughts of Mary Bax Kalder, he sure as hell didn't like talking about her. It was like this even when I was little. Every story was delivered in this tight, compressed voice, a voice built out of timber and restraint, a tone that kept something in.

"Calling who? To say what? I can't just randomly call people. No one knows me there." This one was accusatory. Maybe if he had made more of an effort when I was small to bring me there, instead of turning into the walking dead with grief, maybe then things would be different. "I'm just some strange girl from the city."

I'd gone too far. I watched his shoulders fold in, his head dip a little lower, like he was trying to make his big body smaller. I didn't have the strength to make it better, not now. I started crossing the linoleum, eager for the escape of my room.

"You are Mary's girl. You're not 'just' anything."

I stopped for a moment, back turned to him. Then kept going.

I read a couple chapters of *The Mists of Avalon*, willing time to pass. I heard my dad take Dingles out, but I refused to look through the window. I was tired of seeing him search the corners of the property. It was beyond sad now; it was infuriating. I needed to convince him of Phil. Any more of this searching-for-my-mom shit and he'd lose his mind.

It was hot as Hades in the attic. I turned on the two fans I kept up here and they provided some relief. I still had to strip down—panties and a sports bra—or I'd die. I lay on the cooler floorboards, readjusting the fans to hit me directly, and logged onto Instagram on my phone. Out of habit or masochism, I went to Jack's page. check'em out! #braceless

There was a close-up shot of his mouth, smiling big, straight, white, metal-free teeth, pearly and commercial-pretty. The second image was him laughing, head thrown back, hair all glossy. Jesus. It was too much. So I guess he'd made it home okay from camp. And I guess he had taken my "fuck off" to heart.

"Ooooh, who's that?"

"Christ!" I jumped up onto my hands and knees, my phone clattering on the wood. Phil sat on the window bench, legs crossed at the knee, hands under her chin like an old-timey glamour shot. "Holy hell, Phil, you can't keep doing that to me!"

"Why not." She slid down to the floor. "If I keep doing it, maybe one day, you'll stop being such a jumpy lil bitch."

I sat back on my butt and checked my phone to make sure the screen hadn't cracked. "Probably not. It's just regular human behavior to be scared by scary shit." I was all foot-mouth today, it seemed. She took it in stride.

"Seriously though, who was that?" She indicated my phone with a tilt of her chin.

"Just a friend. Well, he used to be a friend." I shrugged my shoulders. "Where were you today?"

"And what is he now?" She refused to allow the subject change.

"I don't know." I really didn't know. But talking about him with Phil made me uneasy. "Nothing, I guess."

She nodded slow and then clapped her hands. Now that she was ready to move on, the matter was closed.

"I want to be all naked too. Panty party!" She yanked back the lapels of her jacket and shrugged it off. It looked heavy, all thick leather and metal notions, but it hit the floor without a sound.

Her arms looked so thin without the big coat. She snapped open her pants, tearing the buttons free from the holes in one swoop, then paused, hands on her waistband. "Is this okay, then?"

I nodded. I wasn't sure what to say. Her underwear was heartbreak pink and a size too small, so that the bones of her hips stuck out above the elastic band like a geography of want. There was a tiny red rose and a white bow in the front, the underclothes of a young girl. I looked away. There were cuts on her thighs, raised and pale like the one on her wrist. One looked like the letter *A*. She sat opposite me on the floor, in her faded black T-shirt and pink underwear. It was clear she wasn't wearing a bra.

"Can you braid my hair?" she asked without eye contact. It made me feel older. I stood up, found my brush and some hair elastics in the top drawer of my desk, and rolled my chair behind her.

"Wait!" She jumped up and fixed the needle at the beginning of the record already on the turntable. This time it was Dolly Parton. We had two records we could agree on now.

She settled back down, me sitting on the chair and her sitting in between my legs, her back against me. I started to pull the brush through her dark hair. It was thicker than I'd imagined and full of tangles. I took my time working through each knot. "Phil, will this even work? I mean, will braids stay?" I was thinking about her futile attempts to color in her nails.

"Nah, not for long. If I concentrate, it might stay for the night." Her eyes were closed, enjoying the stroke of the brush across her scalp, like any living person would.

I worked carefully and gently, wanting her to stay right here, arms draped over my knees, fingers dangling near my shins. I brought her hair to heavy silk, a little greasy and with split ends, but still beautiful. Then I pulled her head back and started at her hairline, dividing the mass with a pale part in the middle. I was going to do two braids, buying more time.

"Where is your mom buried?"

I was done with the first braid and was just tying off the small end with an elastic that was too big and so had to be looped many times. The question caught me off guard. "Uh, she's here. Out by Soldiers' Memorial. But part of her is here too. She was cremated, so Dad buried half her ashes and kept half."

"Weird. Right? Is that weird?"

I felt defensive, hearing someone else talk about my dad like that, even if it was true. "Maybe. But people keep ashes. That's why they sell urns for them."

"Yeah, but other people don't have their loved ones practically buried in their front yards either. It just seems kind of excessive."

I was rough when I started the next braid. She was quiet for a minute before she asked the next question. "Tell me about her."

"She died giving birth to me, so I never knew her."

"But you know about her though, right?" I realized she was trying to repay the favor of this intimate work of doing her hair, allowing me to talk about what I needed to the most.

"Her mom was Métis and her father was a traveler."

"No shit."

"Seriously. She didn't have any siblings, and her parents died in a fire before I was born, so all that's left are, like, cousins and second cousins, distant relatives." It made me sad to say it out loud. I pictured school-portrait-sized photos of people who vaguely looked like me pinned to a map, all at great distances from where I lived.

"So, you didn't grow up with any Nishnaabes?" So, she was Ojibway. I figured from her tattoo, but this confirmed it. The trick to getting to know Phil was pretending you didn't notice when she slipped up, like letting Roberta spin a story.

"Well, no. But I had my auntie Roberta until last year. She was amazing. She lived in the seniors' home over by the Friendship Centre."

"Wigwamen Terrace."

"Yes, Wigwamen Terrace." I slowed down the weaving of my fingers, trying to draw this out a bit. "She was awesome. Mostly we did puzzles and gossiped about her friends, except no one was really her friend. She thought they were all dinks."

"Ha! I have aunties like that." She slouched in the circle of my legs. "*Had* aunties like that."

I tied the second braid off and patted her on the shoulder to let her know we were done. She stood up and spun in front of me. "Well, what do you think?"

Jesus Christ, she was beautiful. The lines of her face were hard and angular, her eyes clear and bright. She was a young boy in some ways and a delicate woman in others. And there was something about the way she looked at me that made me think of my mother's portrait in the living room below us, so close. I couldn't explain what it did to me, so I just said what I really wanted to at that moment. "Can you sleep over tonight?"

We climbed into the hammock, Phil purposely teetering and hollering, threatening to send us spinning to the floor. We clutched onto each other's limbs and tried to synchronize the sink into the curve. Once we were laying down, the balance threw us right up against one another. There was no personal space to be had in a hammock.

"This is nuts, yo." She threw her hands up and slapped them back down against her naked thighs. But she was smiling.

"I know. I don't really think about it much, it's just me, so . . ."

"Oh, you mean I'm the first gentleman to grace your bed chambers?"

"Indeed you are, kind sir."

We fake bowed to each other while remaining prone, wiggling against the weave, giggling at each other's ridiculous gestures while trying to keep the bed steady. Eventually we settled back down, slowly swinging and listening to Dolly's trials and tribulations on low, just a twangy whisper in the background.

"Tell me a story." I wanted spirits and gods and whatever the hell else dead girls knew. I was desperate to find an anchor. Instead, she gave me the third part of her story—

I left home at the end of tenth grade. I didn't want to leave my mom or my siblings, even though they were annoying as shit. But I had to be somewhere else. Toronto, specifically. I didn't run away. Instead, I begged my mom to let me leave. I told her I was being bullied at school, that I wanted to meet other people like me, that I'd die if I stayed. I had started cutting and I couldn't hide it from her for much longer. She was exhausted and worried so she talked to my auntie Shirley, who told her I could stay with Tay, my older cousin who had a place in the city. Shirley assured her I would be fine, that I would get it out of my system, get bored, and was sure to return by the end of the summer. And in the meantime, Tay would keep an eye on me. She said I would be in good hands.

Tay wasn't there when I got off the Greyhound. I waited at the station with my duffel bag. It was dark before she rushed in, out of breath and dragging a skinny white girl with her. "Holy fuck. I thought the bus got in tomorrow. Good thing my mom called to check. If you talk to them, tell them I was here on time, okay?"

I picked up my bag. "Yeah, sure thing, Tay."

She waved me on and I followed them out onto the street. The first thing was the noise. Cars and people and a streetcar and music from somewhere close. It made me slow. Tay turned back twice to tell me to hurry up before throwing an arm around my neck and pulling me along.

"Jeez, don't be such an old woman. You look like Grandma right now, all worried and shit. Let's go. We got plans, don't we, Candy?"

Candy looked at me with wide blue eyes. "Is that all you have to wear?"

I was in jeans and a T-shirt. I shrugged.

"Don't worry, we'll fix her up." Tay squeezed me. "Look at those fucking cheekbones, wouldya? She'll be a pageant queen in no time!" I smiled and leaned into her, picking up the pace. I missed Tay. She'd left home last year and things got quiet and people laughed less.

We stopped in at a Shoppers to use the makeup testers, and they made me switch out my Adidas T-shirt for a black tank top. Tay undid my ponytail and finger-combed it to volume, then we were off again.

I loved Chinatown right away. The buildings and storefronts were uncoordinated and blocky, like Lego. Red, yellow, green, all painted with symbols and letters I couldn't read. I stopped to watch a half dozen wind-up toys bark and flip and smash into each other in a box outside one door until I got yelled at to hurry up. Some windows had golden-crisp chicken hung from curled claws, others were lined with dusty bottles with cork stoppers. Carts laden with fake jade and smiling Buddha statues rattled as they were pulled inside for the night. And the smells were too many to take in, but I did.

"Jesus. Let's go. We need to get there before Tim ends his shift. I don't want to have to sweet-talk a different door guy," Tay grumbled, guiding me by the elbow onto a side street. I didn't want to leave the hustle and plastic mechanics of Spadina Avenue. Here, the trees acted as green soundproofing, and skinny cats judged us or ignored us from steep front stoops and peeling, wooden balconies. My cousin clapped, as if unable to handle the quiet of this street, and wiggled her flat ass in a tight black dress and short boots with peeling heels. "I'm gonna get chi-blasted tonight!"

"I hope Carmen is there. I don't want to have to go to the booze can to get blow. Not before last call, anyways."

Tay gasped theatrically and covered my ears. "Holy, Candy, my poor little cousin. She's just straight from the country, you know. She don't know nothing about these things!"

"Yeah, just like you were?" Candy rolled her eyes and they burst out laughing. I laughed along even though, I'll admit now, I really was kind of shocked.

At the corner there was a fruit stand, the outdoor shelving and bins empty for the night, a slight smell of rot and a cloud of flies hovering above. On the other side was a coffee shop with green stools lined up uneven at a wooden counter. A few people sat there, and one guy was even playing an acoustic guitar. We turned the corner and a powerful stench of fish punched me in the face.

"Ew, what the hell?" I pinched my nose.

"Oh, you get used to that. It helps cover up the other smells." Candy's voice was all singsongy. She smoothed down her rainbow-colored crop top and passed a hand over her smooth belly. "I'm actually pretty hungry now."

"We'll grab pho after the bar." Tay lit a cigarette. "Almost there."

I don't really remember actual things from that night, just feelings, really. I guess, impressions. We were in a crowded, dark place with a loud band and cheap booze. There were so many people to meet and everyone was friendly. I laughed a lot. I pissed in an alley and smoked weed in another. We went to a different bar after that where the guys we were now traveling with smuggled me in, although I don't think anyone really cared. There was at least one dog in the bar, so, who cares about an underage girl? I lost track of my bag and panicked until Jared, a tall rocker with a blue mohawk, showed me that he had it. Then we all crowded into a narrow laneway and went in a metal door, down a flight of stairs, and into the smokiest room I'd ever been in. It was like descending into a cloud. You couldn't take full breaths. My spit tasted like smoke for two days. Everything in my bag stank. My own hair made my eyes water. Tay and Candy talked to new people and suddenly everyone was really loud and insistent. People had a real need to tell me exactly what they thought in very loud voices and everything was so clear and important. In between grinding their teeth through philosophical arguments about music and the best places to live a "real" life, they ducked their faces to the table and snorted up thin white lines, or shoved keys holding small piles into their nostrils. I was drunk, so it was hilarious. And then it was annoying. And then I was too tired to keep my eyes open.

Jared carried me to the park. I woke up with my face

smooshed against the buttons on his leather jacket. It was early morning and all around us the market was coming to life. Trucks wheezed down narrow streets, pans clattered through the open back doors of a bakery, old ladies in kerchiefs trundled buggies up the sidewalk and the fruit sellers were making pyramids out of oranges. I dozed in and out in the shade while my cousin and her friends shared a twelve-pack. Miraculously, I still had my bag, and I used it as a pillow. I remember feeling like I had just had the best night of my entire life. I felt free, like everything was ahead of me. Like I had so much left to do.

And for weeks, I was free. We partied almost every night. Candy and Tay lived in a studio above the Big Bop night club on Queen Street, and there was always something going on. I met drag queens and drug dealers and go-go dancers and honest-to-god artists. I was there the night the double-jointed guy who mixed LSD in his bathtub accidently got some on his hands and spent the night licking a dominatrix's boots, even though she had taken them off at the door.

Sometimes we were hungry. Sometimes we were sick. But always we were looking forward to what came next. Then Tay got a new boyfriend. At first it was just like, whatever—Candy and I had to find something to do while he "visited" her. The studio didn't have walls except for the bathroom, so privacy was hard to come by. Then he started staying over more and more, and I pretty much set up camp with a tarp and a lawn chair on the roof so I could sleep and generally avoid him. I hated the way he talked to her. Like she was trash. He looked like a bleached skeleton, all skinny and the color of school paste. That's why they called him Ghost. He said it was because he could slip in and out of a place unseen. I knew it was because he was the whitest motherfucker around. Practically see-through. He looked the way he looked at Tay—like there was nothing really to see.

She paused long enough to break the spell. I opened my eyes in a hurry, expecting her to be gone. But she was there, looking somewhere over my shoulder.

"Phil?"

"Yeah, I'm okay. I just don't want to talk about that anymore." She sounded sad, which was more than she usually revealed.

I snuggled in closer. I wished she'd had a smell. "Okay then, tell me a different story, just until I fall asleep."

She cleared her throat dramatically. "Okay, so there was this old Greek dude named Aristophanes. He was buddies with Plato. They probably made out behind the temple after smart-guy meetings. He told this story about the origin of people, trying to explain this need to be with someone, anyone, sometimes. How we are always looking, trying to fit together.

"Aristophanes said that people used to be like eggs—you know, round. And there were three kinds of these eggs. One kind had four legs, arms, eyes, ears, and two faces and two dicks. They were the children of the sun. The other kind had the same, fours and twos of most things, except instead of dicks they had vags. These were the kids of the earth. And the other kind were similar, except these ones, instead of having two of the same, had one vag and one dick—one on either side. They were the children of the moon, which would be the coolest mom to have, I think.

"The egg people, they moved like rolling boulders, like cartwheeling acrobats, they were fast and ferocious. They could go in any direction, could see everything all at once, and were never, ever alone. They were warriors; we were warriors. Someone always had your literal back, and so nothing had limits.

"The people decided they were done with the gods. Like, why the fuck waste all this precious time and good goat meat making offerings to these sky butts when they in and of themselves were so complete, so powerful. There wasn't even anything left to pray for. So some tough eggs tried to climb into the sky to begin a war. They didn't get very far. I mean, the gods still had things like thunderbolts, and they had already killed all the giants on earth, so they could make short work of these eggy fuckers.

"But the gods were pissed, insulted and all. They didn't want to kill them off completely though, because the gods needed their sacrifices. They loved a good BBQ. It was Zeus who came up with the plan. He would cut each of them in half so that they lost their completeness. Two arms, two legs, two eyes and ears, and one damn set of genitals each. Then Apollo, the sicko, he twisted the half-humans' heads around so that they would be forced to face their own emptiness, the loss. And he closed up the hole from where they were severed by pinching closed their stomachs, leaving a belly button behind. Just that tiny round reminder.

"Sure, the plan worked. There were no more cartwheeling, bulldozing attacks from below. They were less tough. But, the two-leggeds were also dying—some from loneliness and a new kind of sad. Others spent all their time searching for their missing half. These people tried locking together with others, holding on with all their might. But eventually they starved to death, doing nothing but holding on to another half-person, trying to be whole. They stopped sleeping, they stopped eating. The gods realized they'd fucked up, and then Apollo, the weird body-mod specialist, he decides he can fix it all by relocating the people's junk, of course. Who doesn't love a good junk move? So he does. Up till now, they were still on the back—remember, the heads had been twisted around to the front so people had to face their loss? So he puts the junk at the front. So they freak out less about their loss and just get back to clinging to one another and eating mastodons or whatever the hell they ate back then and sacrificing lambs and shit.

"And again, the gods' plan worked. So I guess, as long as we can find our other half, even for a bit, we remember more than that round loss. We remember what it's like to be the remarkable whole."

"Phil?"

"Yeah."

"You're a remarkable hole . . . a remarkable *ass*hole." I waited a second and then barked out a laugh. I couldn't hold it in.

"Well, would you look at that?" She flexed her arms and pulled me in tighter, shaking me a bit as she did. "A bad joke in the middle of a serious lesson. You might just be an Indian after all."

It was the nicest thing anyone had ever said to me. I pushed back into her so that each notch of my spine fit into the space between her ribs, lay flat against her shallow stomach, so that my hips were lined up with hers. And even though her breathing was nothing more than a habit, I matched my breath to hers, which was easy, like sliding into warm water, and fell asleep this way, inside the soft arithmetic of two into one.

When I woke up, I was alone. The sun streaked across the hardwood and covered my legs with hot. I stretched out, thinking about Phil's arms holding me in a loose grip, almost casual except for the fact that we were both in our underwear and in my bed together. I put one foot on the floor and flexed my toes, then lowered the other and did the same; same amount of pressure, same sequence of toes. I stood up and walked to the window, already full of morning sun.

And there, on the window bench, held in the safe plush of a folded sweatshirt, was a single brown egg. I clapped my hands and kept them clasped under my chin. This was what it must feel like to get flowers. And I knew exactly the vase to put it in.

I went to the shelf and fished out an empty jar. I grabbed a pair of my best underwear from the drawer—the pale coral ones with the lace back and silk front—they were too big for me anyways; I'd picked them up at a vintage store and the elastic bust on the first wash. I folded them real small and pushed them to the bottom of the glass, making a delicate bed. Then I got a small piece of paper and wrote in careful script *us* and taped it to the underside of the cap. There, it was ready. I put the jar on the seat and grabbed the egg to fit it inside.

"Fuck!" My thumb poked through the shell made epithelial thin from having been emptied. On the bottom was a small pinhole where the yolk had been drained, leaving just a clean shell behind that wouldn't rot. I had underestimated how fragile it was. Cracks snaked from the thumb hole to the bottom. I carefully extracted my finger and gently lowered the shattered shell into the jar anyways, still holding its shape. Maybe I could just position it so that the brokenness was out of sight.

"Shiiiiit," I whispered, screwing the cap on, and held it up to the sunlight. It was still a beautiful thing. Such a beautiful, fractured thing.

RETURN AND FALL

Things with Dad were at an all-time low. I could barely get a standard greeting out of him, and worse, he was rushing. He never rushed. Now there were half-full cups of coffee in the sink when I got up, more socks than usual not making it into the laundry bin, sitting at the end of the hall like forgotten kittens.

I decided I was going to force some interaction on him. It was a Saturday, so he wasn't technically working, which wasn't to say that he was at leisure. Summer was going fast, and between the Jack incident and Phil and now this Penny bullshit, I felt like I'd barely seen him.

I spent some time with eyeliner, which was a near disaster, but I didn't blind myself, so I took it as a victory. I pulled my hair back and wore a plain black dress that was more of a huge tank top than anything. Before I put on my low-top Chucks, I took a Sharpie and wrote on the pale bottoms: PARTON on the right and YOUNG on the left.

"Perfect." I grabbed round sunglasses off my dresser and ran down the stairs, leaving Dingles behind. "Sorry, boy, on a mission today." He literally did not give one shit.

Outside it was a late-summer morning parade—sun and pollen and green and those tiny flies that turn to dust when you try to brush them off. It was a show-off of a day. It was the kind of day that scrubs mud and snow and windy rain from your memories.

I was just past my lawn, stepping onto the path from the front gate that separated our space from the public space when I ran into Jack.

He looked seven feet tall in basketball shorts and a white long-sleeved shirt. He wore blinding new sneakers and his hair was short and faded. He smiled big when he saw me and opened his arms.

"Freddie!"

It was too late to turn and run in another direction, so I stepped into his embrace, my face squashed against his cotton shirt. Oh God, he smelled good.

"Hey, what's up?"

"Oh, nothing." He held me at arm's length and smiled big and forced. "I'm home. Got back a week ago."

I smiled back. "Yeah, I saw in your profile." I tried to be light, to not sound like a girl who had stalked him online, the kind of person who then goes to every person's account tagged in his photos looking for clues.

"You got some time? Let's go get iced coffees." He grabbed my hand and suddenly I could no longer think for myself. Gone was the confidence of the girl in my bedroom, the one who was the best version of anything. I followed him out the gates. I tried not to be disappointed when he dropped my hand once we hit the sidewalk.

We walked down Parliament into Cabbagetown. On the way, he talked about camp—his friends, a sprained wrist from windsurfing, almost getting thrown out for sneaking off in the night to swim. I listened, but mostly I watched him talk. His neck was wider, his shoulders broader. He took up more space, and it changed the way his body moved. He was surer, less concerned with anyone outside of his circle of attention. I kept up his pace to stay inside that circle. We were almost to the coffee shop when I realized I'd left my house to go spend the day with my dad, with a longing to run into Phil, and now here I was, speed-walking down the street with Jack. I was feeling kind of disappointed in myself, that and a strange excitement of being around a person that makes you acutely aware that you have genitals, genitals that you may or may not want to rub against them.

"So how has summer been so far?" We were sitting at a small outside table, two plastic cups of milky iced coffee in front of us. Of course, he meant summer after our fight. He knew damn well how that'd been.

"Oh . . . good, I guess."

"Anything cool happen?"

Honestly, I was going to tell him. I'd like to say that some larger loyalty, some beautifully intricate sense of belonging and love bound my voice, that I didn't even consider telling him about Phil. But the reality was, I was going to tell him.

"You remember a few years ago, when you were really into ghosts and we were setting out those traps and stuff?" I leaned across the table, at the start of a good story.

He laughed, throwing his head back and covering the top half of his tanned face with a wide hand. "Oh God, can you believe that? How embarrassing."

I was caught off guard. "Why?"

"Ghost hunting. Oh Lord. Way to obsess over a TV show. Jesus. I threw all that shit out years ago."

I leaned back in my chair and took a long sip of coffee. Then I told him about the nerdy tour bus company and how lame it all was. And nothing more. We finished off and wandered a bit, heading over to the park. The rest of the afternoon was eaten up by speculation about school, online gossip, and Jack stopping to roll a pinner on the bench by the wading pool. I laughed too much. I covered up the awkward with self-deprecating jokes.

We were almost back at Winterson when the incident came up. We were walking slow, just before the main gate on that patch of sidewalk in front of the south part of the property where the fence was covered in vines and you could see my house. Across the street the high-rise building's balconies were dotted with ferns and flags and drying onesies. The cars drove by faster than they should have.

"Listen, I just wanted to say, about what happened between you and me . . ."

Oh Jesus. I had to cut him off. I wasn't sure I could bear it. *Seven, fourteen, twenty-one . . .*

"Oh, it was nothing." I even waved it off with my hand, betraying myself. "Whatever."

He pushed his hands into his pockets and kicked at the ground, bringing us to a stop. "No, I just, wanted to apologize. For being a complete dick."

I stayed quiet, hoping for more, and also hoping for nothing more than this.

"I just, I was messed up. I think I'm just confused, about, well, you. And me. And everything really."

"How are you confused about me?" It felt like I was fishing for a compliment; I had that same burn of shame but also the need that overwhelms it.

He ran a hand through his hair, watching his feet. "It's just, well, we're good friends."

Best friends, I wanted to correct, but didn't.

"And it's been like that forever. And then all of a sudden, things got weird."

"Weird?"

He sighed. "God, I'm bad at this. Not *weird* weird, just different. I freaked out and I should have just been there for you. I mean, it's not like I didn't want to do it. I mean, of course I did."

"You did?"

He nodded. "I did, and then I freaked out because, well, because you're my friend. You're my Winifred."

He really was bad at this, but it didn't matter. This was more than I could have asked for. Except that I did ask for it. I'd thought about this for weeks. And yet, it didn't feel the way I'd thought it would. It was like not all of me was there. I tried to focus in. I watched him close his eyes when he tried to think of a word. How he kept playing with his newly cut hair and then jamming his hands back in his deep pockets. I noticed twenty-eight and thirty-five and forty-two . . .

"I know. I wanted to call you and tell you about how I got into a fight right after it happened, except I couldn't because the fight was with you." I laughed.

"Exactly! That's exactly what I mean," he said. "I just don't know that it's worth it. Not that you're not worth it . . . ." He reached out and grabbed my shoulders, making sure I wasn't getting angry. I wasn't.

"No, no, I get it."

"God, Winifred, can we just, can we just forget about being mad at each other and see how the rest of the summer goes?"

He held out a hand like we were supposed to shake on it or something.

I smiled. It was so good to be talking to him again. For a while there I thought I would go crazy without proper human contact. Even thinking this made me feel guilty. I didn't mean that Phil wasn't human or proper contact. I pulled myself back to this moment, to this boy.

"Yeah, I'd like that."

"Oh, thank God." He pulled me in and hugged me again, except this one lingered. I let my whole weight rest up against him, from my knees to my collarbone, and when he let me go, I wobbled. For a moment, I thought he was going to kiss me. He just held me there, in that space, and looked down into my face, his eyes still a little red, still smiling.

"Listen, I gotta go. My parents made me get a stupid job for the rest of the summer and I have to be at the community center for four. Come by if you're bored." Then he closed me back in his arms, back into that hug, and I rested my head on his chest. This was so nice, so normal. I didn't realize my eyes had been closed until I opened them.

"Okay, Winifred. I'll text you later." He started waving, walking away. "Maybe you can sneak out tonight? There's a party over at El Akaad's place. I'll bring the weed, you just bring yourself." He jogged up toward Bloor and the subway station.

I didn't wave back. I didn't answer. Because I was too busy watching Phil on the roof of my house, watching us, slowly shaking her head, arms crossed over her chest.

THE POLL

She didn't visit me that night. Instead, I had a dream.

In it, I am sitting at the top of the south border fence, where Jack held me, and I am wishing he would try to kiss me again or maybe not. I can feel the top horizontal pole holding the chain-link wall of fence under me. It's narrow, and so I have to keep my weight even where my butt is on one side and my legs on the other. The pole sits under the top of my thighs.

I am facing the street. The building on the other side of the street is wide awake; every window plugged into the grimy concrete is ablaze with yellow light against the deep night of August. Every balcony is a tooth, off-color and crooked in a residential face. But there are no people, no one watching TV or smoking over the railings.

I can hear the gauzy hush of the dead and insects behind me. It has weight. I want to lean back into that plush sound but I'll tip off. Fifteen feet is too far to fall without consequence. I hold tight onto the bar on either side of my tensed legs.

I know she is there. Same way I know the house is there, the moon is there, the sleepy garden is there, barely corralled by half-buried bricks. Phil is there, at the bottom, behind me. She doesn't have to breathe for me to hear her exhale. And then the ground starts shaking. Except it's not the ground, it's the fence. It starts subtle and then gets faster, more erratic, and I change my grip, hold the pole and the pokey top links that bite into my palms. Someone is climbing.

"Phil?"

There is a response but I can't make it out. It's like humming. The fence sways and I have to switch my balance, flexing and releasing muscles to keep up with the rhythm so I don't fall.

"Phil?"

I sound desperate now because I am. My hands are sweaty. I don't know how much longer I can hold on. It's like riding a mechanical bull, something I've never done but promised myself I would try once age brought bravery. I want to lock my feet into the spaces between the links but I can't move. Even a small change that isn't tied to the sway will send me flying. And I am too scared. The humming gets louder.

"Please stop!"

One hand pulls free and I have to extend my left leg out straight to counterbalance until I can hook my fingers again. The raw wires where they have been cut and tied to the top pole are sharp. One stabs into the base of my thumb but I can't let it go. I swear it'll reach bone. I can hear words now, a song. She's getting closer. The building watches with its toothy grin; silent—there are too many teeth for voice.

"All the king's horses. All the king's men."

She makes her movements big and harsh, slamming her hands and toes into the links like she's pounding piano keys.

"All the king's horses. All the king's men."

"I'm sorry," I try, yelling it down. "I'm so sorry. I didn't mean it." I'm not sure what I didn't mean. The sidewalk looks deadly, all concrete and empty soda cans. And I know I'll have to try to fall backward if I have to fall at all.

The fence rattles. She's got it in her fingers now, using her whole weight to shake me loose. The wire in my thumb tears free and blood fills the spaces between my fingers, making it impossible to hold on. The other hand isn't a wide enough anchor, isn't strong enough to hold me still.

I teeter for a collection of sickening seconds, forward and then back, forward and back, and then I am falling. Head tips, shoulders follow, and then at the last second the fence bucks back and my legs are thrown up. My whole body pulls over itself and then there is just air and air and air. Because soon there will be ground.

"All the king's horses. All the king's men."

I jerked awake on the couch to my phone pinging.

I wiped a hand over my face and picked it up. There were fourteen new notifications. Panic bubbled in my guts. Was my dad okay? Did something happen? I sat up quick.

Two were text messages, the rest were notifications from Instagram.

> Hey, Fred. WTF dude, are you coming to the party?? I think we should work on your birthday wish tonight. I'm your guy. 100%

> FRed, dude, Conner thinkss I'm a morooon 4 not doin it. He says hell do it.

"What?" I opened Instagram. What was he talking about? Doing what? Wait. He couldn't be talking about my birthday—not with asshat Conner O'Dowl? "No, please, no."

The panic bubbles burst and I could barely breathe. I moved

through the screens quickly. On Conner's page was a picture of Jack with a bottle of whiskey in each hand, obviously hammered. Jack missed the chance. Would you smash @WinnishWinter??

"Jesus Christ, no."

Another one was a screengrab from the *Addams Family Values* movie of, of course, Wednesday Addams. Poll time! Who will deflower ole spooky pants? #addamsfamilyvirignity

They were all like that—each one making fun of my request to Jack, each one offering to do the deed, or saying I'd probably eat them afterward, black-widow style. I threw my phone on the floor and pulled my feet up on the couch, hugging my knees. Mrs. Dingleberry jumped when the phone hit the ground, waddled over to the couch and whimpered.

"Oh God. Oh shit. What do I do?"

I'm not sure how long I sat there like that, crying one minute, pulling at my hair in anger next, then laying back in defeat. Worse than the humiliation of the entire party discussing my sexual history, or lack thereof, was the embarrassment of thinking Jack was safe, that he was somehow not like the rest of them. I wanted to die, thinking about my birthday, the way I'd prepared, the way I'd imagined us in the middle of some fucking grand romance. That killed me, that I could get it so wrong. It was an embarrassment that went straight to my core.

The TV was dark and quiet; Dad must have passed through while I was sleeping and turned it off. The kitchen light was still on but the room was empty. There was only the subtle buzzsaw of the dog snoring, splayed out again beside me on the floor. I tried to fall back asleep, but it was no use. I was awake and alone and, once again, a complete joke. Suddenly I wished Phil were here. That none of this bullshit had happened and it was just me and her in my hammock.

I lay there and listened with the unreliable hearing of those in anticipation, every sound assigned to a possibility: Was that her in the hallway? Was she whistling out in the yard? Was she hiding behind the armchair waiting to scare me? Was I being punished? I stayed prone on the couch, not jumping up to look, just listening for a follow-up. Silence.

There were no cracks on this ceiling, nothing to count. I traced lazy outlines of the corduroy lanes on the back of the couch. I tensed and relaxed each muscle in my legs—they were achy from the dream and acute humiliation. I tried matching my breathing to the dog's. I didn't have the patience to master that kind of pause.

I used a fingernail to draw lines in the dry skin of my forearm, corralling them into circles of five. I'd finally started to drift off when my phone rattled. More notifications. My teeth chattered just thinking about them, what they could be saying, who had something funny or crass to say about my stupid broken heart, but I refused to even look in that direction.

If only Phil were here. But now she was mad, and over Jack, no less. What a waste. Tomorrow I would go and find her and explain that he meant nothing, that I didn't even care about him. I would make her listen.

After Jack left me on the sidewalk, I'd gone for a walk around the grounds, looking for her. I walked for almost an hour, even taking the Peak hill in little jumps and wandering the garbage piles and broken-shopping-cart lot. Nothing. Not even a hurled curse word from the bushes.

I'd caught the scent of cedar from a knot of bushes between

the Garrison vault and the Dolag tomb. It rolled down my throat like caramel, slowing my breathing, speeding up my heart; it had to be her. But it wasn't. It was just a newly placed arrangement on the lip of a marble stone, the inscription so new the edges were sharp, MOTHER taking up the entire top curve.

I kept walking, my thoughts turning back to my own mother, the ghost I had called for the day I got Phil instead. I'd always thought if I needed her bad enough, she'd come. That she wouldn't let something as routine as birth, something as pedestrian as death, slice her away from her child like a piece of crust. I wasn't sure if this certainty of her was insanity, and I didn't give a fuck even if it was.

I cut across the grass, headed for the scattering grounds at the back of the property, the hum of the street traffic sliding behind the gloom like blood in a metal vein this close to the northern border of the cemetery. I stopped at the top of the incline and just listened. Squirrels chased each other up a birch, squabbling over a found bagel. I inhaled and a sharp smudge of smoke from a nearby fire wound about my tongue like argyle and lead. I kicked the tip of each foot against the heel of the other and enjoyed the way it vibrated up my calves.

There was a tiny pulse under each fingerprint—a heartbeat like a young bird throbbing for food—so I picked a large dandelion and rolled the pulpy stem between my fingers until they were covered in weed milk.

When I was young, I'd tried to earn my mother's trust, like you would a stray—I was so sure she was hovering around nearby. Maybe if I left a plate of shortbread cookies by the apartment door, maybe then she'd show up. But then what? Could I scoop her up like a handful of ashes and keep her in my pocket to replace the absence of her that had settled there like an abscess? Could I dig out the spot first? And what would do the job—coffee spoon for grief, a silver fork for the ache?

Before Phil there hadn't been as much as a misplaced fog. I rubbed the sticky tips of my fingers on the front of my dress. They felt skinned—electric and raw.

I walked over the brittle grass toward the back fence separating the scattering grounds from the thin forest behind. I'd never actually seen anyone scatter ashes here. It was an odd choice, and I couldn't wrap my head around how peppering a corner of a graveyard planted with bones was anyone's idea of a fitting rest. Even stranger, the west edge was delineated from the urban sprawl by a row of townhouses; their identical backyards open to Winterson. Here were the swing sets and plastic playhouses of children, leaning against the chain-link fence like red dresses at a funeral, gaudy in all their vitality, hemmed in by black grief and gray fetishes of death. I couldn't understand who would buy these properties.

And then there was the act of throwing grains into the air, to get caught in the wind. I imagined little Susie Kwon making mudpies iced with Isabella Monroe's remains, little Johnny Rice yelling "Olly olly oxen free!" with Mr. McDermott's cells coating his new adult teeth.

I crunched down the grass, imagining the blades snapping underfoot like tiny glass test tubes with a thousand strands of DNA inside, sucked from the tomb up. It made me uneasy, this small, intimate destruction. It was better when it just melted away, when it morphed to dust under the pressure of flame that kept touch at bay, removed from the landscape of regular life.

"Now what, eh?" I'd yelled to hidden ears. "How do I get

you back?" I wasn't sure which ghost I was asking anymore.

I lay on the sofa until the sun pushed against the blinds and the birds started yelling around the yard. Somewhere over the hill I heard Floyd start up the mower, like a terrifying rooster signaling the start of the Winterson day. Then I got up, kicked my phone under a chair, and took the stairs to get dressed.

More soggy Froot Loops. I really had to eat breakfast quicker.

"First tour's this week."

I jumped. I hadn't heard Dad come into the kitchen. "What day?"

"Thursday night." He grabbed a Pop-Tart from the open box on the counter, offered me a weak smile and left for the day.

I brought the full bowl to the sink. Okay, it was Monday. I hoped I'd be able to find Phil by then and warn her. Plenty of time. I set out right away.

The grounds were quiet in the weight of the early August heat. It was just after morning rush hour, so even the road was quiet. And in the lull I heard a hundred different calls: cicadas, grasshoppers, frogs, bees. I took the path that wound behind the chapel and into the back lot, listening. No footsteps, no cursing, no Phil. I went all the way to the Peak this way, eyes searching, ears scouring. I pushed through the overgrown branches and into the clearing. There was nothing but a semicircle of unvisited graves and that balled-up blanket kicked against the willow. I felt the Froot Loops working their way back up.

"Phil?" I whispered at first. Then repeated it, louder.

A squirrel launched itself from an elm into a cedar. That was all.

"Fine then." I sat on the edge of the incline, like that first day, settling into the soft grass and digging my feet in. The dream of the fence had kept that moment of unbalance close in my limbs and I wasn't taking any chances. I closed my eyes and called out, mouth closed, voice quiet. I thought about her face, the way her hands moved like boneless things, her hair. I thought of the way her feet always pointed out when she wasn't standing on them. I thought about her scar. I thought about the strength of her skinny arms, closed around me. I thought about the red lines cutting into the tops of her thighs from her underwear. I thought of her fingers . . .

"What?"

I opened my eyes. Her face was pushed right up to mine, an inch away. I cupped my hand over my mouth to hold in a startled scream.

"Holy shit, Phil!" She was on her hands and knees in the dirt, as if she had scuttled up the incline that way, coming to a sudden stop before collision.

"What do you want?"

She sounded agitated. I refused to move back, to be the weaker one. I answered her calmly. "I just came to see you. You haven't been around."

"Neither have you." She relented, pushing herself into standing, arms akimbo. Now she blocked out the sun.

"What the hell do you mean?" But I immediately knew what she meant—my walk with Jack.

"Must be nice to just wander off whenever you feel like it." Suddenly she was smoking, though I hadn't seen her light one.

"Can't you wander off?" I genuinely didn't know.

She laughed, walking a few steps back down the hill.

"Wait!" I called after her. "Where are you going?"

She flipped me the middle finger over her shoulder and kept walking. "I'm wandering away."

I had these weird feelings—maybe indignation, or frustration? And also guilt. And definitely panic. I didn't want her to go, not like this, not mad at me.

"Seriously? What is your problem?" I shouted. Fuck it. I stood up, brushed the seat of my shorts and started to follow. "Honestly, I'm not allowed to go anywhere? What am I, a prisoner?"

She turned back so suddenly I almost banged into her. "Am I a prisoner? Pretty much. And if that's true then you're the one who put me here." She was shouting, red in the face. "You know what, just go home." She pointed up the hill.

"Am I a dog now? You can't tell me to leave." I felt tears building. I'd never seen her like this. And now I was taking my anger out on her; I knew it but I couldn't stop.

She stopped talking then and walked away fast, faster than I could match without running, so I ran. She cut into the tall weeds, through the bushes, and into the sparse woods. The water smelled like old metal and something rotting. I caught up to her when she stopped by a stack of pallets surrounded by empty green bottles.

"What do you want, Winifred?" She put her hands on her narrow hips. She looked tired.

"I want to know why you're freaking out on me?" I bent over, hands on knees, trying to catch my breath. There was something about the air down here. It was too heavy. It was all the humidity of every day of the whole summer collected in a dirty bowl. I needed her right now. I wondered if she knew I needed her.

"Is he the same boy on your phone?"

Frustration was becoming the dominant feeling. "Yes, but he's nobody, he's an asshole. I'm not even talking to him anymore. He went to this party Saturday night and was talking shit about me to everyone. It's just . . . you know what? You wouldn't understand. You're not even alive." I regretted it as soon as I said it.

"Fuck you." Her voice had lost its edge. Instead she sounded hurt.

"What's the big deal? It's not like we're together or anything!" I knew it was a big deal. But I couldn't find a way to take it back so I left it there, stuck in the viscous air between us.

She smiled with irony. "Right." She kicked one of the bottles over. "Who cares? Not me."

This hit me hard in my throat. I wanted her to care. I needed to be more than the girl who called her in. Together we were an egg; she'd shown me that herself. One of the tears I'd been building escaped.

"I'm so confused." I walked a slow circle.

"And I'm so dead, so we're pretty even." She was smoking again, or still, I couldn't remember. Her movements were erratic today, like a collage joined together at the wrong angles.

I remembered why I had come in the first place. I forced a large breath. It was like blowing on hot soup. "Listen." I had to tell her before she took off again. "I just wanted to let you know that there's going to be a ghost tour here on Thursday. At night."

"What the hell is a ghost tour?"

I told her about Isaacs. I explained how it was really important because otherwise me and Dingles and Dad would have to pack up and leave. I warned her to stay away unless she wanted to deal with a bunch of paranormal tourists. And then there was quiet. I was nervous. Maybe she would disappear for good now.

In that space I had time to look around, to look anywhere except at her. There was different trash and the trees had grown to a tangled mass but this was the place she had shown me that first day. This was where she died. Breathing was hard. She was too quiet.

Finally she spoke. "I don't want you to leave."

I released the breath I hadn't realized I was holding. "I don't want you to hurt though."

"I won't. Just don't call for me and I'll be fine."

She looked at me and I saw something soft behind the hardness. I knew then that when she showed up it was because I'd brought her forth. Every time she walked over to my apartment, each time I "ran into her" on a walk, even when I was confused in Jack's arms on the sidewalk—every single time I had thought of her. I was the magnet. Maybe she was right. Maybe I was keeping her prisoner.

I knew what I had to do. I had to get to Penny to make sure she backed right off, because what if she could call her too? If I was going to be a jailer, I could at least make sure it was not an impossible prison to escape.

Phil left me there without saying goodbye. I climbed back up the hill and went home. I must have started a message to Penny a dozen times only to delete every word. How could I get through to her when me not wanting a thing made her want that same thing even more? Instead, I scrolled through her profile. Her last update read "At the Lab tonight. Come by if you're in the hood." She didn't mean it for me. After all, I was definitely not one of her friends and she definitely did not want to hang out with me at a bar. But at least I knew where to find her.

Leaving the grounds was hard. I had to count every one of my jars and records, straighten every paper tacked up on my walls, and triple-check my pockets to make sure I had the right subway fare. But by eight o'clock, I was actually ready to go. My dad wasn't home so I didn't have to explain other than to leave a note on the counter: "Gone for a walk. Back soon." I left out the part where I was headed to a bar.

I kept my head down on the train and focused on the stops— how long it took to get to each one, how many I needed to pass before I got to mine. When I got off at Spadina, I was hit with a wave of anxiety. Not because I was going to see Penny but because this was the stop I used to get off at to go to Roberta's. And she wasn't here anymore. She would never be here again. I felt fragile in her absence. I tried to push past it, rushing up the stairs and out onto the street.

I found Penny on the patio, alone at a table surrounded by arguing couples, laughing girls, and self-important bros. She didn't see me until I was already sitting down. The table legs were uneven and her beer sloshed in the pint glass when I folded my hands on the surface. She was already annoyed. I looked at her fingers first; there was no sign of Roberta's ring. *Probably pawned it*, I thought. I tried to look like I belonged there, like I wasn't intimidated by all these loud people and music and Penny herself. I wished I smoked so I'd have something to do, something to occupy my hands. Instead, I pulled them off the table and put them in my lap.

"I need to talk to you."

"Obviously." She looked around me, like I was so small

she could make me disappear by focusing just past my ear. Maybe I was.

"I just need to make sure that we're good."

She laughed in a small hiccup. "We're never good, little cousin."

"Yeah, and I don't even know why." I really didn't. I could find no clear moment, no defining incident that had set us off in this downward direction. It had just always been like this.

She took a sip of her amber beer. "Well, that's because you're just so good, aren't you? So sweet you just can't even imagine what made big bad Penny want to drive you out of town and leave you on the side of the highway like a box of puppies." She sneered and made her voice high and whiney. "Poor lil Winifred."

"Jesus, lady, what is your problem?"

"You're my problem." She set the beer back on the table calmly. Being an asshole made her calm. "And all people like you."

"People like me? And what kind of people is that exactly?"

"Can't-do-no-wrong kind of people. Spoiled people. Privileged people."

"And how the hell am I privileged?" I pointed at my chest. "How exactly? Dead mother. No friends. Living in a cemetery? How is that being spoiled?" I wished I hadn't said so much. Every piece of information was a bullet for her. I knew she'd throw the "no friends" bit back at me sooner or later, and since Jack, it would really hurt because it would be absolutely true.

"You had her!" The calm was kicked out of her body now and her voice grew louder. "You always had her."

"Roberta?" I was genuinely surprised. "She was *your* mother. I only had her part-time, at best."

"Yeah, but she thought the sun rose and set on you. Her girl." She made air quotes around the words. "I was always a disappointment." I saw in her face that she wished she hadn't handed that bullet to me. I left it on the table for now. She covered the loss with more swallows of beer.

"I mean, look at who got the fucking ring." She slammed the empty glass down.

"And look who has it now, so who even cares?"

"I do!" She leaned forward so we were both inclined toward the very person we wanted least to be closer to.

I retreated, settling back against the chair. "Listen, I didn't come here to fight."

"What else do we ever do?" She leaned back too. "So what's even the point?"

The waitress stopped at the table and put down two shot glasses of clear liquid. "You want anything," she asked me without looking up from her tray.

"No, I'm good."

She shrugged and walked away.

"Jesus, you coulda just got served and you turned it down? What kind of teenager are you, anyways?" Now it was Penny's turn to be disappointed. "Are we even blood?"

"Not sure," I answered honestly, and we both laughed a bit. The agreement made us uncomfortable. She took both shots, one right after the other. I decided to get right to it. I sat up straight, but before I could begin, she started talking, the liquor making her need to share.

"Your dad, he still quiet as all hell?"

"Yup. Every day."

"What a waste."

I didn't answer.

"He's another one, thinks he's too good. Actin' like he's a goddamn priest or something."

I sighed. *Here we go, always having to attack anything she knew I loved.* "What the hell is that supposed to mean?"

"It means no man goes that long without want."

I knew what he wanted. He slept over it every night. But why did Penny care what the hell my dad did or didn't do? She pulled a pack of smokes out of her purse and stood up, her metal chair making a terrible screech on the cement.

I followed her out of the patio area and onto the sidewalk. She teetered a bit trying to light her cigarette, the lighter refusing to catch. I didn't offer to help.

"My father has nothing to do with us. I don't even know why you have to talk about him." She always had to bring it to this place, where I was so mad I couldn't find my way out of it, which only seemed to amuse her more. "And I don't think you should say anymore."

She stepped back, her hands up in front of her. "Ooooo. What are you going to do about it?"

I turned on my heel and paced in a circle. What was I going to do about it? I had come here to reason with the unreasonable. I'd known damn well it could come to this.

I took the lighter out of her hands, flicked it, and lit her cigarette for her. "Penny, I don't want to fight with you again. I just came here to make sure we had an understanding."

She took her lighter back and shoved it in her back pocket, catching an eye full of smoke so that she rubbed her mascara down on to her cheek. "About what?"

"About the . . ."—I looked around—"ghost."

But she was a dog with a bone. "I offered, you know. After your mother died. I came around. Tried to babysit and help out. But no, he didn't need my help."

"Jesus, Penny, seriously . . ."

"I even tried to offer him company, you know?" She pushed her boobs together with her palms. "*Company* kind of company. But oh no, no one was good enough. Not for him and not for you."

I couldn't speak, but my mouth was open. *Penny and my dad?* My stomach hitched around a pocket of air that grew hot. It was uncomfortable to even put them side by side in my thoughts.

"Then coming around Roberta's all the time? Being all nice and quiet, like he wasn't a giant asshole who made me feel like shit." She was louder than she needed to be. A few heads turned to look from the patio. She caught them and waved them off. "Mind your own damn business. Jesus, can't a girl have a conversation with her little cousin without bystanders? Christ." They quickly turned away from her volatility.

"Was this even about me, ever?" So then there was a moment or at least a time where this began, and it wasn't even anything I did to her, that I could have done to her. She'd been rejected. It was that simple. And I had to suffer for her humiliation.

"Oh, Winifred, it's always about you, though, isn't it? Roberta's girl, Thomas's precious girl." She sneered around her smoke.

"Listen, Penny, I'm sorry you got your feelings hurt." I wasn't. I was shocked, if anything, that she'd even thought about my dad, at all, in any way. I tried speaking low, trying to make eye contact while she wobbled around, unable to stand still. "You can hate me if it makes you feel better, but I am still your cousin. And I'm asking you if we have an understanding about our . . . business."

She finally grew still, locking her eyes with mine. "You really want this, eh?"

I nodded. "Yes, I do."

"You think all want is the same?"

"What?"

"You think some want is bigger than others?" She flicked her butt into the road. It looked like a falling star before it sparked on the asphalt.

"I'm not sure I understand."

She put a hand on my shoulder. "I'm not sure you understand either, little cousin. And I'm not sure I can explain." She headed back onto the patio, hip-checking a redhead with an enormous beard sitting at the first table.

"Just stay away from the cemetery tours," I shouted after her. "Please."

She turned a bit and threw up a peace sign. And there, against her collarbone, hanging from a silver chain, was Roberta's ring.

Maybe she wasn't heartless after all. If she cared enough to hold onto the ring, maybe she cared enough to give me this one small victory. I had to believe it. It was the best I was going to get from her, this small belief hanging on the thinnest of chains.

ENDINGS

When I got out of the subway, a text came through.

Freddie—
*Dude. I am SO SORRY. I was wasted. I don't know how it even
became a thing. Conner saw my phone when I was texting you
and I thought I could talk to him about it—I mean, probably
because I was wasted already. There's no excuse. But I honestly
didn't try to hurt you. I really was just thinking about you after
we hung out. And I was really hoping you would come to the
party. And I was hoping we could get together. But, obviously
that's probably not going to happen now. I just hope you don't
run out and replace me. I care about you—a lot. Yours always. J*

He was worried about being replaced? Because he wanted to
be the first man on the landscape or what? It wasn't even really
about me at all, or us. And maybe he had been replaced. Maybe
the first man wouldn't be a man after all. Even I was shocked
when I deleted not just the message but his whole contact.
Walking through the front gate, the fences felt less imposing. If
I jumped, I was sure I could touch the top links.

When I got home, Phil was waiting for me at my window. I let her in, ready with excuses about where I'd been. She didn't even ask. Instead, she settled on my floor and started talking, like she was under a deadline and had to get all the words out.

"My mom, she used to get me to come home real easy," she started.

"She would just put the porch light on. It worked for years. I'd be running the road with my cousins and, 'ping,' once that light popped up, I knew I'd better get the hell home. My mom was small but Jesus Christ, I knew not to cross her. She had this wooden spoon she hung by the front door. Heat for the Seat, she called it. I never got it. My brother did—only the once. I just didn't want to see her face if she was mad. She'd get all disappointed.

"It worked, that light, until I was fifteen. That's when I left for the city. That's the last time I saw her. But at least I never had to see her disappointed." She waited until I sat at my desk and then continued her story—

Me and Tay and Candy, we lost the apartment when Tay used the rent money to go on a bender with Ghost. By the time she got back, Candy and I were on the sidewalk with a few boxes of crap and a futon mattress rolled up with bungee cords, and she was different somehow.

"What the fuck, Tay?" Candy was angry. She hadn't had time to put on makeup and she cowered behind a paper fan. What if someone from the clubs saw her like this, without her eyelashes and eyeliner-inked beauty marks?

"Shut up, it's my goddamn pogey check that covered the rent anyways. Don't think you have a say in anything, freeloaders."

I'd been quiet, grinding my teeth trying to keep back the angry words while I guarded our good garbage against being tossed in with the regular garbage. I knew my mom had been sending money to cover my room and board, but I thought now wasn't a good time to make that point. Tay's face was gray and shrunken. I checked her wrists for a hospital bracelet—anything that could explain her ghastly appearance.

"We don't need a place anyway. We can stay at the Native women's shelter until Ghost gets his new place. There'll be room for all of us." Now I knew for sure she'd lost her damn mind.

"I can't go there," Candy whined. She pointed to her own face to indicate the obvious.

"We'll just say you're my cousin. They won't ask for proof. They can't. It's self-identification, dummy."

"What does that mean?"

"Means it's basically the racial honor system." Tay laughed. She looked over at me.

"Doesn't sound very honorable for us."

"Jesus, who shit in your Corn Flakes this morning?" She dug around in her purse, looking for a cigarette.

"I didn't have Corn Flakes this morning," I answered. "You'd need an actual bowl and spoon for that."

She ignored me. We picked up a few boxes and had to leave the futon at the side of the road.

The shelter didn't work out. You had to be clean. There was a curfew. And I was too young to be officially allowed to stay there without child services swooping in. So we couch surfed. Our belongings were whittled away, one thing at a time—to the pawn shop, to friends in exchange for crashing or a bowl of ramen, and then just abandoned outside of a Salvation Army when we were too exhausted to carry them anymore. All we had was the weight of three bags and Tay's habit.

Rainy days were the worst, and not just because of the wet and damp. They used to be my favorite back home. On rainy days Amos told stories and Mom let us drink tea. In Toronto, they added a desperation to our usual hustle of "accidently" falling asleep at a party (*might as well let her sleep, we'll leave first thing*) or crashing rough in the park after the booze can gave us the boot when it was clear we weren't spending money. Rain made me homesick. Rain pushed poverty into your bones like new teeth erupting.

Ghost showed up now and then, and then Candy and I were left on our own. We were barely a week into this new phase when Candy decided "fuck this" and called her parents from a pay phone. That bitch had a nice house waiting for her in the suburbs not an hour away the whole time.

"Tourist," Tay sneered after her as she climbed into her father's Buick, all scrubbed clean in a Coffee Time bathroom and wearing the track pants she only put over her short dresses when things got dire. The door slammed and Tay screamed her worst insult—"You're not punk at all!" Candy meekly waved from behind the soft-tinted glass.

"Tay, it's time for me to go too. This isn't exactly working out." I had to say it right then, just rip the bandage off while she was already mad.

"What? Phil, you can't leave me too! We're family, bro." I wasn't expecting this. I was expecting spit and F-bombs—she usually reacted with what Amos used to refer to as "piss and vinegar." I wasn't prepared for a plea.

"Come on. Whaddya going back to? There's no gay people up there, you know as well as I do. And summer's not over yet—there's two more weeks." She guided me away from the curb, like I was going to just jump into a passing vehicle and disappear right then.

"You idiot, there's gay people everywhere," I threw back.

"Listen, Ghost is gone to see a place this afternoon. And he won't really be around once we get it anyways. He's got a new job starting, so it'll just be you and me. We can party again. Like before."

"Tay, I'm tired and hungry and shit isn't fun anymore." I suspected she wanted my mother's money transfers more than she really wanted me kicking around.

"Phil, give me three more days. That's it, just three more days. If we're still shit out of luck then, I'll bring you to the Greyhound station myself."

Her eyes brimmed with tears. She looked pitiful with her messy hair and runny mascara. She'd lost so much weight in the past month her pants barely clung to her extravagant hipbones.

Okay. Three more days. I could do that. As long as it didn't rain.

She stopped talking. Something about her voice right then reminded me of Roberta, when Roberta was near the end. Dementia and pain had knocked all the movement from her limbs, erased the most important lines on her face, the ones that made her Roberta. I went to her apartment every night, switching off with the day nurse. It was the only way we could keep her there. Dad would come with me, but he left often, trying to give us space and privacy until she was asleep and it was safe to crash out, one of us on the couch, the other on a blow-up mattress beside it.

"Bring me my purse." Her voice was hoarse. It was a fight to get her to eat or drink so she always sounded like she was at the end of a marathon run.

I did as I was told, grabbing the reusable grocery bag she'd been using as a purse for the past few years. I placed it gently on her chest, making sure the pillows under her head were fluffed enough that she could see inside.

She took out a length of toilet paper and unwrapped from its core a metallic lipstick case. She rummaged around for another minute, finally pulling out a square of mirror. Then, hands shaking, neck straining, she tried to apply a layer of coral-cream lipstick.

"Here, Auntie, let me do it for you." I reached for the tube but she pulled away.

"No. We all gotta prepare ourselves, dammit." She looked at me with eyes that let me know I could have been the nurse or maybe just some kid who'd snuck into her apartment. "You'll see, you."

"Where are you going?" I was hoping for another memory. She'd been doing that a lot lately, reliving these moments from her life as if she were in them right then. I didn't mind, especially if they were good memories. Maybe she was headed out on a date with her husband, Gordon. She'd talked about him a lot in the last two weeks, sometimes even *to* him. "Gigi," she'd say, hearing the nurse putting the dishes away in the cupboards, "get them damn kids out of the kitchen. Or they'll be no bread for you."

"When you walk out that door, you gotta be your best. You gotta be better."

"Better than who?"

She stopped again, sighing a bit this time at the interruption. "Everyone." She squinted her eyes and moved her hand slowly, trying to trace the shape of her lips.

"You gotta be ready. Get your lipstick on, your best earrings in, and make sure you remember to close the door behind you. You don't want anyone getting in, including yourself. You gotta be in control or things get messy."

She was making less sense now. I put her "purse" back on the dresser and sat on the bed.

"And then you gotta take his hands and look him straight in the eye and then you say where you wanna go. Or else the Jesus knows where he'll take ya."

I laughed. "Is this dating advice?"

More exasperation in her voice. "No, stupid. It's death advice. Don't get blown all here and there. You're still you after, just in a different place. Now pass me my powder."

Phil didn't stay long. This time, instead of winking out, she just kind of faded while I sat at the desk. Watching her grow transparent and then into nothing made me think maybe there was a moment where I could hold her tight enough to stop it. But I didn't call out to her; I didn't ask her to stay. Maybe I should have. Instead, I waited until the room was empty, then I went to go brush my teeth for bed.

The next day would forever be the day that I became acutely aware of my breasts, because that's exactly where the pain settled in and stayed when I found Mrs. Dingleberry in a patch of sun on the living room floor, not breathing.

Dad and I used to joke about how no one would ever know if Dingleberry died, he was so often comatose, unmoving. But as it turns out, I did know, as soon as I entered the room. The air was different. The sunlight was different. I was different. I was without him for the first time in years, and it was rending.

And even though I knew, I still crossed the hardwood, dropped to my knees, and lowered my belly so that I curled around him like a chalk outline, trying to wish hard enough, trying to have enough influence to make him take a breath. I lay there, breathing slow and even as a guide for a full minute, as if he were just forgetful. When that didn't work, I begged.

"Hey, Dingles? Buddy? You need to stay with me." My voice cracked. "Can you stay with me, please? Please?"

I ran a hand down his greasy back, from his ears to his tail, both somehow harder, both without twitch. Even his fur felt different, and I was struck by the absurdity of a whole personality rammed into this small body. I got up on my hands and knees and looked into his little face, smooshed up and usually wheezing. It was so still, lips pulled back a bit to reveal a row of perfectly white Chiclet teeth. This made me the saddest, this small, even row of good teeth in a mouth that would never need them again.

Then panic set in, the feeling that you've been left behind on some important day, that you may not ever make it now because you've woken up too late. And I cried, soft and desperate, cracked open and with abandon, the pulsing core of that heavy grief in my breasts.

INVASION

I stayed in bed for a few days. I didn't want to eat. My father delivered crustless cucumber sandwiches, mumbling "just enough to keep Children's Aid at bay." I couldn't move Dingles's sleeping pillow out of my room, but I couldn't look at it, either, so I covered it in laundry as a compromise. By the end of the week I was able to go back outside, but it was strange not pulling a squeaky weight behind me. Dad moved the wagon to the storage closet on the main floor so neither of us had to witness its emptiness, waiting there by the door.

Phil came back to my room, but in many ways we were starting over. Mostly, she just climbed into my hammock at night and rocked us both until I was asleep. There was no music, no more dancing. But it was enough. It was clear that something had changed between us, and we were trying to figure it out. I continued to ignore Jack's calls and texts. Just seeing his number pop up on the screen was enough to make me nauseous. I closed all my social media accounts. There was nothing there for me anyway.

Thursday afternoon the cemetery was getting ready for our first tour bus group. Mrs. Prashad, who wanted nothing to do with the whole unsavory affair, left early. "It's not digni-fied. This is a final resting place, not a reality show circus," she insisted. Mr. Prashad picked her up in their tan Subaru, their three daughters scrubbed and silent in the backseat like beautiful mannequins at a children's clothing store.

Mr. Ferguson instructed Floyd to be "extra diligent" with his tidying. In response, Floyd yelled at the mourners who were wandering through, telling them to "pick up the pace" and "use the damn garbage cans." Dad and I cleaned up our front lawn, since it was visible from the main gate. We put old shovels, watering cans, and my rubber boots in the unused office space that made up the first floor. I gathered up the teacups I'd left for the rain at the beginning of summer and placed the stack just inside the door. Dad was more anxious than usual, grabbing his hammer and finishing nails to repair small imperfections in our low white fence.

From about four o'clock onward, I did my very best not to think about Phil, just in case I accidently "called her." We'd agreed it was the safest way to go, so she could stay wherever the hell she went when she wasn't with me. She wasn't sure exactly where that was. "It's more of a feeling than a place, I guess."

The last thing we wanted was her getting caught up in the tours. I focused in on the one true distraction I had, Mrs. Dingleberry. Earlier today, Dad had come up to my room and given me what he thought was a gift of comfort, in a small jar just the right size for stashing on my shelf.

"It's his ashes." He handed over the container rubbed gray with loss. "So you have him forever."

I took it from him with a small "thanks," but I couldn't put him on my shelf; he didn't belong there. For now, I had the jar in the bottom drawer of my desk. One of us was confused about the ways we live with the dead, and I'm pretty sure it wasn't me. Then again, I was the one hanging out with a ghost, so who knows.

As instructed, we put on our most somber attire. The staff memo stated: *dark preferably, nothing to stand out or draw attention to the personhood of the employees beyond functioning pieces in the Winterson machine.* We had a hard time figuring out what that meant, exactly. So we pretty much wore what we wore for big funeral days: suits for the men, a simple black tunic for me, and for Floyd, cargo shorts, a jangle of keys, and a faded plaid button-up with the sleeves cut off.

At eight o'clock, the tour bus drove up in a cacophony of air brakes and exhaust. It was black with tinted windows. Across the side in an electric-green font shaped like lightning bolts was "TORONTO HAUNTED GHOST TOURS," and in smaller letters underneath, "Isaacs Inc." I watched from our front door, standing on the threshold in half safety. It felt like that bus took up all the space, all the air. It made my stomach itchy from the inside. So that when Dad came up behind me and pushed at me with his shoulder to nudge me out, I resisted.

"C'mon, Win. They want us there in case anyone needs something."

I gave in, dragging my feet while I followed him down the lane.

The bus crawled with a low roar until it was lined up with the chapel, then it stopped, the final hiss and release like a predatory sigh. It settled there, nuzzling down toward the freshly hosed driveway and relaxing on its wheeled haunches. There was a moment when we could hear an amplified voice speaking on a mic from inside—final instructions, I guess, or a last-minute ghost story to get them in the mood, more likely. And then the door slid open, folding in on itself and slapping the metal siding. I flinched.

Chess Isaacs himself was the first man out, sunglasses on in the growing dark, a ridiculous floppy black cap on his head like an old-timey squire. That was as far as he went in terms of costuming. Other than the hat he wore plain black trousers, black loafers, and a green golf shirt, the same electric shade as his logo, which was embroidered in black stitching over his left breast pocket. A short girl with stick-straight hair and narrow glasses followed him, clutching a clipboard and dragging a small trolley: his assistant. He made a big show of going over and shaking Mr. Ferguson's hand while the rest of the passengers lumbered off, clutching cameras and iPhones and backpacks full of water and extra sweaters.

Dad and I watched them spill out and pool around the front of the bus, stretching their backs and shifting their loads with a strange sense of forced excitement. It was weird to have so many live people here, not grieving, not saying goodbye in that quiet, useless way mourners did, but straight-up living. It was garish. We bit our nails and straightened our clothes in the odd shape of this new phenomenon, all this new life.

"Okay now." Chess was loud, extra loud now that he had a headset secured over his pancake of a hat, his voice booming out from the portable speaker on his assistant's trolley. "Everyone? Everyone, if I can get your attention, please?"

He gave them a moment to assemble into a loose group around him and Mr. Ferguson, who shuffled nervously, clearing his throat as if he too was about to speak.

"Welcome to Winterson Cemetery, the newest addition to the Toronto Haunted Ghost Tours roster. This is Mr. Ferguson;

he is in charge here." He gestured to Mr. Ferguson, who gave a feeble wave to the group. No one waved back, though a few took pictures. "He and I have had many a long conversation about the ghost that haunts this place. And make no mistake, there is at least one confirmed ghost with multiple sightings over the years."

He held up a finger to indicate the one spirit and then used the same finger to point at different tourists. "And you, and you, and you all know what that means. If there is one confirmed ghost it means there is likely more. As we discussed on the way over here, if there is one active phantom, there is usually a portal."

God, my dad really did not need to be hearing this crap right now. The last thing a hopeless romantic needs is hope.

"We're going to wander these historic grounds and I will give you some background on the different areas and some of the older and more interesting graves you'll encounter. And, of course, we'll also visit the locations of the sightings themselves. And who knows"—he raised that finger again and paused for dramatic effect—"perhaps we'll see the ghost itself. Though I must caution, it is rare for a spirit to appear when confronted with so many living souls."

Nervous laughter and a few more pictures, the flashes throwing shadows down from the pointed steeple. With them here, the grounds did seem haunted. A young boy in a Blue Jays cap yawned, already bored by all the talking. His father punched him good-naturedly in the shoulder and, when the boy looked up at him, made the standard "ooooooo" ghost noise. The kid rolled his eyes in response. I did too.

"Okay then, let us begin!" Chess clapped his hands once

and the sharp percussion was picked up by the mic, sending it echoing over the front grounds like a slammed door. He started walking north, his assistant and Mr. Ferguson on his heels.

We watched the group follow, older couples with actual cameras first, families whispering anticipation and possibility to their children in the middle, couples with their phones, holding hands and already snapchatting the evening taking up the rear. Floyd spat in front of the bus and lit a cigarette, then slipped off into the gathering dark. Dad and I faltered, not really sure where we should head.

"I'm gonna trail a bit," he said.

"Do I have to come?" I was anxious to break away.

He shook his head and I grabbed his hand, giving it one squeeze before letting go. It fell back to his side. But in that moment when I clutched his wide palm, I felt the tension and knew he was doing more than trailing. He was going to be watching and listening along with the rest of them. It made me impossibly sad.

I knew I couldn't trust being anywhere near the Peak. I had to keep my mind as still as possible, free of any thoughts of her, so I went into the chapel. It was a small, tidy space. Wooden pews enough to hold eighty, a simple altar at the front painted red with a pulpit for eulogies, and a triptych of windows behind. To the right, there were a few rows of candles with a change box for offerings. There were no dramatic Catholic crosses, no bleeding statues or weeping virgins. That's probably why I didn't come in here much; it just seemed so pedestrian compared to the gothic pain that blew through the chapel on any given day. That and the fact that the windows were uneven and two were of different sizes; they were impossible to count to satisfaction no matter how many times I tried.

I sat in the back row. It was cooler in here with the marble floor and vaulted ceiling, the dark wood curving down like the bones of a whale. It felt safer in this stomach than being outside right now with so many interlopers, with the heaviness of my father, pretending he was just playing reliable staff member in the midst of his personal crisis.

I picked at slivers while I waited for the tour to end, the kind of slivers that had been shoved into my brain over the past few weeks. Was I still angry about Jack? I'm not even sure it was anger so much as pure humiliation. Once he was deleted, once I'd made that decision to carve him out, all that was left was my anger at myself, my stupidity. I'd honestly thought we were going to do it and that it would mean something, that he'd cradle my head or stare into my eyes or wipe the blood from my leg with his T-shirt after. How naive could you get? That's what killed me, that I was willing to be so vulnerable and he didn't give a shit.

But why did it have to be all romantic anyways? Why had I made it any different than rubbing one out before I fell asleep at night? I wasn't dying to have sex with someone else, really. I was just dying to feel something.

I was glad when Floyd walked in, interrupting my thoughts, because they were starting to veer toward Phil.

"Holy Christ, your asshole cousin's out there makin' a racket." He laughed. "Ho, you shoulda seen that Isaacs's face when she rolled up. Ha! Worth it." He held onto the back of the pew behind me, chuckling.

"My cousin . . . wait, Penny? Why is she here?" I was on my feet.

"She's hijacked the damn tour. Doing a séance or something. Oh, it's rich, let me tell ya." He wiped his face with a dirty bandana and shoved it back in the side pocket of his shorts.

Cold blew along the marble floor and collected at my feet, climbing up over the scabs and scrapes of my legs, slipping into my guts. I reached over and took hold of his shoulders.

"Floyd, where? Where is she?"

He looked startled by my grip, my stare. I felt the way people do waiting for news of a car crash.

"By the Peak. Can't miss her."

I ran as fast as my shaking legs would carry me.

ANCIENT INDIAN BURIAL GROUNDS FROM 1990

I could hear her now, from the other side of the trees.

"This is Native land and I am your guide in this territory. My people have been here for thousands of years and only I can properly coax out the secrets held here." She didn't have a fancy mic and speaker like Isaacs, but man, Penny could holler.

"And now I need to tell you that this is a burial ground, for at least one of my people. And to call forth that spirit, we need a name." She passed her eyes over the group, letting that sink in.

"No," I whispered. "No, no, no."

She raised her voice and called out, "Philomene. Philomene Dorothy Elliot. We call on thee."

She banged her hand drum four times. "We ask the guardians who sit in each direction to release your spirit. We ask the four stages of life to come together. We ask the four colors to blend into a door for your release."

Pushing through the branches, I saw bright flashes from cameras and steady strobes from the phones set to video. They illuminated my cousin—party-girl Penny, city-dwelling Penny who wouldn't so much as go without WiFi—standing in a circle of white candles in a full friggin buckskin dress holding a hand drum and stick, like the kind of stick made for modern drum sets, with the tapered end wrapped in leather.

She paused. "I must ask again that you please not take any video or photo recordings of this sacred ceremony. Or I will be forced to stop right now." She held her ground, not lifting the drum while she waited. Cameras were lowered and those who faltered were group-shamed into listening. No one wanted to miss this "Authentic Indigenous Experience."

She was calling Phil. How the hell did she know her name? I sure as hell hadn't told her. Or wait . . . maybe I had, at least the Phil part.

"Philomene, we beseech you to come forth from the bosom of the Creator, and to manifest now, here, with us." More drumming, this time fast and low, not at all a real song, gaining speed and volume. She ended this spurt with a guttural sound— half scream, half sigh. "Born March 5, 1975, who in 1990 met her untimely demise, overdosed, right here." She pointed down into the ravine with that stick. "Here on our grounds. Body not recovered for months. Poor, sweet Philomene, we ask for you to visit us now. Come forth!"

I pushed through the outer layers of the circle. "No, Penny, stop!" I was shushed on all sides. All the while, her words were bursting like fireworks. *Overdose. Body.* I felt like someone was taking my clothes off in public. I needed her to stop. Right now. "Penny!"

She looked over the heads of those gathered and yelled, "Everyone focus." And then she began drumming again— untrained, chaotic drumming. The kind of drumming created just to drown out a frantic voice. "Focus in on Philomene together!"

"Win! Win, are you okay? What's going on?" Someone grabbed me from behind, hands practically holding me up. It was Jack. Jack was here. I didn't have time to think or explain.

"We need to get her to stop. Now!"

I tried to break free but he wouldn't let go. Instead, he held onto me and pushed us ahead, maneuvering through the crowd to the front. Some people stepped aside and others resisted, but with a nonstop stream of "excuse me's" and refusing to slow down, we made our way. I was frantic, walking on tippy-toes to see over heads, to watch my stereotype of a cousin, to peer over the incline. Right when we broke through the first onlookers, all holding hands with their heads bowed, swaying to the rhythm-less song Penny was pounding out of that loose-skinned drum she'd probably bought at a tourist store, the noise stopped.

"Look!" she cried, pointing again with the stick, except now it was shaking in her unsteady hand, her turquoise thumb ring a blur of blue and silver.

At the bottom of the hill there was a swatch of ground illuminated by the orange street lamp from the other side of the thin trees, where the street beyond connected at the edge of a deep ditch. In that tall grass, right where I had seen her the first time, was Phil, flickering like a faulty bulb. And she was looking directly at me, but not just me—me and Jack, him still standing behind me, his hands over my shoulders.

Someone screamed, and a murmur passed through the crowd like a collective breath. There was the shifting and swishing of fabric as the banished phones and cameras were retrieved. People pushed against one another, trying to see.

"What? What is it?"

"I don't see anything. Move!"

And Penny raised her arms, drum in one hand, stick in the other, the myriad cheap beaded bracelets she wore tinkling against one another like wind chimes. She opened her mouth, "Philomene Doro . . ."

And that's when I tackled her to the fucking ground. And Phil winked out like a flame. And all hell broke loose.

We rolled around, all buckskin and Converse and spit. The drum flew out of her hand and thumped against the ground, probably the best sound it'd made all night. I heard the whoosh of breath knocked from a body and wasn't sure if it was mine or hers until I couldn't refill my lungs and she had a chance to catch me with a right hook right in the chin. I grabbed at the multicolored loom necklace draped into her cleavage and yanked. It came free in my hand and I held onto it like a small trophy. Her eyes were shock and murder at the same time. She was no stranger to brawls, reacting before she could even figure out who to swing on. And then we were being pulled apart. I landed one kick in her thigh before I was out of reach, leaving a muddy star print on the soft skin of her dress.

Also used to performing for an audience, Penny recovered just as fast, struggling back to her moccasin-covered feet, dusting off my print and accepting the drum someone held out to her. "Thank you." She was quick to calm, at least in front of the group. Me, I was in tears, struggling in the arms of my father, who slowly backed away until we were on the outer rim of the circle.

"My apologies," she managed. She fixed her hair, pushing strands back into the top of her thin braid. "Spirit sometimes takes over and does strange things to people."

She shot me a look that I knew meant I would be dead later, if she got the chance to catch me without my dad. And then Isaacs was there with his stupid flat hat and crackling speaker.

"Okay, folks. Well, we have run out of time, I'm afraid. But I am so pleased that we were all able to witness an actual Native American ritual and to have the great good fortune of seeing a specter! Round of applause for my uhh . . . colleague here." He swept his arm out to indicate Penny, who took a deep bow.

Even with the fight, or maybe because of it, the crowd erupted in applause and whistles. Isaacs and his assistant had a hard time corralling them back into line to get to the bus. They were too busy shaking Penny's hand, taking selfies with her, and aiming cameras over the edge into the now empty spot below. Before he joined the group, pushing the last of the stragglers along, Isaacs spoke to those left—Penny, me, my dad, Jack, and Mr. Ferguson.

"Listen, I'm not sure what just happened, but we need to have a meeting. And you"—he indicated Penny—"you need to be here. Tomorrow at noon."

It wasn't a question.

"C'mon, Win. Home. Now." Dad steered me out of the clearing, Jack at his heels, leaving Penny behind to clean up her mystical shit and get out of our cemetery.

I cried all the way home, ignoring Jack, who tried to explain to my dad that he had dropped by when he heard about the tour, but my father wasn't really in the mood for conversation— not ever, but especially not with me falling apart. I'm not sure if it was the loss of all the adrenaline I'd had a minute ago or the image of Phil, pained and alone at the bottom of the hill, but I was inconsolable. Dad kept his arm around my shoulder through the grounds, into the house, up the stairs, and into the kitchen, where he deposited me into a chair. He lifted my chin with his calloused fingers and examined my face.

"You hurt?"

I shook my head. Other than a bit of soreness on my jaw, I was physically okay.

"Tea then." He went to the counter and plugged the kettle in. Jack settled into the other chair.

"Winifred, what the hell happened? Who was that?" Jack leaned across the table.

It took a minute to smooth out my breathing before I could answer. "My cousin. That was my cousin. She's such an a-a-asshole." Tears pushed through again before I could grab them.

They waited for me to calm down and soon I had milky tea in front of me and their undivided attention.

"She was trying to call out Phil, the ghost I was telling you about." Dad crossed his arms over his chest, leaning back against the counter. "I gave her Roberta's ring . . ."

"You did what?"

"Dad, I had to. That's what she wanted. But not to call the ghost, to NOT call the ghost." I took a sip of warm tea. "I mean, at first I wanted her to call her, to get her to be here so we could do the tours and make money to stay, but then I didn't want her to. Because it hurts her."

"Hurts your cousin?" Jack was trying to put the pieces together.

"No, hurts Phil." I finally fully noticed that he was in my kitchen. "And why the hell are you even here?"

There was silence in the kitchen. I was exhausted and all I wanted to do was get up to my room and ask Phil to come. I needed to talk to her.

"I know what this sounds like and Dad, I know you don't believe in Phil, but she's real and she didn't want to come tonight and now Penny made her." He was paying attention, but the look in his eyes was all pity.

"Win, I know I've been . . . off lately, and that's gotten to you." He uncrossed his arms and hung his head. "I'm sorry."

"You didn't see her? Either of you?"

I swung my gaze to Jack, who stared down at his own hands, laid out on the table. He slowly shook his head.

I didn't care if they didn't believe me. I needed to be alone and I needed to see Phil, now.

"Okay. I'm tired. And upset, I guess. I'm just gonna go to bed." I stood up.

"You sure? I can hang around for a bit. Maybe watch some TV?" Jack offered.

"No. You need to leave and, please, don't come back."

"Win," my dad started.

"No, Dad. He needs to get out of our house. And neither of you wants me to explain why." Jack looked back down at his hands.

I headed for the stairs. I heard Jack get up from the table and say goodnight to my father, who did not answer back. I felt heavy. Tomorrow I had to see Penny again. Tomorrow I had to come up with an excuse that did not involve the fact that there was a real ghost here they could exploit, but an excuse that would still keep the tours coming, if they even wanted to after tonight's little performance. Suddenly, I really was tired. As tired as I'd ever been in my whole life. Everything followed me to bed.

My jaw ached and my pride hurt and the sting of fresh humiliation wore holes in my skin. Why oh why was this the summer of humiliation? So instead of sleep, I cried. And then I was angry for crying, imaging Penny smug and bejeweled in Roberta's coveted ring somewhere close. I needed to figure this shit out. I needed to figure out how to pull my con artist cousin out of Phil's proximity. I had to keep Phil safe. Then again, maybe this would be settled for me tomorrow at the meeting. I was sure Isaacs would tell Penny to stay away. And Mr. Ferguson wouldn't want her bullshit on the grounds. That gave me some comfort. I just hoped those fools would think to bring a restraining order with them. They would if they had any idea who they were dealing with.

"Something's wrong with that one. Shoulda had one more just to balance things out." Roberta watched Penny snoring on the small love seat while I set her dyed hair into curlers. "Comes from her damn dad, I think."

I laughed quietly. If Penny woke up, I didn't want to be blamed for anything she might overhear. Not that she needed to have any reason to blame me for just about anything.

"She hates me." It wasn't a question; I was just making an observation.

Roberta slapped the kitchen table with an open palm. "Screw that. No one hates you." For all the dramatics, her response lacked the strength of conviction. "You don't give no one no reason to hate you."

"It's because my dad's white." I shrugged my shoulders. It didn't sting anymore. You can get used to anything. I once walked with a sliver in the bottom of my foot for a whole month.

"That doesn't even make sense. Plus, she don't know much. She'd probably try to smoke sweetgrass if I gave her some." We'd laughed conspiratorially and I had felt momentary relief.

And yet, there Penny had been, in a borrowed buckskin dress, banging on a shop-bought drum. For someone who didn't know much, she sure looked real to anyone who didn't know any better. And if there was one spirituality Penny followed, it was money.

I remembered Phil's face, looking up the hill at the people and the cameras, at Penny's ridiculous get-up, at me and Jack standing together. I had to find a way to explain this to her, to make sure she understood I hadn't sold her out. I mean, in a way I did, by telling Penny about her to begin with, but that was before . . .

The way she'd flickered there, popping in and out—a small attempt at escape, over and over in the face of so much focus. How the hell did Penny know her full name? Maybe it was just more made-up bullshit like that bullshit song and her bullshit ceremony.

"Philomene Elliot." I whispered, eyes closed.

Did Phil muscle the final push into death herself, or had some-one done it for her? I thought about the lines cut into her skin. Suddenly, the glass panes in my window frame rattled, clattering against the wood like nervous fingers, hard, quick. A bronchial wind blew into the room in a gut-punch exhale, lung-wet and flecked with voice. It raised goosebumps under the sticky layer of humidity coating my limbs. My teeth chattered. Every open space on me, in me, was filled with a sharp despair that boiled to rage and I snapped my fingers into fists. I clenched the muscles in my calves until they were pinched with cramps. Then the rage simmered to fear and adrenaline threatened to spill over, tipping into blood and nerve. Finally, the feeling changed to sound: a

cutting lilt like a whistle then a kettle on the boil then an elec-
tronic alarm set to warn a town of attack. I jammed my fingers
into my ears. Then it became a scream so biting I felt nauseous.
It took up all the room, slid slick and cold around each cell.
Sound stopped. All sound. I had no heartbeat, no click in my
jaw. I couldn't hear my own gasps. And then there was color,
extra, crawling color—midnight plumes and the darkest eye.

It was Phil and her grief, her betrayal, her zero-to-sixty dead-
girl rage. I covered my face with both my arms and tried to offer
her tantrum haunt a clothesline of apology draped between my
isolation and hers—

*I'm sorry I'm sorry I'm sorry I'm sorry I'm sorry I'm sorry I'm
sorry I'm sorry*

But she offered no ears with which to hear me.

THE INVISIBILITY OF
CHILDHOOD

Mr. Ferguson's office was crowded. He sat behind his desk and Isaacs took the armchair by the fireplace. Penny was in the second of the matched set. I sat on a straight-backed wooden chair by the door and Dad stood beside me. There wasn't enough air for all of us to breathe. I held my breath for long minutes.

"So, you are related to Mr. Blight?" Mr. Ferguson asked.

"No." Penny scoffed. "I am somewhat related to his insane daughter, through our mothers." She wore her pedestrian clothes— long jean shorts with rips in the thighs, a white peasant blouse, and those jelly shoes. A beige purse sat at her feet like a well-behaved poodle, its spaghetti strap a tail wrapped around and tucked in under itself. She had put makeup on, so her scowl was bright pink. I could tell by her tone that she also thought she was being summoned here for a reprimand. I was surprised she'd even shown up.

She pointed a bright red nail at Isaacs. "Your customers loved my presentation last night. I think I should get a cut of the take."

And there it was. She came by to demand payment for her break-in-looter-style séance. Classic Penny.

Isaacs laughed. "Slow down, slow down. Just who in the hell are you, first?"

"I am Penny Pinch, local Toronto psychic. I mostly do online and over-the-phone consultations but I'm looking to branch out into appearances. I took a course at the Native Theatre downtown in June." She pushed her sunglasses up onto her head, challenging him with her heavily lined eyes.

"Interesting. And so you are Native then, I take it."

"Well, I'm not Chinese."

I sighed. Awesome. So awesome that everyone in the room knew I was related to this jackass.

"Well, it's just that, you're right. People did love the presentation, most of it anyways." Here he looked in my direction, long enough to catch my look of confusion. I was willing to take my lumps, but only if I could watch Penny get hers.

"And how did you know about the ghost in the ravine? This"—he held up a piece of paper in his hand, squinting— "Philomene Elliot?"

At her name I jumped in. "That's not the point. I don't think we should even talk about that. It's all BS anyways."

"Win . . . ," Dad warned, placing a heavy hand on my shoulder.

Penny looked at me, one eyebrow raised. I could see it in her eyes that she'd decided to pick at my obvious scab.

"Well, since you asked." She swung her gaze back to Isaacs. "She came to me in a vision."

"Ho ho ho." He unfolded his legs and leaned his elbows on his knees. "You can't scam a scammer. How did you really know?"

She locked gazes with him, measuring and calculating. He didn't even blink. "Okay, a little birdie whispered her name and then I went to the archives at the Reference Library to check out any bodies that may have been found in this area. And voilà. A body found down the back ravine, obvious signs of trauma, more junk in her body than even possible to shoot and old cuts all over. I'm sure you've heard about all this, Winnie, eh?"

There are ways that we comfort ourselves that researchers say go back to the womb, that time before time, when all we had was ourselves and a thunderous heart in the deep, red sky. Without the standard-issue womb, with all its design benefits and cushiony interior, I sought reassurance in the ridges and curves of unorthodox geometry. I had to bend legs and hold a bulbous head and rock myself to sleep. I had nothing to hold me back but the even numbers of my mother's heart. And this is how I sat now, folded into girl-shaped origami in a wooden chair, hearing the list of Phil's death march. Hands each wrapped around the opposite elbow, my stomach pulled back into a bone-ringed bowl, shoulders lifted to earlobes. *Two, four, six, eight, ten, twelve.* I remained quiet, mouth too full of multiples to open in this room.

"I am, after all, not a scammer, but a businesswoman. It's imperative to do your research. But then you must know that, Mr. Isaacs, as a fellow businessman." She smiled, catlike, calling him into her elevated status from the wingback.

And he smiled back! What was I watching? She was turning this her way right before my eyes.

"It doesn't matter what you researched. You broke in here, hijacked the tour, and caused a fight. People were freaked out!" I jumped to my feet. Even my loud voice was small in this room where I registered as less. Penny could smell the blood in the water. And she just smiled at it—at me, at all of us.

"Yes, Winifred, people were freaked out. That's generally why people pay money to go on ghost tours to begin with, to be freaked out." She spoke slowly, as if I were an especially dim child. "And, if you hadn't lost your temper last night and pitched a fit, everything would have gone off smoothly."

I had no response.

"Chess." She spread out the *s's* like an uncoiling snake. "I can assure you no other tour has an Indigenous element, not like I am offering. And it goes over big as an 'added bonus,' especially with the out-of-towners who think Canada is still 'our home and Native land,' but who never get to see one of us in the flesh because, you know, pesky colonization."

He laughed nervously, unsure if she had told a joke.

She carried on, straight-faced. "We could really capitalize on it." His worry that he had overstepped boundaries into ignorance made him more agreeable than ever.

"Absolutely."

Jesus, it was like she really knew him, knew what made him tick. Maybe she had just been around businessmen before. He seemed one of a type. I watched him steeple his fingers and lean his lips against them, subtly nodding. Oh my God, was he actually considering bringing Penny into Winterson on a regular basis? I turned to Mr. Ferguson. He lowered his gaze to his desk calendar. I'd swear he was distracted, reading his upcoming appointments. Did he not give a shit about the cemetery? About us, even?

"No one wants to see your touristy Indian crap." I couldn't stand, my knees refused to hold my weight. Phil, laying in the mud. Phil, with blood drying in stripes across her graying skin. Phil, in my bedroom last night as a scream beat black and iridescent in the tunnel of an angry breath.

Penny didn't address this next part to me, and maintained eye contact with Isaacs, but make no mistake, it was definitely for me. "And of course, I am also the one who can bring the real ghost of Winterson out to play." Her smile got wider. I saw teeth in there.

"Yes, there is that." Isaacs took a sharp intake of breath and clapped his hands together. "I didn't see the specter in question myself . . ." He looked over to Mr. Ferguson, who frowned and shrugged. "But there was certainly enough of a reaction to convince me."

He turned toward me. "Winifred, is it?"

Isaacs waited for my father to nod, which he did, folding his arms across his wide chest as warning.

"Yes, well. I think we can all agree we cannot have a repeat of last night's fiasco. The fight—it cannot happen again." Now his voice was deep, and he inclined his head while he shook it, at me. He was shaking his head at me? I could feel Penny's smile without looking.

"But, again, I do think we can all agree that what Ms. Pinch— Ms., is it?" He double-checked, posture straight to bring him to his full diminutive height. She smirked a response. "That what Ms. Pinch provided to the group last night was not only completely unique on the market but was, in fact, highly successful. You should have heard the chatter on the bus headed to Morningside Gardens. They were excited. Hell, I was excited."

Penny gave a quick, immature clap, a burst of staccato self-righteousness that poked into my brain. Defeated. Tears weighted my face and I hung it toward the thin carpet. It would be near impossible to protect Phil, to keep safe everything that was important to me—not with Penny around.

My father put his hand back on my shoulder and shook a tear loose. It balanced on the end of my nose. I left it there so I had something to concentrate on, to keep the rest from breaking free.

It was Penny's turn to stand. Her shadow fell over me, over the entire room. She put her hands on her hips. "Alright, boys, shall we dismiss the children and talk numbers?"

Their silence let me know I had been effectively removed from the conversation, if I had ever even been in it to begin with. I swiped at the tear, sniffed, and, head still hanging, made for the exit, my father behind me. I opened the door to the afternoon and then hesitated there, with one foot out, the other in.

"When is the next tour?" Penny asked.

"Thursday. Every Thursday, fifty-two weeks a year. And with any luck, we'll have enough interest to add a Saturday to the schedule by Halloween. Oh." His voice grew louder; Isaacs couldn't hold back his excitement. "We are definitely doing a Halloween special! The potential, ladies and gentlemen, is without limit." Here he spread out his arms, demonstrating the expansiveness of his reach despite his truncated body.

Next Thursday. I walked out into the blinding bright. Next Thursday.

"Win, we'll stay away from her. Stay in on those days." Dad walked slightly behind me. "And we can still stay here with the tour money."

"Dad, that's not it. Not it at all." I sighed, stomping off heavy over the gravel to the main path. I was eager to be alone. "I'm going for a walk. Alone."

It was a lie, of course. I went straight for the Peak. To Phil.

TEAR ME APART

I walked down to the ravine, following the sound of the water trickling over rocks and garbage, the flow pushing a bent shopping cart to clang against its own frame.

"Phil?" I yelled. "Phil, I need to talk to you."

I heard my voice breaking. Not now. Not now. I had to be strong. I had to get through to her. We had six days to figure shit out.

"Phil!" I wandered through the first low bushes into the clearing. I stood in the middle, kicking tipped bottles out of the way, and planted my feet firm. I closed my eyes.

"Philomene Dorothy Elliot."

"Oh, look who's a real hero now. Fuck a Ouija board, eh? Who needs it when you can summon the broken dead all by yourself."

I opened my eyes. She was standing by the tree, the tree where her body was found.

"Phil, listen. I really, really need you to listen." I took a step toward her and she winked out into nothing. *Dammit.* "Don't make me call you again!" I yelled.

She popped back into the clearing, standing on the warped

pallets. "Yeah, real big man now." Her arms were crossed over her chest.

"Phil, for Chrissakes. I need to talk to you. Seriously."

"Oh, it's serious, is it? What are you going to do if I won't listen, call your boyfriend down here?" She jumped down, her feet kicking up dirt like smoke. "Oh no, you'll probably get your corny cousin to drag me out in front of an audience again."

She was pissed. She was pacing. Her frenetic energy made me nervous even though I knew her. Or maybe because I knew her. "He's not my boyfriend. He's not even my . . ."

"In fact, why are you even wasting all this good supernatural shit? Shouldn't you go gather a crowd?" She cut me off, waving her arms above her head, her shirt pulling up to show a few inches of stomach and an outie belly button that hit me deep in my own gut. "Hey! Hey, everyone! Come down here quick! Come see the amazing dead girl. Don't forget your cameras!"

"Enough. That wasn't me."

"Oh, wasn't it? Wasn't that you I saw on the cliff in the arms of your boyfriend?" She kicked a bottle and it exploded against the trunk of the tree. I winced, glass falling around us like fireworks.

"It's not like that . . ."

"It's not? Okay then, how in the hell did that crazy bitch in the buckskin like E. Pauline Johnson know about me? Know my name, even?"

I wasn't ready for this part, the part where I had to admit it was me, that I held some of the blame. I looked at the ground. I could feel her eyes on me. "That was an accident," I told her. Except that wasn't exactly true.

"An accident?"

"I mean, I didn't even know your name, your full name, until then. I may have mentioned you to her but not all that. She found all that out on her own."

"All that? All what?" Her voice was loud and sarcastic. "Oh, you mean the part where she told a bunch of tourists how I was attacked and shot up into oblivion? How I rotted down here, alone, for days? Just those things. Minor things." She was pacing again, in a wide circle, around me.

"I had no idea."

"But you do now. Does that make me more intriguing to you? More attractive to you? You're into trauma, aren't you?" She pushed these things out at me like physical shoves, and I was losing balance.

"I would never, never have told her those things, told anyone." I realized I was crying. I seemed to have so many tears these days. "I told her not to do it!"

"Wait, you told her not to what? What did you tell her?" She moved in close, bending at the waist, looking up into my face. "How much came from you?"

I stumbled through it, trying to explain that before I really knew her, the idea of an actual ghost here at Winterson was a godsend, one that I had to try to use. I explained that there were sightings, but that they were just me messing around in the cemetery. And that I was going to ask my cousin to help me make sure the ghost was seen, and not me—the real ghost. I couldn't make it sound any better than what it really was. I'd sold her out.

"But that was before," was the best I could do.

"Before what?" She was quieter now, smoking in that way she did—without smell, the cigarette seemingly eternal.

My feet moving in the dirt set loose little tornados of dust.

"Before I loved you." The burn in my face was intense. I wasn't sure which way I meant, which kind of love I was professing. I waited for her response in agony.

And then she began to laugh. It was a cruel sound that made my insides fold up, crumple actually, like paper.

"How in the hell do you know what love is?" She flicked the cigarette into the tall grass. "How do you know what it even means?"

"I know about love." I was even quieter than her.

"No, you don't. Your dad, he knows about love. He knows what it's like to give everything, your entire life, to love. He understands the nights spent patting the empty bed beside you looking for a missing shape. He knows what it's like to sleep over the ashes of it."

I was shocked. How did she know so much about him? I'd never even considered that she went anywhere but where I was.

"I know about love. What it is to miss a place you can never go back to. To remember your mother's voice every night before you pass out. I know that want. Love is want. It's loss. It's everything." She put her hands on her slight hips and turned her back to me.

We stood there, so much space between us, for silent minutes. And then she told me about the last hours, when she breathed to live and not just out of habit.

Two days after I promised to give Toronto, to give Tay, one more shot, she left me at a Shoppers Drug Mart on Queen West to go meet Ghost and find out about the space. "His buddy knows the landlord. It's almost for sure—guaranteed!" She pocketed a black eyeliner and a bottle of Tylenol before she took off. I waited there for an hour but security started following me around, so I left.

It was crazy hot out and I stood on the sidewalk for a minute using my hand as a visor, then headed to Kensington. Tay always ended up in the market. She'd show up sooner or later and I could nap in the park if there weren't too many kids screaming around. I ended up staying in that fucking park the entire day, my stomach eating a hole into my guts. I didn't have money for a hot dog or a bag of chips and certainly not for the bus ticket home.

I picked all the old nail polish off my nails. I had a conversation with a homeless guy who told me about his time in Nam. I slept on and off through the kids and the tourists and the hippies and then at midnight—

"Phil!"

It was Jared, the punk we hung out with off and on. He reached down and gathered me up in a huge hug. He smelled like cloves and sweat. I was so lonely it was the best thing I'd ever smelled. I recognized a few of the others with him, a short kid named Flip who liked to get high and show off kickboxing moves; Rachel, a bald girl who didn't talk much; Dezi, who sold counterfeit purses in front of the Chinatown mall and coke on the side. They were with three other guys I didn't know. They looked familiar, probably just from around the market.

I made bad decisions. I drank shitty rum and smoked a crooked joint and when one of the other guys—Bo was his name—offered me a pill, I took it. Didn't even really think about it. Didn't have to. I'd spent the day in the park and I didn't know where my cousin was and I was determined that tomorrow I would be heading back home without ever having so much as kissed a girl.

We went to the booze can for a bit, met up with some other people and laughed too much. Those hours are blurry. I remember watching two guys give another guy head in the washroom, drinking a warm beer and accidently swallowing a cigarette butt that had been floating around in the can, arguing with a tall girl with white hair and black bangs and being carried up the stairs and into the alley by Jared, who said he was stopping me from going full savage. I remember Bo and his friend Lazy saying they were headed to a house party in the east and telling me to come. So I went, jumping into the backseat of a cab, where I think I fell asleep. We were getting out of the car before I noticed I still had Jared's jacket on.

The party was in a high-rise, and since you can't get away with too much surrounded by so many neighbors, it was shutting down by the time we got there. Lazy stole a bottle from the liquor cabinet and we opened it in the elevator on the way down. Then we crossed the street and walked along the fence, through tall grass and under low branches and ended up near a creek.

This is what I remember from then: That the stars were bright but cold. That it wasn't just the three of us anymore; two more guys from the party had joined us. They were quiet and had small eyes, like the kind of indent you make with a fingernail in the ball of your hand when you make a fist. I remember that the jokes got mean and the movements more aggressive, then I realized no one knew my name. I tried to tell them—*My name is Philomene Elliot, daughter of Rose and Manny Elliot, granddaughter of Amos the storyteller*—but my tongue was too big for my mouth and my lips were too cold to coordinate. My eyes rolled too much. I couldn't do the one thing Tay said to always do—look like you're in control. Like you could stab a motherfucker, even if you might puke in your own hands. I don't know when it happened, but suddenly I was alone with Lazy. *Maybe the others just went for a walk*, I thought. And smiled at the thought of three men skipping through a field, maybe making daisy chains. I imagined them coming back with yellow crowns and sticky fingers. I laughed a little.

I remember the click of the lighter, over and over, while Lazy tried to hold it steady to the bottom of a spoon. I remember how he spoke too close, like his voice was already inside my head as he rolled up my sleeve. I remember watching the needle but not feeling it. I remember the sound of buckles and buttons and breath and effort. And after, I remember crawling toward the sound of the water. And then I was alone, and without other eyes watching me, my own eyes began to watch and I noticed for the first time that the sun was coming up.

It was morning, on the day I was going to go home. I should have been on a bus sliding along dark highways toward my family. I should have had a bag of Cheezies for breakfast, knowing that there would be soup for lunch when I arrived. Now it was just my last day. Ever. And then, before all the color in the world sucked down some drain I couldn't see but knew was there, it started to rain.

I'm gonna tell you a story about this old guy who lost his voice. I heard Amos. *Was his own damn fault—he yelled so hard it got thrown all the way to the other side of the lake.* I loved that story.

S'why you have to think before you open your mouth, before you decide to be loud at someone else. You never know what you're gonna lose of yourself. He sounded so far away.

Anyways, off he goes. Gets into his canoe there and starts paddling to the other side . . .

The last thing I remember is being homesick. Sick for home.

So sick for the place where I was profoundly loved.

He's paddling so hard he forgets to breathe, him. He holds his breath and works his muscles and soon he's out there in the middle surrounded by nothing but his missing breath to match his missing voice—one comes before the other you see.

I'm not cold. There's no temperature anymore. I hear water trickling over shopping carts and garbage. I hear footsteps headed away from the clearing, coughing, bottles . . .

And he's surrounded now by stars, so many damn stars, it's like every relative and every ancestor he's ever had. And they begin to sing, a soft song, a song for the dying and newly gone . . .

The light collects into these pinpoints, dull, like I'm seeing them from under the water. Soon there is nothing to see but stars.

And then, one day, out of nowhere, there's you, Win.

She turned back to face me. "Love is being a fucking ghost haunting a girl because you want to know how her day went, to make sure she's okay. And it's still feeling that same way after she stabs you in the back."

"Haunting me?" Not Winterson. Me.

She looked over her shoulder. "God, you're an idiot."

"Maybe. Maybe I am, but I just wanted to keep my home. You say my dad understands love, so you can understand why I had to keep him here, close to my mother."

"He sleeps over her ashes! Carries them around in a goddamn suitcase. What makes you think he needs to be here?" She threw her arms out and spun, indicating the land around us. "This is nothing. It's not her, it's not you, it's not me."

I wanted to be held. I felt alone and isolated even just eight feet from her. She wasn't moving any closer so I wrapped my own arms around myself, cupping my shaking shoulders. Winterson meant nothing? How could I even bring myself to accept that after all these years, after all I'd done to stay?

On her last day, before they came with a stretcher and an oxygen tank, loaded her in the back of an ambulance and brought her to the hospital to die under fluorescent lights, Roberta told me a long, meandering story about her home. It was the most complete narrative she'd managed in weeks.

"When you go to the shore in November, the sand is different. It's thick. Before the ice but after the heat. It's like squeezing a bag of brown sugar with your feet. And the water, it's different too, quieter. It's like her mouth is full and she can't talk real good. But she can still hold you, like."

Her eyes were cloudy and her teeth weren't in, but she sounded younger than she had in years. She spoke with a slight smile.

"It's not that this part of the shore is much different than any other part of the shore. It's because the water here is where my grandmothers are. Their bones are rubbed smooth here. Their songs are held under the rocks at the bottom. Their hair is tangled in the weeds along the side over by Langlade's place. That's what makes it special. It's us, after all."

I always thought I suffered from a kind of acute homelessness because I didn't have that land, because I'd never walked that stretch of shore. But then, she'd worked so hard to make sure I had it in the stories, that I had us: Roberta, Mary, Faith, all of us. She'd spent whole afternoons drawing maps in my head while also trying to force pieces into the puzzle where they didn't go until I took them out of her hand.

Maybe my dad didn't need Winterson, but I did. There was nowhere else that I belonged—not in school, not in a condo, certainly not with Jack.

"I can't leave, Phil. I can't go. What are you going to do?" Again, I had an image of her and Floyd, chain-smoking, riding tandem on his mower, a duct-taped bicycle helmet over her long hair.

"Jesus, Winifred. I don't know—maybe go somewhere else? Maybe go anywhere else. You think I like this? You think I want to keep waking up by this tree, this garbage?" She picked up an empty shopping bag clotted with dirt, then let it fall to her feet.

"Can you leave?"

She sighed heavily and leaned against the tree. "I don't know. But what choice do I have?"

I tried to think it through. I could beg Penny, throw myself on her mercy, to get her to stop. Who was I kidding? Penny had no mercy. If she did, she'd have it surgically removed. I could try again with Isaacs, convince him Penny was a real-life scoundrel. I remembered the way his eyes lit up, talking about the potential money to be made, and not-so-subtly checking out Penny's long legs. Every potential was another piece that didn't fit in the puzzle. I couldn't make them fit, and there was no one to take them out of my hand.

"I'm going now. Kindly leave me alone."

I jumped out of my thoughts. "Going where?"

"Just leave me alone, Win." The way she said it made my heart sink. It was less angry, more tired. I wanted her to be angry again, anything but this tired indifference.

"Phil, I swear I'll make this better. I'll find a way. Please don't leave, not like this."

She stood up, arms heavy at her sides. "Oh, don't worry. For the low-low-price of a tour ticket you can see me." She paused. "When exactly can you see me next?"

I tilted my chin toward my chest. "Thursday."

She clapped her hands. "Thursday, ladies and gentleman. That'll be the next show." She took a sarcastic bow, folding at the waist, sweeping an arm out in front of her. Then she straightened up, snorted, and walked into the grass. "And Win?"

"Yes?" I looked up, hopeful.

"Don't call me ever again."

And then she was gone. And I was truly alone.

HANG THE BELLS

I didn't call her. She didn't come. The few times my depressed daydreams about her got to be too much, that same ill-wind blew into my room and I willed those dreams away. In between, I tried to force the pieces.

Can we talk?

I typed on Messenger.

Please?!

Penny responded by blocking me.

I visited Mr. Ferguson.

"Does your father know you're here?" He fiddled with everything on his desk—the calendar, a framed photo of Mrs. Ferguson, the cup of pens—trying to show me he was a busy man with no time to spare.

"No. He doesn't need to. Penny is my relative and I feel responsible for her being here. It's my responsibility to get her out." I sat across from him, moving nothing, hands folded in my lap, legs crossed at the ankles, trying to show him I had all the time in the world for this. I wasn't going anywhere until he listened.

"Well, uh, you see, Winifred, this isn't my decision. I signed a contract with Isaacs and in it, it clearly states that he has control over the way the tours themselves are run." He picked up a folder that said "Burials, September," as if that's where the actual contract was filed.

"But there must be something we can do. This is our home."

"No, Winifred, this is our place of business." His voice was softer when he said this, soft but firm. "And we have to do what's best for business."

I left. There was nothing I could say to dissuade him. All I managed to do was make him increasingly uncomfortable with my eventual pleading.

I posted anonymous reviews to the Toronto Haunted Ghost Tours website.

"Horrible display of cultural mockery" read one. "I won't be doing these tours until the fake trickery is canceled" read another. Each one was removed within an hour of being posted.

And then I sat down with my father—my last resort. It was Wednesday and I had officially run out of options.

"Dad, I really need to do something about Penny." We were in the living room after dinner. He swiveled his easy chair to face me on the couch.

"Not sure what can be done."

"Well, something has to be done. We can't just let her get away with this." I leaned forward, bum on the edge of the seat.

"Get away with what?"

"Dad, seriously? With her stupid little fraud." I was impatient by this point. Impatient and frustrated with being brushed aside.

He rubbed his chin and lifted up the baseball cap he wore so that it rested high on his head. "Thought you said there was a real ghost. How can it be fraud?"

"I cannot believe you are on her side!"

"No. I am not. I'm just saying."

I threw myself back into the cushions, on the verge of sulking. "There is a ghost, for reals. But I don't want Penny here making it into a show. Phil—the ghost—doesn't want her to do it. It hurts her."

He was quiet.

"I don't know how to explain it, but she doesn't want to come here all the time. She doesn't want to be called out. It's, like, painful. And considering the way she died, I get it."

He was silent for a minute, and when he answered, his voice had an edge of gentleness to it. "Maybe you don't want to be called out. Maybe you don't want to be reminded of Penny and Roberta and your mom."

I couldn't believe it. My own father! "Dad, what the hell? This isn't about me. It's about Phil and it's about us."

"But, this is good for us. If we forget it's Penny, it's good for us. Good for Winterson."

Did he think I was so petty that I would blow a chance to stay over Penny being a part of it? I mean, sure, I didn't exactly like that she was getting paid at our expense, but as if I couldn't put that aside, if this was only about feeling salty, as if I couldn't let Penny think she had won if it meant we could stay. It made me angry. I spoke from that anger.

"You know what, you're not the only person who knows love."

He looked confused.

"You're not the only one who lives with a dead love, who can hold out hope of being visited. The ashes, Dad? I thought we'd buried them all at the plot. But I can't even have something for myself."

It was as if I had reached across the space and slapped him on his cheek, like I had struck him as hard as I could. Because really, I had. I didn't have time to feel bad about it—that would come later. Tomorrow was Thursday and I couldn't sit by and let this shit happen again. If I did, I would lose Phil forever.

I stomped out of the room, went upstairs, and put Neil Young on full blast. I had to think. I sat with my back to the closed stairs hatch, expecting him to come up after me, to yell or punish me, even just to ask me to turn down the music. He didn't come, leaving me alone with this puzzle.

The next day we avoided each other. It was easy because by the time I woke up, he had already left for work. I was full of nerves. The hot water in the shower did nothing to calm them. I wasn't hungry but I forced down a piece of white bread folded over a thick layer of Cheez Whiz. It stayed in my throat along with my voice. I made sure the front door was locked so no one, especially not my dad, would wander in at lunch. Then I carefully cleaned the knife I'd used to make breakfast, using the time to think, reconsider, and resign myself to the plan I'd crafted. Then I started getting prepared.

When you're excited about something, an afternoon can drag on forever. When you're dreading something, it can flash past in a blip. On this day, it was noon and then it was six and there was nothing in between. Dad came home at 6:20 and didn't bother calling me for dinner. I heard the door, then the sink, heavy footsteps across the floor, and then his bedroom door click closed. I was grateful for him staying out of the way, but a small part of me stung. I thought about my words last night, his face after I'd thrown them. I pulled my feet up onto the window seat and hugged my shins to my chest. Oh God. Why did I keep breaking things?

I watched the grounds below, the small front yard and the sprawl beyond. It was still bright out and a handful of visitors left through the front gate, too animated to be mourners. I watched Floyd carry his spade to the sidewalk and start dragging it over the concrete, severing ant hills from their underground tunnels, scooping litter into piles. This was his version of sweeping. The screech and gnash of the metal was piercing.

I kept thoughts of her out of my head. Whenever she popped in—her smile, the way she blew smoke rings through smoke rings, her hand-poked tattoo—I started counting. There were fourteen slats in each section of the low white fence around our yard; twenty-nine sections across the front. My heart beat loud in my ears and I counted that too, until the steadiness of its cadence brought me to a place where I could think without consciously counting and hold back thoughts of Phil. I switched to counting birds, which is a challenging thing. You never know if a bird you think is a new number is just one you've already counted swooping back.

At 7:15, I stood up, let out a breath that shook at the end, and stretched. I needed to be limber. I needed to be alert. I needed to get my head out of the game and just act. I picked up my backpack, crept down the stairs and through the kitchen, and down to the front door.

Outside, the sky was starting to streak with darker clouds, a green hue lifting up from their hem; sign of a storm to come.

I didn't need the sky to tell me that. I could feel it in my rib-cage, where I carried a smaller storm just itching to bust out. I slung my backpack on and walked fast across the lawn and into Winterson proper, toward the Peak.

The strings of bells Jack had made years ago were tangled, so it took some doing to set them right. I draped them like gar-land, down the side of the incline, ending at the bottom, before the ravine. I panicked when the flashlight didn't turn on. Then I opened up the back and put the batteries in the right way and it clicked on, shining through the dense twilight before I switched it back off. Every noise made me jump down here—each bird alighting, every car swooshing by from the road—and I hid in the trees, listening. I had to concentrate. It was 7:52 and the tour bus would be arriving soon. Also, being this close to Phil made it dangerous. It's almost always impossible to tell yourself not to think of a thing and then not immediately think of that thing. So I stayed focused on the task at hand.

I unfolded voluminous white fabric from the bag and shook it out. Then I took off my clothes. Almost ready. Almost time. I was crouched at the base of a cedar when I heard Penny above. She was on her phone.

"Best gig ever. An hour of my time and I end up making five times what I would if I took an appointment. Yes, I brought cards this time. Damn right I'll be handing them out—I don't give a shit what the short guy has to say. I'm on my hustle." Laughter. Even when she was happy Penny sounded like an asshole.

"No, I'm not giving them any real songs. Why would I give them anything real? Fuck that. It's all gibberish. They don't want real anyways."

I doubted Penny had anything real to give anyone. She was always about Penny and no one else.

"There's a TV show in this for me, I know it."

She ended the call and I risked peeking out and up the hill. I was shocked to see her stretching, limbering up, the same way I had done in my room. Maybe we were both exacting a plan. Maybe we were both just doing our best. Doubt bubbled in my stomach and I clutched at it. God, I did not need to have to run to the toilet now. There was no time and I would stick out like a sore thumb, rushing to the washroom like this. I wouldn't make it back on time. I breathed deep, eyes closed, and rubbed my stomach. I counted slowly by twos; I needed the comfort of even number by even number. I wished Phil were here with me. I needed her unquestioning bravery.

A wind picked up, spiraling in the clearing.

I panicked. The wind rustled the trees and the bells gave a soft tinkle. "Shit!"

Penny looked up from braiding her hair, listening. If she noticed the bells she might investigate and the whole plan would be shot, not just for tonight, but forever. I'd never get another chance.

Shit, no. I pushed Phil from my mind with an image of Jack, specifically Jack and me under the willow. My embarrassment snapped down over Phil's face and she was gone. The wind died and Penny went back to braiding, humming the theme song to *Rocky*.

It was almost showtime.

THE RETURN OF MARY

The bus growled into the cemetery. It farted and squealed to a stop in front of the main chapel. I heard all this from the ravine, echoing down like the arrival of a monster. But the monster was already here, standing at the top of the hill in a borrowed buckskin dress two sizes too big so that it slouched off a shoulder, revealing a black Wolf Pack T-shirt. She cleared her throat repeatedly, sang notes off-key, and banged that lifeless drum, loose and concave. Her tote bag rested against the smallest gravestone on the edge of the semicircle. A braid of sweetgrass poked out the top. She'd stepped up her game this time.

My stomach had settled into the buzzing flight of a thousand butterflies, bodies fat, wings wide. I thought I might throw up. The flashlight was slick in my fingers from the evening humidity and nervous sweat. When I let them, my teeth chattered. One shot. I had one shot.

Chess Isaacs's voice leaked out of the bass-heavy speaker, muffled words ping-ponging off mausoleums like verbal balls, careening and weighted. I tracked the group like this, listening for his descriptions, the words becoming clearer as they walked closer.

" . . . thousands of bodies, some ancient . . . . Small child, Victorian-era cape . . . . Reports of noises at night . . ."

Penny rolled her shoulders, using her hands to push her head down and rotate it on its stem. Then she shook out both arms and, reaching for her phone inside one capacious sleeve, took a quick selfie, throwing up deuces and pushing out her lips.

More words now.

"The best spiritual interpreters are the ones who themselves are ancient . . ."

If I hadn't been trying to hold my quaking muscles to my clattering bones I would have rolled my eyes.

"Toronto Haunted Ghost Tours is proud to partner with local experts to bring you the most authentic experience possible." The voice was clear now. They were here. A quick wave of nausea pushed its way through me.

"Ladies and gentlemen, may I present to you, Ms. Penny Pinch."

"Thank you, Mr. Chess Isaacs, for understanding the need to bring me in for you. Indeed, this is a one-of-a-kind, once-in-a-lifetime experience you are about to embark upon. No other outsiders have ever been let into our sacred ways— until tonight. Tonight, you will be let in." She held up her arms, the drum in one hand, the stick in the other, and waited for the applause that started slow and then grew, dutiful, and with some embarrassment.

"I am Penny Pinch, or, as I am known in my community through ceremony, Far-Sight Woman."

I couldn't believe the absolute bullshit coming from her mouth. I didn't know how she could say these things without laughing; they weren't true at all. She was known as "Asshole Who Takes Advantage of Her Mother," or at best "Lazy Dick

Who Freeloads on Grocery Day." These names were given by Roberta and without a ceremony.

"I will be your guide and together we will call forth the spirit of a girl whose body was found right here on this land." She went to her bag and removed the braid of sweetgrass, holding a Bic lighter to the end until it smoked, and then handed it to a middle-aged man wearing a fanny pack. He beamed—the chosen helper. Ironically, he wore a Washington Redskins cap over his balding head. He laughed without sound and looked behind him into the crowd but held the braid with both hands, as if it might be snatched by a passing eagle.

The tours were held at dusk so that the lighting was moody and partial. People are more afraid when they can't wholly rely on their senses. Back here, the street lamps offered circles of orange in the trees. It made the rest of the space shadowed by comparison, with the edging of backlit branches like lace on blue velvet. I released a deep breath with my chin tilted up and saw stars, small and bright, pushing through the heavy sky. *Here we go*.

"I am going to play you a summoning song given to me by a Tibetan monk, and while I do, I want you all to focus. Focus in on the energy of this place and the feminine spirit. If you close your eyes and suck back into yourself, and then push all that focus outward, we can bring her forth. When the song ends, I will call her to us."

Heavy swipes on hide; the hollow notes, like an echo in a bell jar, thudded to the ground. She began to sing, low and badly. I stood now, smoothing out the front of the dress, the flashlight at my bare feet. I tried to count her beats by twos but they were too uneven. I counted my toes instead, peeking out from under the white hem.

"Okay." She spoke over the last fading notes, quick and sloppy. "Let's get started." She placed the drum on the ground and turned to face the incline where I waited at the bottom. I crouched back down, hand over the flashlight switch. Deep breath. I reached out and took hold of the end of string dangling from a low branch. I pulled hard and the line of bells tinkled.

"What's that?"

"Do you hear bells?"

"Where's it coming from?"

Penny paused, and then launched into step two of her homemade séance. "We call to each direction and the guides that sit in each doorway. We beseech you to allow the spirit we seek to come forth."

I reached down and clicked the switch on the flashlight. A spotlight of blue-white striped from the bushes out into the clearing. There were gasps, low murmurs. Good, they'd noticed. I stood straight, hands by my sides, trying not to grasp the cotton in clenched fists. *Glide, Win, glide*, I reminded myself.

Penny continued, shaky but louder. "We ask that her soul be released from your bindings so that she may walk this plane. We call Philo—" She was cut short when I stepped out from the trees, into the narrow stream of light, in my mother's long dress.

I'd had two choices, really: I could have worn the cape from the first sighting or the dress from the last. But the cape was too small now, barely coming to my waist, less theatrical. So I'd packed the dress, white and folded like a flag of surrender into my backpack.

"Oh my God! Look!" It was the man in the Redskins cap. He pointed at me with the braid of sweetgrass. There was rustling and exclamations and still I kept walking—one foot in front of the other, trying to keep my gaze forward but stealing looks up the hill, long enough to see the man point, long enough to take in the look on my cousin's face. *One. Two. Three. Four . . .* Almost there.

"Everyone, everyone please calm down. We don't have very long with a spirit once it shows itself, so we need to focus." Penny's voiced was edged with annoyance. She saw right through this. I knew she would. But she was a professional, and I never doubted she'd stick to her script. The next part was a directive hidden in her crowd banter. "It will leave us soon, *very* soon. We have to stay still and focus."

This was perfect. If no one was willing to listen to me, then Penny would have to do all the work of showing her true self. If I was going to give everything up, toss it all away, the least I could do was take her down with me.

I had made it halfway between the bush on the west side and the trees on the east when I stopped, center stage. As I lifted my head and turned to face the crowd on the hill, I saw Phil on the other side of the clearing, her bright eyes, her army pants, faded and faltering like a reflection in water. She watched the same way they did—mouth agape, unsure of what she was seeing.

What she was seeing was me understanding what home was, me doing what I'd said I would, protecting it at all costs. I smiled, looked directly at Penny, and opened my mouth to speak, to come clean as an obvious fraud and discredit Penny and Isaacs in one fell swoop . . . and then, he yelled.

"Mary?"

It was my father. I snapped my mouth shut. He pushed his way through the crowd, emerging from the glow of two-dozen cell phones held up to capture the miracle of my haunting. He stood beside Penny for a moment, eyes locked on my figure standing stark and still, his chest beginning to heave with labored, excited breathing. I froze.

"Mary! I knew it was you. I knew it."

He started down the rocky hill, throwing himself at an alarming speed, falling once on his backside and quickly righting himself. "I knew it. Oh, Mary. Mary!" His voice was full and loud; I'd never heard him this way before. It was the sound of stone smashed open on stone, of pearls being plucked from oyster shells, of agony turned inside out.

I was here to out myself, to tell them it had all been a trick, to make sure my cousin never came back for Phil, even if that meant losing my home. I'd never wanted *this*, to give my father even a moment of the kind of hope he'd kept locked up in his heart and under his bed. I never wanted to break him. I should have worn the cape.

He got to the bottom, his face open in a way I'd never seen before. His eyes adjusted to the dark, to the glare of the flashlight, and changed a bit.

He had run here to pull his wife into his arms, to look into her eyes, to see his suffering reflected. He wanted to know he was not alone, that he had her, finally and forever. But it was just me. It was always just me.

His frantic smile pulled in on itself and his forehead wrinkled. He slowed his pace, catching himself on the last of the downward run's momentum. He was seeing clearer now and he was confused. He tugged at his beard, his voice getting softer. "Mary?"

And then I did the only thing I could do when you're caught playing ghost during a cemetery tour with your asshole cousin running a séance and your dad fit to burst over the chance you are actually your dead mother—I picked up the length of skirt around my feet and ran.

"Wait!" he yelled, giving chase.

Fuck. I ran as fast as I could, ignoring the sharp rocks and bits of trash under foot. I ran straight into Phil's clearing, jumping over bottles, moving headlong into the trees. And then an arm that had carried me onto the bus, that had allowed me its length to swing from, grabbed me around the waist and I was nearly folded in half in the capture. We both tumbled to the ground.

He pulled himself up to his knees and held my chin in his hand, turning my face to him. "Winifred?" He said it like an exhalation, like something sitting on his lungs until he couldn't grab breath. He said it like an ending.

Movement in the bushes. I hoped it was Phil, revealing herself, coming to me. Isaacs pushed through first, the Bluetooth microphone still over his ears, positioned in front of his mouth. "Oh shit." It reverberated behind and up the hill.

A few of the tourists followed him, out of breath, their camera phone flashes held aloft as shining surveillance eyes. Penny hadn't bothered. She was already packing up at the Peak, always one to know when the time is right to skip town. Even she couldn't convince anyone she wasn't a part of this.

I pouted, like I'd planned, even with the great miscalculation of my father, and spoke to Isaacs, and the growing crowd in general, the words I'd decided on while waiting for the show to begin. "Penny said this was the only way. She said we'd get a TV deal out of it."

Then I turned to my father and in a low tone I whispered, "I'm so sorry." He looked away from me.

LIFE OUT OF DEATH

I was twelve and had just gotten my first period. My dad wasn't sure what to do besides buy me one of everything from the "lady aisle" at Shoppers Drug Mart and give me a wide berth. I rode my bike up Bloor Street to Roberta's on the third day, despite Dad's wonderings if it was okay for me to ride a bike. Apparently, his knowledge of menstruation was limited to rumors and innuendo from the 1970s. I locked my bike out front with a few scooters and one rusty walker that had been there since last winter.

"Hey, Auntie." She buzzed me in and I took the stairs up to the second floor.

"Hey, my girl." Her head was hanging out the door, as she watched me approach down the hall. "Watch out for all this garbage in the hall. Marchand doesn't know how to use the damn chute, or he's just too lazy."

There was one green bag, half full and tied up neat outside her neighbor's door. "Auntie, Mr. Marchand has a broken hip, remember?"

She waved this off. "He's got two. What, are they both broken?" She went back inside. I carried the offending bag to the chute, stuffed it in, and waited until it tumbled all the way down. There was something so satisfying about that sound, of bags somersaulting through metal corridors to the basement. Then I went into her apartment.

It was a sunny spring afternoon and the windows were thrown open to let in the cold, clean breeze. I could see the dust swirling just above our heads, sent spiraling in the current. Roberta was wearing a ski jacket. "S'cold in here but we need the new air."

I made us tea and sat at the kitchen table with her, in front of our latest puzzle. "So." I took a sip. "I got my period."

"Ever good!" She was genuinely happy for me and patted the top of my head. It was such a starkly different reaction to my father's well-meaning panic. Today he'd asked me if I wanted to make a doctor's appointment.

I clicked in a corner piece and we mused over the fragments in silence for a minute. "But why exactly is it good though?"

"Huh?" She lifted her chin from where it rested on the flat of her palm, held up by a bony elbow on the edge of the table. "Because you made it; you're a grown-up."

"Yeah, but how is that good?"

"Means you have new responsibilities. And now you can get wise, like your old auntie." She was trying to ram a dark blue piece into a black patch, her tongue pushed out past her lips. I gently took it out of her hand and replaced it with the right piece. "Lookit there, I got it!" She clapped.

"Because I bleed?" I snorted.

"No. Because you can make bigger decisions."

There was another moment of concentrated silence. "A lot of good that did my mom."

"Eh? What's that?"

"All growing up did for my mother was bring death."

"Your mom used to wear this pink one-piece, it had blue stripes across the front. She thought that thing made her look like an Olympic swimmer. Anyways, she wore it until it was always up her ass crack." She chuckled. "Boy oh boy, we had to burn that thing halfway through a summer so she wouldn't put it back on. She was madder than hell.

"The bottom was all pulled, looked furry like with broken threads, because she sat on the dock in it and all the loose splinters and boards ruined it, always catching the fabric. But she refused to get a new one and she refused to stop going on the dock. Even after we told her she'd need a tetanus shot if she got cut on a nail.

"Back then we had the whole shore on the north side of the bay. Oh man, the parties we had. Guitars and fires and slider soup and kids jumping around. You can't even imagine it. And your mom? She was the one who'd start and end it, even when she was just a tiny thing. She'd dance and swim and play the spoons. She had permanent round marks on her thigh, I swear it, she played them so hard."

"What does this have to do with anything?" I was impatient, irritable. Normally I'd stay quiet during these stories.

"Just shut up, you. I'm telling you because you're here talking about how life isn't worth death. And I'm telling you your mom didn't believe that, not for a second. She played on that dock even though it ruined her favorite suit. She sang even though her voice was like a cat in heat. She danced until the dirt was a cloud to her knees. It's worth it. It's always worth it." She reached her skinny hand over the puzzle and slapped the back of mine, which is as close as she would get to holding it. "You're worth it. She'd have been the first person to scream it. And now you have to make bigger decisions. That's not hokey, it's science, sure as shit."

Was it worth it? Giving everything I had like this? My dad was still turned, facing the woods, on his knees, resting his panting weight back on his feet. I could hear Isaacs in the middle of a speech about "no refunds" to grumbling customers and the "removal of frauds." He said it loud and distinct, so Mr. Ferguson had no doubt of what was to come.

Penny screamed from the top of the hill, a thousand miles away, "Fuck you, Winifred Blight! You're no relative of mine!" And then Floyd was chasing the stragglers out of the clearing with a rake. "Nothing to see here. Get lost now. Before I dig you yer own hole! You too, big head."

Eventually, it was just me and my father and the ghost of my mother, which was just me after all. We were sprawled on the ground of the clearing, an orchestra of crickets rubbing tone into the empty, a soprano of cicadas stirring the still air around us.

"Dad . . ."

"Why?"

"Dad, listen. I didn't mean for you to be here, I didn't mean for you . . ."

He stood and raised his voice. Another tone from him I hadn't heard in all my memories. "Why would you do this? How could you be so cruel?"

"I just wanted Penny to go away. But no one would listen!" I was yelling too, but tears made my voice less striking. "No one! Not even you!"

"So you pretended to be your mother?"

"No, I didn't pretend to be my mother. It was an accident. I was the kid they saw before." I struggled to my feet in the twisted dress now muddy and fringed with blades of torn grass. "I was the reason it started—the rumors, the tours—but not on purpose. I never pretended to be anything other than me." I pointed to my chest, finger digging under my collarbone. "Me. I was only ever me."

"So then what in the hell is this, then?" He gestured to me, to the dress, then down the path to the hill.

"I had to get rid of her, Dad. She was hurting Phil."

He put his hand on his forehead and turned away. He seemed shorter than usual. This small act of disappearance made me angry. He couldn't get smaller when I needed him to get bigger. "Dammit, Win, enough with this."

"Enough with what? Oh, you can think that Mom has come back from the grave and that's perfectly sane, but I can't tell you there is another ghost without being a liar? How does that even make sense?" The crickets put down their bows. The cicadas exited stage left.

"It's not like that. You don't understand." He was tired already, all the hope and adrenaline kicked out of him. But I was just getting started.

"No, you're right, I don't understand. I don't understand because I was raised in a cemetery with a dead mother and a half-dead father. How could I understand anything?"

He turned to me and I saw tears in his eyes. The sight of them knocked the breath out of my body. I had more to say, but then something else entered the clearing with us. Shame. Deep and red and slithering. I was ashamed, of my words, of the dress I wore, of the way my father kept turning away. I had brought all our shame into this space and now it was swallowing me whole. I had to run again, to get away from him this time. But there was nowhere left to go. This was it; we were at the end of the known world.

We faced each other, a girl in a dirty dress and a man broken by what it could have meant. He should have stomped away. He should have struck me, like he never had before. He should have left me there to die behind a tree. Instead, he took quick steps, like a loping gazelle, and gathered me up in his arms so that my feet dangled from my ankles.

"I'm sorry, Win. I'm so, so sorry."

And I was a pearl ripped from the darkness of a hard shell and tossed up on a platter. I was out in the open. And it was terrifying. I held on to him for dear life.

In time, I asked him to go ahead, told him I needed the walk. He left reluctantly, ready to meet Isaacs's wrath, though to be honest I was pretty sure my dad would just punch him in the nose if he tried. What was there left to lose? He could shoulder Mr. Ferguson's soft disappointment. I stayed in the clearing, not thinking of anything but myself, my dad.

When the crickets took their seats and began tuning their instruments, I left. I didn't bother going back for the flashlight or the empty backpack. Though I did hear the bells in the trees like children laughing when I climbed up to the Peak. I didn't look back.

I stepped carefully on bare feet, avoiding the hard grass and the gravel edges of the pathway. All of the sudden I felt fragile. I took my time. It was full dark now, in that way summers in the city get dark—incomplete, with the promise of something just beyond the next bend. Sweat and tears smeared dirt over my cheeks and I left it there. My hair was matted and the dress torn at the waist and I couldn't be bothered to feel anything about it.

Instead, I thought about the future now that I'd poisoned the present by tracking in the past. Was Dad already packing up our small apartment, dragging the suitcase from under his bed to the top of the stairs? Would we bother taking Dingles's wagon with us? Would we leave in the truck that was used so rarely it hadn't had a chance to pick up our smell? And where would even we go? Where was left? Mostly, I wondered if I had done the right thing when I wasn't even sure what the right thing was anymore.

There is a blanket that surrounds cemeteries, so that if you were to poke your head through the gate from the sidewalk, the sound is muffled to keep out the noise and exclamations of the living. It's there to keep the dead from getting jealous and returning to demand silence. And to keep the cemetery separate to stop the living from thinking about the soft erasure of death. It's a barrier that is exact and boundaried and unmoving. When you spend your life living inside of it, the outside world can be too much. There is too much to hear, to see, to count. I walked on bare feet in a tattered dress through this very silence, knowing that I had ripped open a hole in the boundary, that soon I would be on the other side. That soon I would cross the fence, whether I liked it or not. I remembered falling from the fence in a dream, the way the ground rushed up to meet me halfway.

I walked the path around the chapel, the long way, not wanting to face what was on the other side. I kept my head down. I was too heavy to count and the anxiety tiptoed up my legs like a column of ants. But I had stayed away long enough—the bus was gone, the yard was empty, not even Floyd puttered about.

I imagined he was somewhere saluting the end of the reign of tourists with a mickey and a smoke. That made me smile, to think of his small, impolite joy. I stopped and looked over at my home. It was dark and half hidden, like a gray mushroom at the base of a tree. I walked even slower now in the freedom solitude offered.

I left the main path where it split into the driveway down to the now closed gate. I walked up onto the soft grass of our mowed lawn, in through the opening left in the ornamental picket fence. And just then, just as I left the line between work and home, it began to rain like a kettle tipped over above the house. I ran to the door and grabbed the column of teacups, setting them down in the grass. Every cup sang, the water plucking scooped notes out of ceramic. It was as if tiny fingers were pressing gently on the highest keys of an untuned piano. It was a symphony attended by frogs and slugs. It was a going-away song, sad and beautiful, like Neil Young playing Rachmaninoff at a child's funeral.

I walked as slowly as I could, listening, letting the rain run in rivulets through my hair, down my back. I went to the side door and stood for a moment under the small metal awning. It was a drum now, stretched tight and even, as if it were held over a hot element. It was a traveling song, low and even—a song of what was to come next.

I pushed open the unlocked door and entered the dry heat of the main floor. There was no dog there to shush, no companion to carry up the stairs. I was suddenly overwhelmed with exhaustion. It made it almost impossible to lift my own weight up the first flight of stairs. But still, I turned around and came back down once I hit the kitchen, heading back to the door. I looked out into the dark expanse of the side yard and then flipped the switch on the wall. The porch light snapped on—the best way to call someone home.

That night I dreamed. I was in an open field, low buildings in the back like bruises fading on the wall of far-sky. Above, the entire sky, and below, an expanse of grass is illuminated by an enormous orange moon. It looks like a silent film prop hung by cigar-smoking laborers standing on ladders. I am wearing my black dress and an elaborate crown made of woven bark and cloudy gems, with chewed lace draped down over my forehead. Someone is walking out of the dark toward me.

"Phil." Her name is a stone rubbed smooth by water. I suck on it, hearing the way it rattles against my molars.

There is no answer. The figure is small, long arms and hair and a skirt that smooths out the tall grass like a comforting hand over fevered skin. Pressure builds and releases, builds and releases. My ears pop. And then she comes into the circle of light.

"Mom?"

She smiles, that flashy smile that was all teeth and mischief, the one that never quite made it into photographs, the one Dad had tried once to explain by saying "it was like a fox had a really good joke he couldn't tell."

She stops and just stands there, the moon and the field and the silence between us. I can't move, am sure of it. My feet have grown roots. I am a statue, a lithopedion in her presence, stuck, unmoving.

"Mom, I need you to come to me," I say, except my voice is just wind with a small gurgle like rain in a gutter.

She just smiles bigger, and raises her arms, hands open and forward. I pull, yanking my right foot from the ground, and take a step. I laugh. This has volume. I focus on the left foot, and it too comes loose. I make my way like this, one plodding foot at a time, across the space between us. And then I am there, in the circle of her arms. She closes them over me, pulling me into her chest. She isn't warm or cold or solid or mist. And when she releases me and I look for her face I see only mine. It was just me. It was always just me.

And the moon grows brighter and the grass begins to braid itself and I open myself and speak words and hear words as if I haven't said them at all.

"Welcome home."

It was the sun that woke me up, streaming into my room like a great spotlight of heat. I opened my eyes slow. I felt like I'd run a hundred miles. My legs were tight and my feet were cut. The sun caught the round of a glass jar on the window seat, where its light collected and broke off onto the walls. So many colors and lines to count, but I didn't.

I swung my legs over the edge and put swollen feet on the floor, then hobbled to the window. There, on the ledge, was the jar with the egg in it. On the shelf where it had sat was a perfect circle of clean with dust around the edges. I held it up and turned it. Still, the egg sat in the middle, on my best pair of underwear folded in the bottom. Except now it was intact—whole. The puncture was gone and in its place was a small spray of hairline cracks like a map of rivers across the curve of a pale globe.

It was almost perfect.

BOXES

The thing about ashes is that there are none. That's just what we call them to be polite, to be gentle with the grieving. Everything that was body—skin, marrow, small bones, hair, scars, tattoos of hearts and harlots, everything—is gone. All that's left is the larger bone fragments—femurs and coccyx, sections of ulna. And those are ground up into dense beach sand and sealed in a bag that's put into a box. And that box, which is now about the weight of a bowling ball, is taped shut. And we call this *mass*, this gray sand, ashes. As if the person was simply transformed in a bath of flame, poetic and pagan, as if the leftover pieces weren't ground down under extreme pressure with mechanical ease, as if there wasn't an on switch and an instruction manual to the fire. Having a silent and pained man in a blue suit hand them to you makes it even more mystical. You feel like there has been a ceremony, that perhaps now you are part of it for having received the six-to-eight-pound package.

And maybe that's not wrong. Everything has a part to play. That's just science, sure as shit.

We packed up our place into boxes, many of them these same boxes from the crematory. Why not? We knew they would hold.

And this was the kind of goodbye that required a bit of common sense and ceremony. I wrapped each jar in my collection in flyers from Canadian Tire and Walmart and made them snug like glass eggs in a carton. I rolled up the hammock and jammed clothes into duffel bags. Dingleberry's old clothes went into a plastic bin that was placed at the curb, where I had found them to begin with. I put a sign on a piece of cardboard, poking out the top— "FREE DOG/BABY CLOTHES." They were gone by noon.

We avoided the cemetery staff, Dad and I both being fans of the Irish goodbye, but people came by anyways. Mr. Ferguson brought my father's paperwork and gave him a stiff handshake that lingered too long and made my dad rub the back of his neck with his free hand until it ended. Mrs. Prashad brought over a reusable grocery bag stuffed full of old issues of *Cosmo* and *Glamour* for me to take with us. And Floyd gave me his best knife.

"Hopefully you'll run into some bears on your way to BC. This should do it." He handed it over handle first, and only when my father had left us alone. I threw my arms around his neck and gave him a hug.

"I love you, Floyd." He pushed me off, mumbling some words about silliness and feelings, but I saw him pull out a crusty handkerchief to wipe at his eyes as he walked away.

It took two days to fully empty the apartment. We didn't have a lot of stuff and there were things we didn't want to bring— the couch and the easy chair and the kitchen set whose chairs were prejudiced against new owners, having taken on the exact shape of our butts—so we had to make a few runs to the dump. We would start over once we got to my father's parents' land, the eleven acres on the coast of British Columbia that was willed to him, land I could only imagine as feral and green. God, I hoped so. I hoped there were strings of lacy moss and giant ravens that carried whole ermines in their beaks. Ravens as big as minivans. I hoped there were more trees than people. Trees like tombs. Dad said there was an old camper on the lot and that we'd figure out what kind of house we wanted and then build it together. I imagined him cutting the wood with karate chops.

The day before we started packing was the last day of summer vacation. Jack rode his bike over on the way to his shift at the rec center.

"Say it ain't so." He threw his arms up, bike leaning against his side at my door.

"So." I replied, walking outside and closing the door behind me. He lay his bike on the ground and followed me. We sat on the step, side by side.

"I saw clips of the shit that went down last week. Crazy!"

I was mortified. I put my forehead against my knees and wondered how long it would take before the doomed tour made it onto YouTube. Not that long, as it turned out.

"Did you really pretend to be a ghost?"

"Apparently."

"But you did such a shitty job." He punched my arm lightly. "And after that ghost-hunting phase and everything, you'd think you'd know better."

"I know. I did it on purpose." I waved off his next question. "It's a long story."

He grew more solemn. "When do you leave?"

"After the weekend."

"Where you headed?"

"BC, near the coast in the middle of nowhere. My grandparents left my dad some land. We're going to build." I surprised myself with the discernable excitement in the answer.

"Listen, Win . . ."

"It's okay. I don't want to talk about it."

"But I really am so sorry . . ."

"Seriously, I don't want to talk about it. It happened and we just need to move on."

"So, we're good?"

I paused, searched around inside before I answered. "No. But we're not bad. It's just that it doesn't hurt anymore. It's not big enough to hurt."

For something that didn't hurt, he sure looked like he'd taken a blow. And I honestly didn't care. His face was not the one that unlocked me. His words sure as hell wouldn't be the ones that undid me.

He shuffled over on the concrete and put an arm across my shoulders. I leaned into him, resting my head on his sweaty T-shirt. He smelled like summer and clean skin and flexed movement. It made me miss the small curves and skinny grip of another.

"I'm going to miss you."

I sighed, closed my eyes. "I'm going to miss you too. More like I already miss us, the old us." It was true, despite everything that had and hadn't happened. We couldn't recover, and I'm not sure either of us wanted to.

We sat like that until his phone reminded him he had to get going or he would lose his shift. We hugged, awkwardly, and then, toward the end, with a fleeting sincerity, and I watched him pedal off, his wide back hunched over the bars, his shirt catching the wind like a jersey cape.

I was glad he'd come by, glad we had a moment to say good-bye, to honor everything we'd been and meant to each other. But even still, there was an absence I couldn't ignore. He wasn't the one I needed to talk to. He wasn't the one who'd stayed away no matter how many nights I lit up the yard with the sad yellow beacon of the porch light.

On our last night in Winterson we ordered in a pizza. It wasn't really an indulgence as much as a necessity; every pan, dish, and fork was packed away. We ate in the empty living room with a single floor lamp lighting our picnic. We took turns taking chugs out of a big giant bottle of Dr Pepper and wiped our greasy hands on the towel we'd laid down over the hardwood. The room was empty to the wainscoting. Even the boxes were downstairs in the main room, ready to be piled and bungee-corded into the back of the pickup. We had sleeping bags rolled out, each with a pillowcase stuffed with clean clothes. Dad kept the TV hooked into the wall for the night. It sat on the floor, so we had to lay down to watch it. Halfway through *Pretty Woman*, Dad's breathing got slow and even. He was never one for romance movies. Which was pretty ironic seeing as how he was the most romantic person I'd ever met—old-school romantic, the kind who gives up their entire life for love. Even Romeo and Juliet got to die on the same day. Imagine if one of them had had to live with it forever?

I was just drifting off when I heard footsteps upstairs. I sat up, scared. Had someone come in the window? I pictured Penny crawling into my room with a knife between her teeth like a revenge-hungry pirate. *You're no relative of mine, aarghh!* Then it wasn't just steps anymore; someone was jumping, and it sounded like they were wearing heavy boots. If the pictures were still on the wall, they'd have fallen off. How was my father sleeping through this? And then I knew who it was. I slid out of the sleeping bag and ran up the stairs.

The hatch was already thrown open but the ceiling light was off. I stuck my head in and swiveled around like a periscope.

"Well, I guess this is one way to dump a girl." Phil was sitting on the window ledge, legs crossed at the knee, bouncing her foot and examining her nails, as casual as the dead could be. I scrambled up into the room, excited. But once I was there, within the same four walls as her, I grew anxious.

"I am really sorry, Phil."

"Sorry for being such a shitty ghost?" She laughed. "You should be sorry. My God, that acting stunk."

I ventured a smile. "Yeah well, it's never really been my thing. I once threw up a whole half a hotdog before giving a speech in the seventh grade. Like a whole unchewed, undigested piece. Fell right on my shoe."

"That's really uh . . . disgusting. Really gross." She stood up, jamming her hands in her pockets.

"So, I'm leaving." Saying it out loud made it hard to focus. I was leaving. Holy shit. I was actually leaving.

"I can see that."

"Phil, remember when you told me you were haunting me and not Winterson?"

She watched me in the dark, the diluted dark of the city at her back, illuminating her outline against the window. She nodded.

"Listen, does that mean that you can leave? I mean, does it mean your tie is to me, and not here?" I pointed to the floor.

She laughed, a hand over her narrow belly. "Oh man, you've been watching too many movies."

"That's not how it works?" I laughed at myself. "No? *Ghostbusters* lied to me! Oh man, what a waste of a childhood. Who do I sue?" I shook a fist in the air.

"Win, I don't know for sure how it works. But I know I am not getting in the pickup with you and your dad." I hadn't really thought it through, but the idea of her perched on the wide front seat with us didn't seem so impossible. She lifted an eyebrow at me, seeing into my thoughts.

"Yeah, I know, duh." I tried to keep it light. "Because you can just teleport yourself there in a second." I snapped my fingers. It echoed in the space like the breaking of a fortune cookie or tiny wee bones.

"Phil?"

"Yeah."

"I don't know what to say."

She crossed the floor and gathered me up in her arms and we fell, into each other, onto the bench, in the soft light from an incomplete darkness. I kissed her face, the raised scar on her wrist, the smooth fingertips that tapped at my window. She put a hand over my chest, on my neck, into my hair. I think we were both crying or laughing or maybe just gasping like a fairy-tale fish pulled off the line and tossed on a rock. We struggled against the limitations of physicality, mine permanent and hers borrowed. But we managed to translate the frustration and want into something like love, or at least the language of it. I wanted to lick her skin. I wanted to find a way to push her inside of me and carry her there like a child without a womb. I knew there was enough space. It could be done. We kissed and it was so soft, so light, and then it was something more. We lay on the floor together, trying to find ways to make all our pieces fit, so we could be a complete picture.

I was dozing off when she left me. I stayed awake just long enough to hear her speak words in the language, into my hand,

and to cup my fingers over it for safekeeping. I would remember them later. I would unwrap their meanings on the road or sitting in a tall tree surrounded by Cadillac-sized ravens. She sat for a moment, on the edge of the window bench and watched me breathing. She changed her mimic to match my cadence and then we were both breathing the same, clear as math.

She gave a low whistle before pushing through the window in a movement that was as hidden in the open as her smoking. There was a moment of the kind of quiet people pay money for, total absence of all noise and thought. And from down below in the yard, there was the sound of Mrs. Dingleberry's wagon, grinding under his considerable weight, slicing through the squishy gray muck on the gravel paths like rubber spoons into cereal. This sound made my breath feel huge, like it reached every part of me, all the way to the backs of my knees. I hugged them to my chest, tears sliding grateful into the shallow bowl of my collarbone. They were together now.

The next morning, I woke curled up on the bench: a single, complete, girl-shaped egg balancing on the edge of the day. I was alone but I wasn't afraid. Something like excitement pushed itself into my movements. Something like love made the mechanics easier. It was almost perfect.

ASHES TO ASHES

We double-checked the bungee cords and the rope and pushed on the boxes from all angles, testing out the sturdiness of our design in case there was an accident, or we were set upon by road bandits.

"Important shit in the front." Dad exhaled, stretching out his back. Then he loaded a folder of papers and IDs and a photo album onto the bench seat, in the space between us.

"I'm already here. I'm the most important shit," I joked.

He smiled. "Okay then, one last run through."

"Dad?"

"Mmm."

"Can I just stay in the truck? I don't want to go back in." I held one of my jars between my thighs. That was all I needed with me right now.

He closed the door and walked to the house. He looked out of place in his travel clothes, a pair of ripped jeans and a gray shirt with some band I didn't know on the front. Portishead? Clearly, we had different musical tastes. Good thing I was the one who made the playlist for the trip.

He came back out carrying that blue suitcase from under his bed: my mother. The silver casings caught the sun and sent light stabbing in through the windshield.

"Shit." My heart got suddenly heavy and ratcheted down a few ribs, unable to stay aloft. He adjusted the folder and my backpack and settled the suitcase on its bottom so that it sat upright between us, like a small barrier.

"Dad?"

"Mmm?"

"Can we stop by the scattering grounds before we leave?"

He glanced over at me and then put the car in reverse. We trundled the truck over the main road, following the wider path to the western perimeter. He left it idling and I climbed out.

"Aren't you coming?"

He watched my face for a moment, gauging his leeway. He looked back to the dashboard, then over at the suitcase, then pulled the key out of the ignition and followed me, closing the door with the suitcase still on the seat.

I walked to the edge, the small jar covered by both my hands. I waited to feel him step beside me. We both looked down the gentle slope of grass and dirt patches, the screams of children in their backyards beside us.

"I have to leave something here." I waited for a response. None came. "Where it belongs."

I unscrewed the top of the jar; there was a suctioned pop as it released.

"Mrs. Dingleberry, you were the best dog I could have ever asked for, and I didn't even ask for one."

He laughed softly beside me. I smiled at him.

"We want to leave your ashes here on these grounds you so loved, where you slept through every walk and growled when we took you out in the winter. Where you amused visitors with your fashion choices and made all of my days better."

Dad reached over and put a hand on my shoulder. Then I tipped the jar as the wind picked up and let all the gray sand fall at our feet before it blew in small rivers around the rocks and dusted the grass down into the green expanse. I would have liked to imagine him watching us, chubby paws crossed over one another, an intelligent tilt to his wrinkled head. But the reality was, he'd have slept through the whole thing.

"See ya, boy." Dad's voice was heavy. I touched his hand, still on my shoulder, and put the cap back on the jar. We stood there for a moment as the wind picked up and watched little twisters of Dingleberry whip and careen over the field.

"Well, let's go." I turned toward the road. "I'm ready to leave."

We walked back to the truck beside each other, with matched steps. I paused at my door, hand pulling on the handle. "Are you sure you don't want to leave anything here?"

Dad paused on his side of the truck, then leaned on the roof with his forearms, the keys in his right hand clattering against the hot metal.

"Nah, this isn't the right place."

I sighed. Where would he put her in a trailer? I imagined the suitcase under a fold-down table, roped to the roof under a barbeque tarp, kept in the middle seat of the truck as we got groceries, or when he brought me to school, or attending my graduation, a corner-store bouquet of roses leaned up against the suitcase in the seat beside him. "So then, what is the right place?"

"We're gonna take her home. Up to the bay, before we head out west." He kicked at the gravel with his work boots. "Where she belongs."

Maybe it was the sun, but I could swear I saw tears in his eyes. Then again, it could have just been the ashes of our fat dog blowing in the breeze.

We settled into our seats and I attached my phone to the radio. "Alrighty, get ready for the Ultimate Road Trip Playlist."

"Oh good Lord."

"Nope"—I held up a finger—"the Lord has nothing to do with it. No Christian rock on this list, my good man. But there are a few gods . . ."

I found the file and hit shuffle. The first jaunty notes pounded into the cab through refurbished speakers.

"Oh no . . ."

"Oh yes!" I hung my arm out the window and banged on the side of the door. "Here we go!"

I sang as loud as I could: to Floyd, who was sharpening his blades behind the shed, still a bit upset after our goodbye; to Mrs. Prashad, who I'm sure rolled her eyes at her desk; to the ghost who would always be my first love and who, maybe, if I wished with the right kind of want, would return to be my last.

"Jolene, Jolene, Jolene, Jooleeeeeeennne . . ."

My voice was clear—bad but clear. Because I could finally take full breaths. My back was straight and my head was up. And my dad, he drove with an arm out the window, fingers tapping out the beat on the mirror in spite of himself, a smile on his face. We were leaving. We passed through the open gate. Phil was right: I wouldn't walk out of here; I was driving out, with my dad. And then, turning onto Parliament and joining a stream of cars, we left. We were headed for the next thing and we would have lettuce instead of bones in our garden, bushes instead of mausoleums, and a girl instead of a lithopedion. Soon, I would learn the words that Phil had put into my hand, the ones I carried in the shell of my ears as we wound our way out of the cat's cradle of the city. I'd hold those words in the space behind

ACKNOWLEDGMENTS

This book wouldn't exist without family and friends. To some of the best friends I've had over the years, Susan Blight and Janine Manning, thank you for your humor and light, and for sharing your stories and your tea. A special—and huge—thank you to Lynne Missen and the Penguin Random House team. As always, enormous gratitude to my excellent agents Rachel Letofsky and Dean Cooke at CookeMcDermid for their patience and for always having my back.

Thank you to my daughters for being complicated, bright, challenging, courageous, vulnerable, and extraordinary. And for allowing me to love you through it all.

my molars—across the highway, sitting at diners with a plate of fries, sleeping in motel rooms lit neon through the closed window—and when we got to our new house, guarded by ravens as big as Buicks, I'd pull them onto my tongue, shaping my mouth to make the right noise and pause. And once I could speak them, I'd fish the sky, using those words as bait to yank grannies out of the dark, like slick trout still dreaming of home.